HAYLEY HOPE IS GONE

MICHELE DOMINGUEZ GREENE

Storm

Ebook ISBN: 978-1-80508-812-7
Paperback ISBN: 978-1-80508-814-1

Cover design: Blacksheep
Cover images: Shutterstock

Published by Storm Publishing.
For further information, visit:
www.stormpublishing.co

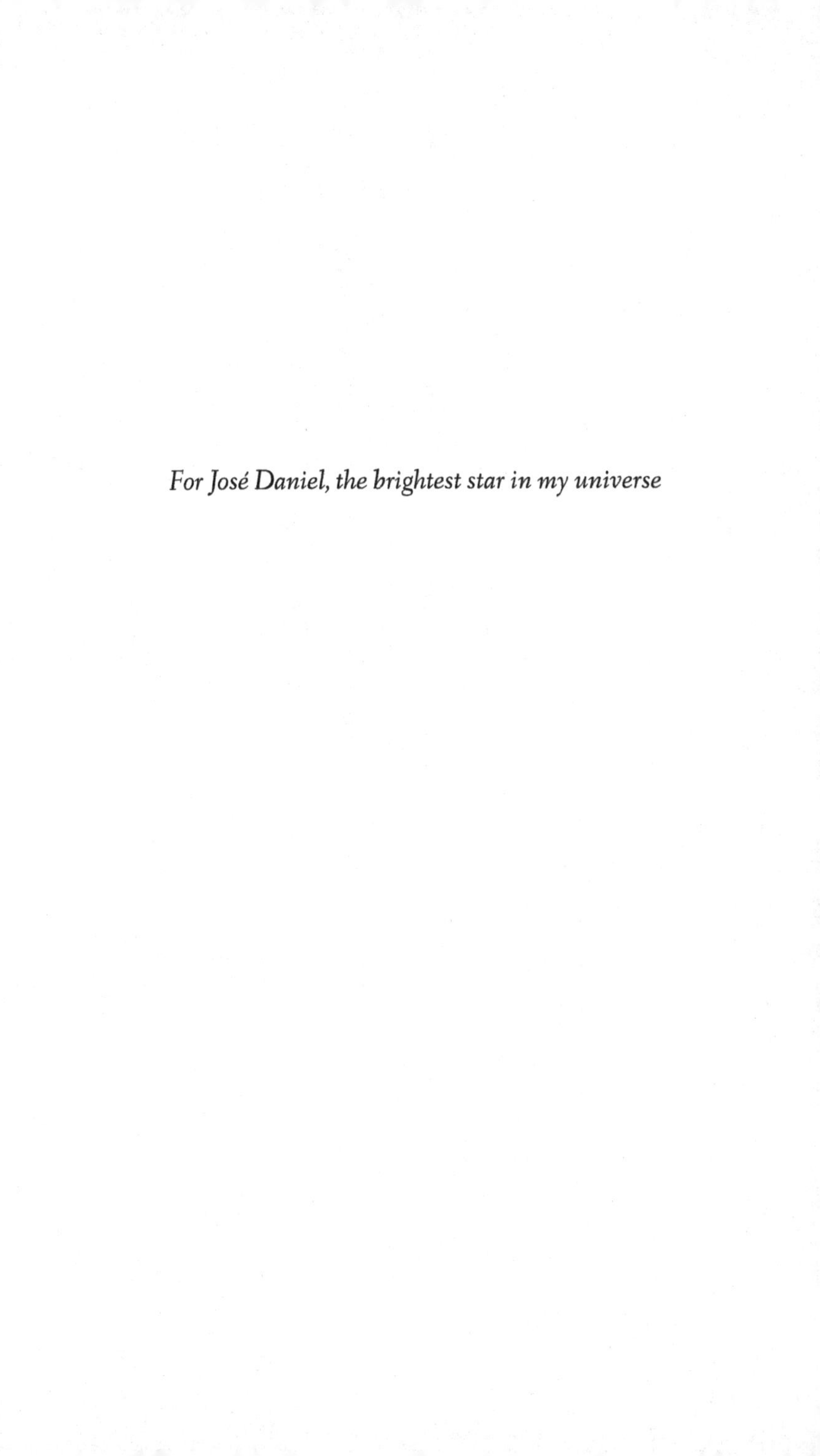

For José Daniel, the brightest star in my universe

PROLOGUE

The moon was full, a hazy mist hanging over it like a gossamer curtain, almost transparent. No birdsong echoed, no screech of a Steller's jay, no caw of a black crow to cut through the thick darkness. The trees stood as stately witnesses, staring down from the rough terrain, dispassionate and unmoving. Indian summer had arrived. There was no breeze, just a slight chill in the air. The water of Lake Arrowhead, dark as obsidian, lapped against the hulls of the remaining boats anchored peacefully in the small marina. No teenagers ordering burgers from the Jax Beach Hut, swimsuits dripping wet, their hair a tangle of curls, sticky with lake sludge. The portly men in Tommy Bahama shirts who sipped margaritas on their boats, moored and bobbing like a baby's bassinet, were gone. Deserted and silent, resort towns lose their luster as summer fades.

It was quiet, too quiet. Then the footsteps, padding in the dirt, along the chain-link fence that guarded tiny Papoose Lake, formed by the concrete dam where the trout gathered in the spring. A quartet, moving as silently as a snake, prodding the girl forward as she stumbled, unsteady on her feet. They guided her, keeping her upright as a key slid into the padlock and the gate was pushed open. They moved to the south edge of the small lake, beyond the storage shed, not visible from the highway that linked the different neighborhoods of the small town: Tavern Bay, Shelter Cove, Orchard Bay, Point Hamiltair.

The group stopped and settled, some feet shifting in uncertainty. The girl's eyes were wide, her pupils dilated as she looked at the dark water. The ropes around her wrists, fastened tightly. One of the others stooped to wrap another line around her thin ankles. She giggled, under the influence of a narcotic and unaware. Then a hand lurched out and shoved her over the concrete edge, her body hitting the surface of the lake with a sudden splash. They stood watching her thrash against the depth, her voice struggling as the water rushed to fill her open mouth. She sputtered and writhed, freeing her legs and kicking hard to stay afloat.

"She's floating," one hissed.

"I think... she's trying to keep from going under..." another one whispered, barely audible.

The girl's eyes darted back and forth to the faces, hidden by dark hoodies, a low-set brim on a hat. They stared, not moving, not breathing.

"Help..." her voice croaked out a weak plea.

One of the figures grabbed a long metal pole resting against the storage shed. The pole extended into the water, tapping against the girl's chest. She smiled in relief and tried to grab onto it with her tied hands. But the pole dug into her breastbone and pushed her under, holding her there. The water moved furiously for several minutes. And then it was still. The group stood on the concrete dam, in silence or shock. No one spoke. They waited. The surface of the water was like black glass. The girl was gone.

ONE

Emily drove the winding curves of California Highway 18 that headed up to the picturesque town of Lake Arrowhead, nestled in the mountains above San Bernardino. In the passenger seat, her father, Michael, gazed out the window, a contented smile on his face. He'd been looking forward to this trip for months. Now that she'd been placed on disciplinary review by the FBI, following the Josie Vance kidnapping case, she had time for this type of trip.

Her superiors at the FBI in Los Angeles would take several weeks to decide if her break with protocol was worth losing her job as the head of the CARD team. Child Abduction Rapid Deployment had been her specialty at the Bureau, her success and commitment informed by the fact that she was a kidnapping survivor, having been taken by a child predator and held for five years. When Josie Vance was taken by the same man who'd abducted Emily years earlier, she was the only one to figure it out and defied orders to pursue him and bring the little girl home safely.

Lake Arrowhead was just a few miles from Arrowbear, where only months ago Emily had faced down James Tibbs, the man who'd kidnapped her as a child. The confrontation had ended with Tibbs dead and Emily finally free of the shadow that had haunted her for decades. As she drove, following the rhythm of the winding road, she took deep breaths, as if testing what it felt like to no longer carry that weight. Without the secrets, the constant drive to prove herself worthy, who might she now become? For the first time, she allowed herself to believe that she didn't have to work tirelessly to earn every good thing in her life.

Her husband, Antonio, had been her rock; he'd stood by her through the revelations about her true identity, the demons brought up by the Vance kidnapping, and they had emerged stronger for it. They had survived what would have capsized many marriages. Now that he was off for a family reunion with their twin daughters in Arizona, it was the perfect time for a little father-daughter trip.

Emily gazed out the window at the passing landscape, seeing the Strawberry Peak lookout tower that she and her father had hiked to countless times during summer breaks to take in the stunning view of the valley below. She smiled at the thought of the lazy afternoons they'd spent fishing for trout in the secret spots that only locals knew about. They'd hiked the backcountry for hours, her father pointing out the rock formations that had stood for thousands of years. She could almost smell the sage that turned pale purple at dusk.

On the fourth of July, they'd floated out to the middle of the lake in a big pontoon boat, watching multi-colored explosions of light in the sky. Now it was one of the few concrete memories Michael retained as early onset dementia claimed more and more of his brain. He'd honeymooned there with his wife, Andrea, and could remember what they ate the first night they arrived. But he couldn't remember his attendant's name at the El Sol memory care facility if she was out of sight.

The road steepened as they neared Lake Arrowhead. Bright

yellow Scotch broom burst from crevices in the rocky hillsides, while fragile Indian paintbrush stood tall and spindly, their deep orange petals catching the sunlight. Emily eyed the massive chain-link fencing that covered the rock face beside them—the only barrier between drivers and potential deadly rockslides. The highway narrowed to just two lanes with no divider, hugging curves that dropped straight into nothingness beyond the guardrail. Not a route for nervous drivers. But with each switchback conquered, with each mile gained in elevation, Emily felt the weight of the world below lifting. Up here, above the clouds that blanketed the valley, everything felt cleaner, lighter—as if they'd ascended beyond their troubles.

She wouldn't have to spend a moment plotting to find a missing child or face a distraught family with an update that the investigation was not moving fast enough for them. Or worse, delivering the news from which they would never recover. There would be no tragic disappearances, no heart-stopping loss of a young, promising life.

But then she met fifteen-year-old Lillian Knox. And discovered she was wrong.

TWO

Emily and Michael arrived at their rental house, a beautiful French country–style chateau, aptly named the Maison du Lac. The rental had been arranged by Savannah Granville—once Savannah Pratt, a girl Emily had befriended during those teenage summers at the lake. The property sat within a gated area called the Old North Road Estates, off one of the main highways that ran through Lake Arrowhead. Adjacent to the small marina, with boats bobbing in the sunlight, the Maison was just a short walk from the lake's edge.

Michael stepped out of the car. "Wow! Is this place really ours?" he asked.

"For the next ten days!" Emily replied, unloading their duffel bags.

Inside they found big, soft couches covered in patterned chintz, the fresh flowers overflowing in vintage crystal vases. A floor-to-ceiling pine bookcase was built into the wall, filled with a wide array of books to fill the lazy days of summer. Emily found a bedroom for Michael with a small balcony that over-looked the lake and put her bags in the room next door.

"Are you hungry, Dad? I can make you a grilled cheese sandwich," Emily asked.

"No, honey. I think I'll lay down for a bit. I didn't sleep too well last night," he said.

She helped him into a pair of pajamas and settled him under a big, white coverlet. He needed extra naps lately and any change in his routine taxed his brain and sometimes caused anxiety. Emily had arranged for an in-home caregiver to be there every day to help out, and to handle the cooking since that was not in her skill set. She could go face to face with a serial killer and take him down, but an omelet always became a blackened catastrophe. She had hired a woman recommended by the long-term care facility at the small community hospital, Lynne Smenck, who had experience with dementia patients and Michael's dietary restrictions.

Back in the day, Emily and Savannah Granville became fast friends. Vannah was always up for a hike to the Pinnacles or water skiing; they'd gone to the local Blue Jay Cinema to see every new movie, eating stale popcorn and slurping giant Cokes in the back row. Emily remembered her as a smart, willful teenager full of energy and ready for any adventure. Now, she was married with four children. She had never left the mountain and married a local boy right after high school.

The whole trip seemed like a page out of small-town life, and Emily looked forward to the slow pace of a mountain getaway. After unpacking their belongings, Emily scanned the Maison du Lac and found seven small, hidden cameras. A habit from her FBI work, where she'd discovered how disturbingly common they were in vacation rentals despite being illegal in California. She located the WIFI router, turned it off and put the cameras in a Ziplock bag, stored them under the mattress in a guest room and turned the WIFI back on.

She slipped out the front door and walked a winding path

to the lake's edge. The garden was filled with mountain laurel and lilac, and blue vinca flowers spread out like a magic carpet. Emily stopped and turned around, sensing something or someone behind her. She saw nothing, just the mustard flowers swaying on their delicate stems. The area was known for mountain lions and bears at this time of year, but she doubted one of those apex predators would be following her in broad daylight.

The house came with its own private dock where a small metal rowboat bobbed gently against the moorings. Emily peered inside a weathered storage bin nearby and discovered several kayaks and colorful inner tubes tucked away for guests' use. She walked to the end of the dock and sat, letting her legs dangle over the edge. The sunlight danced across the water's surface, creating patterns of light that seemed to shift with each gentle ripple. As she gazed out across the expanse of the lake, Emily felt the tightness in her shoulders begin to release, the knots of tension from months of work slowly dissolving in the mountain air.

As she headed back, she saw the neighboring house, a looming modern structure with enormous windows and a large wraparound deck. A teenaged girl stood watching her, her thick dark hair falling past her shoulders. Beside her was a gray-haired woman, holding the deck for support. Emily smiled and waved; the girl seemed stunned and nodded in greeting before leading the elderly woman inside.

Lynne Smenck was scheduled to arrive at twelve thirty, so Emily prepared Michael's list of medications, diet plan and his daily schedule for her to follow. She texted Antonio to let him know they had made it safely and he sent back a video of the twins singing "Happy" by Pharrell Williams, outside a Burger King. Emily laughed; they loved eating forbidden junk food on a road trip.

Michael emerged, rested and relaxed. Emily prepared him a quick lunch then, precisely at twelve thirty, the doorbell rang.

She was surprised, expecting Lynne to buzz them from the electric gate outside on the highway.

Emily opened the door, and a woman with iron-gray hair and reading glasses dangling from a beaded chain around her neck stepped in. She offered a warm smile that didn't quite reach her eyes as she extended her hand.

"Mrs. Ray? I'm Lynne Smenck," she said, her grip surprisingly firm.

Emily tilted her head slightly. "Pleasure to meet you. How did you get through the security gate?"

"Oh, I've lived here long enough to know all the codes for all the gates." Lynne waved her hand dismissively and gave a little conspiratorial wink. "It's part of being a local!"

Emily's FBI instincts flickered briefly—unauthorized access to gated communities was a security concern—but she pushed the thought aside. "This is my father, Michael Ray."

He looked up and waved from his spot at the table in the breakfast nook. Lynne went over to him and shook his hand, careful not to stand too close to him, and speaking in a quiet, even tone. He seemed easy and comfortable with her, which was a huge relief. They spent the next half hour making small talk and when Michael seemed relaxed enough, Emily said, "I have to run to the store, I forgot your favorite coffee creamer. Will you be okay alone here?" He gave her a smile and a thumbs up.

"Oh sure, we'll be just fine. Maybe we'll take a walk to the lake in a bit," Lynne said.

Emily headed out, eager to do a bit of exploring of her old teenage haunts. As she drove toward the Village, the commercial hub of the town, she saw a public memorial next to tiny Papoose Lake. It was a tributary of the larger Lake Arrowhead, surrounded by a chain-link fence and not open to visitors. There were photos and messages, votive candles, a teddy bear affixed to the metal wires. She wondered if perhaps a child had drowned.

Once she arrived at the Village, she wandered around the two-level commercial zone. She remembered a thriving shopping area but now, most of the stores were empty. Old signs for previous businesses had been left hanging: Tasty Bean Thai Restaurant, Little Tykes Toy Store, Ava's Attic. She felt a melancholy pang when she saw that the small amusement area, Candy Cane Park, with its bumper cars and go-karts had been closed and dismantled.

On the second level, she picked up her dad's coffee creamer in the supermarket and as she was checking out, she saw the dark-haired girl from the house next door buying multiple cans of Beefaroni and instant ramen. The young girl locked eyes with Emily for a moment then looked away, hurrying outside with her bag of groceries. As Emily walked to her car, she saw the girl working on her phone, in frustration. She looked up, scanning the area nervously, as if she expected something bad to happen at any moment.

Emily approached her casually. "Aren't you my neighbor over on Old North Road? I'm staying at the vacation rental with my dad. I think I saw you earlier on your deck?"

"Oh, yeah... I saw you," she said, distractedly.

"I'm Emily."

"I'm... uh... Lillian," she said, grabbing Emily's hand and quickly letting go. Her phone pinged, she received a message and scowled.

"I hate this shitty town... we don't even have a decent Uber..." she muttered.

"Do you need a ride?"

"No, that's okay," she said quickly, "I'll get an Uber in a little while. It always takes time up here."

A pickup truck pulled into the parking lot with a group of

teenaged boys in the open bed. When they saw Lillian, they began to hoot and gesture at her, suggestively.

"Hey, nutcase! Cast any spells on anyone lately?" one boy shouted.

"Want to go for a swim in Papoose Lake?" another one taunted her.

At this, they laughed and a few of them made low, rumbling sounds, challenging her to react. They appeared drunk and clearly underage. Emily saw a Sheriff's Deputy in his white SUV a few spaces away, but he didn't pay any attention to the boys. Lillian's shoulders tightened up and she looked at her slip-on sneakers, keeping her head down. The boys clambered out of the truck and moved in toward her. Emily stepped closer, instinctively protective.

"You sure you don't want that ride? You're safe with me. I work in federal law enforcement."

"For real?" she asked, her eyes widening. "That's cool," Lillian's posture relaxed slightly as she tucked a strand of dark hair behind her ear. She glanced over her shoulder at the boys, then leaned closer to Emily. "I need to talk to you about something."

They walked to Emily's car and the girl climbed quickly into the passenger seat. Emily watched the boys disperse and retreat toward the market as they realized Lillian was no longer an easy target. She held her bag of canned pasta and ramen between her knees and crossed her arms over her torso awkwardly.

"So, do you live here full-time or are you on vacation like we are?" Emily asked.

"Full-timer, unfortunately. This town is a hellhole, I can't wait to get out," she said.

"A hellhole?" Emily asked, surprised. Half an hour earlier she had considered it a paradise.

"It's just... the people who live here. You guys are flatlanders, so it's just a pretty vacation spot to you. But it's different when you live here," she said. Her shoulders hunched slightly, as though carrying an invisible weight. "Everything looks nice on the surface, but underneath..."

"Flatlanders? Is that what we're called?"

"Yeah, but without tourists this stupid town can't survive. They should be happy that anyone comes up here to spend money," she said, staring out the window, avoiding eye contact.

"I noticed that the village is pretty empty. I came up here when I was a teenager, and it was really busy. I used to ride the bumper cars in Candy Cane Park," Emily said.

"Yeah, that's been gone a long time. If you came as a teenager that was like a million years ago. It's not the same place it was," she said sadly. Emily winced inwardly at the "million years ago" remark; at thirty-eight she guessed her teenage years were like the late Jurassic era to Lillian.

She continued, "It was cool when I was little, I guess. But once everyone started getting older, they became assholes. And the grown-ups are worse than the kids..." Her voice trailed off.

Emily knew that being a teen in a small, insular town had to be hard, with everyone knowing your business. And kids always draw lines, it's easy to end up on the wrong side of the social divide. She glanced at Lillian, who kept her eyes glued to the window. She was an odd one. She wore all black; a loose, flowing shirt decorated with safety pins across carefully placed tears in the fabric with leggings featuring the same deliberate rips at the knees. Her black slip-on sneakers were tattered and had been colored with markers. On her wrists she had a cluster of woven bracelets; her nails were bitten short but painted purple. She was remarkably pretty, with a tumble of dark hair, streaked midnight blue, and fair, luminous skin.

"How old are you?" Emily asked.

"Fifteen. But I feel a lot older than that," Lillian said, half to herself.

As they passed Papoose Lake, Lillian sat up in her seat, straining to see the memorial items left at the fence.

"I saw that on my way to the store. I guess someone had an accident or something?" Emily asked.

Lillian nodded. "It happened last month. It was my best friend, but it wasn't an accident," she said quietly.

"Oh, I'm sorry to hear that. Was she your age?"

"Yeah. Her name was Hayley Hope."

THREE

Emily pulled into the big turn-out next to the gates for Old North Shore Road and put the car in park, the engine idling. Lillian stared at her with youthful intensity, as if Emily might be able to fix everything. Emily knew what it was like to be fifteen and adrift, grasping onto anything or anyone who could keep her from going under.

"What happened, Lillian?" Emily asked gently.

"It was Hayley." Lillian's voice cracked as she spoke her friend's name. "They say it was a suicide, but she didn't kill herself." She leaned forward, eyes suddenly intense and pleading. "They found her floating in Papoose Lake. They covered it up. I keep telling everyone, but no one listens." She slumped back. "They act like I'm nuts," she said.

"Who are 'they'?"

Lillian paused, uncertain about talking more. Emily saw the doubt and fear in her eyes.

"You said you're in federal law enforcement?" Lillian asked, tentatively.

"Yes. The FBI. You can google me if you want to confirm it. My full name is Emily Ray."

This information seemed to reassure her; the defensive set of her shoulders relaxed.

"It's just..." Lillian's voice hardened with conviction. "She didn't kill herself. She had plans—real plan. She was going to get out of here." Her eyes lit up momentarily. "She wanted to go to college, and she was going to direct movies. She talked about it all the time." Lillian shook her head firmly. "And she wasn't depressed or on drugs or anything. That's just what they want people to think."

"Who do you think killed her and who do you think covered it up?" Emily persisted, studying Lillian's face carefully. She needed to determine if the girl had valid suspicions or if these were just the desperate imaginings of a grieving teenager unable to accept a tragic reality.

A big Chevy Suburban pulled into the turn-out and the driver rolled the window down.

"Emily? Emily Ray? It's me, Savannah!" the driver shouted, excitedly. It was Savannah Granville—Emily's former summer friend who had arranged their lake house rental. She had three children of varying ages in the backseat of her large SUV.

When Lillian saw her, she visibly recoiled, shrinking down into her seat and turning away, as though trying to make herself invisible.

"Did you get checked in and settled?" Savannah asked, climbing down from the big SUV. When she came around the hood, Emily saw she was heavily pregnant.

"Yes, the caregiver is there with my dad. Everything's great. Look at you! How many is this?"

"Numbers five and six. Twins again! You just call me if you need anything. My mother-in-law owns the property management business, but I help sometimes, so consider me a special concierge service for your trip," she said, with a girlish, upturned cadence to her voice.

"You look pretty busy there," Emily said with a nod to the kids in the car.

"Oh, you know, it's mom life! I was passing by on my way home to make my husband's lunch so I'm glad I ran into you," she said.

Emily turned to introduce Lillian, but she was gone.

"I gave a neighbor's kid a ride home from the store, but she got out, I guess," Emily said.

"She probably took the stairway down. You know how teens are! My Bella is a handful," she said with a little laugh.

"Well, my girls are still in elementary school so we're not there yet."

"Get ready for the drama, the meltdowns, the push and pull. But worth every minute. Boys are so much easier!" Vannah said, with a grin at a bored teenage girl in the backseat, whose response was to roll up the window. "Let's make a plan to meet up, soon! I can't wait to see your dad again!"

"Absolutely, I'll call you tomorrow."

Emily looked around for Lillian, but she was nowhere to be found. Back at the house, she found Michael and Lynne working on a puzzle at the big kitchen table. It bothered her that Lillian had vanished so easily and silently. She wondered if the girl had developed that skill out of necessity.

"Do you know the girl who lives next door? Lillian?" Emily asked.

"Yes. Lillian Knox. She lives in that big house with just her grandma who's not in good health these days. That's what I hear. She's a troubled girl," Lynne said, shaking her head.

"She lives by herself with her grandma? There's no one else there?" Emily asked. The older woman she saw on the deck earlier didn't seem hearty enough to take care of a teenager.

"Well, her parents travel a lot. They're photographers for some big magazine or something. There's a Mexican lady who comes by to clean, but that's it. At least that's what people say."

Emily recalled Lillian buying Beefaroni and instant ramen noodles at the store. Michael and Lynne were engrossed in the puzzle, so she headed for her bedroom, settled at the antique desk by the window and fired up her laptop, searching for "Hayley Hope."

She found a mention in *The Mountain News*, the local newspaper. It was filled with fluff pieces extolling the fabulous amenities and thriving mountain communities, no mention of the vacant storefronts and failed businesses in the Village. There was a brief article about Hayley Hope with what must have been a school photo of her. Emily zoomed in on it; she was a beautiful girl with wavy, blond hair and a big smile. The article described her as a suicide victim and a freshman at Rim of the World High School, where she was in the Media class. There were scant details, just the basic facts that she was found in Papoose Lake—there was no funeral service listed. She was buried at Mt View Cemetery in San Bernardino and was survived by her divorced parents, Dina and Ryan Hope. She ran a background check on Dina and Ryan; they both had multiple arrests for drug offenses and domestic violence.

Emily then searched for the surname "Knox" in Lake Arrowhead and found Lillian's parents. They were indeed professional photographers who worked for major magazines, including *National Geographic*. Their professional bios claimed that they regularly went on photo safaris and shot major photographic exposés all over the world. There was no mention of a daughter. A fifteen-year-old alone at home without adequate supervision was a situation for Child Protective Services. But Emily's own experiences in the system flashed through her mind—the overcrowded homes, the overworked caseworkers, the children who sometimes ended up in worse situations than they'd started in. No, Emily decided she would not make that call until she understood the whole truth of Lillian's circumstances. Sometimes well-intentioned interventions could do more harm than good.

She felt suddenly tired, the altitude and thinner mountain air sapping her energy. Collapsing onto the bed, Emily pulled the muslin summer coverlet over her body. Despite her exhaustion, sleep remained elusive as Hayley Hope's smiling image lingered in her mind. The arrest records painted a clear picture: Hayley hadn't enjoyed an easy home life.

Being on leave from the CARD team didn't magically shut down Emily's investigative instincts. Her brain refused to power down like a computer with the flick of a switch. For years, protecting vulnerable children had defined her mission, her purpose—walking away from that intensity wasn't simple. Antonio would likely chide her if he knew her thoughts, reminding her about getting too easily triggered, becoming too deeply entangled in situations involving at-risk kids. This vacation was supposed to be about unwinding, stepping back from the high-pressure life she'd created for herself. But old habits die hard.

Abandoning her plan to take a nap, Emily found Michael downstairs in the den watching television with Lynne. He was laughing and calm, which meant the transition to a different space wasn't triggering any major confusion or stress for him, so far.

"I'm going to take a short hike," Emily said, feeling that old familiar restlessness creeping over her. She had to exercise and recalibrate.

"Oh, you should take the path that leads toward Tavern Bay. It's lovely and you'll end up at the beach club," Lynne advised.

Emily remembered Tavern Bay, one of the handful of beach clubs that the Arrowhead Lake Association maintained for people who lived in the areas that had lake rights. People who lived outside those boundaries were not permitted, unless they were guests of card-carrying members. Emily remembered how important those distinctions were to young Vannah Pratt, how it made her group of friends feel special and superior.

The whole thing had always baffled Emily. Lake Arrowhead was the size of a quarter, and it certainly wasn't considered exclusive by anyone in the sprawling cities down the hill. But in small towns small things become important.

Emily slipped on a fanny pack for her phone and earbuds, heading for the hiking trail, but she didn't go towards Tavern Bay. She circled back towards the marina and Papoose Lake. As she passed Lillian's house, she saw her. Lillian wore a pair of big, over-ear headphones and was waving a smudge stick around the room, leaving a trail of smoke. Emily would stop by and speak to her on her way back.

The marina was dotted with boats; many had been taken from their slips for winter storage. She walked along the steep road toward MacKay Park, to the fence that ringed Papoose Lake. It was on the east side of Lake Arrowhead, formed by a concrete dam. There was no swimming allowed, access was restricted and the gate to enter was secured with a heavy padlock. The fence was high with circular razor barbed wire along the top.

She lingered, looking at the collection of messages left on the fence. Most were handwritten outpourings of grief or guilt or both. Several bouquets of dried wildflowers were attached to the chain link; the stuffed teddy bear she had seen from the road hung limply by one sad arm. The smiling photos of Hayley were faded from the sun. She had been at enough crime scenes involving water to know what it must've been like, the day they pulled her body out. A cluster of police cars, a coroner's tent, large tarps blocking any public view. The somber officers and sheriffs, not knowing where to look as a distended, unrecognizable pulp of a young woman was brought to shore. Water deaths were horrible, on par with shotgun blasts.

These impromptu memorials always affected Emily more than the organized rituals of loss after a death. They had the raw, un-curated sense of sorrow felt by the community. Several of the religious candles had tipped over and she knelt to straighten them. As she stood up, she saw a Sheriff's white SUV idling by the entrance to the marina, the driver watching her. She stepped off the concrete and headed down the incline toward MacKay Road, where she was no longer visible.

From the road, she looked back at the tall fence around Papoose Lake. The circular barbed wire was sharp and forbidding. It could shear the skin off any part of a body that brushed against it. How did Hayley Hope get over it to drown herself?

FOUR

Lillian Knox stood by the window, looking at the Maison du Lac across the way from her house. The new visitor seemed nice enough—she'd protected her from Danny Granville and his friends in the Village. But she regretted confiding in Emily Ray, once she saw that she was close friends with Vannah Granville. She did her best to keep her distance from the Granvilles as much as she could. But even though she tried to stay away from them, they didn't stop bothering her. She knew they came around her house, moving things on the deck to freak her out. They'd scared her grandmother once and then she was upset all day.

Lillian had left a few messages for her parents, but it would be several days before they responded. They were in a remote village in Africa for *National Geographic*, and they were obsessive about work when they were on assignment. When she was younger, she liked that they had confidence in her and left her alone with just her grandmother. She felt very grown-up, but now the situation was different. Grandma Evelyn's confusion had gotten much worse, and she needed help with most things. Lillian knew that her parents were unaware of the decline; they still thought of her as the sprightly, sharp-as-a-tack school-teacher she had once been.

But Evelyn couldn't work the stove most days, she left the burners on, and Lillian had to disconnect the gas line if she was gone for any length of time. Evelyn needed help getting dressed and she didn't remember where things went in the house. Now, it was Lillian who had to take care of her, not the other way around. As long as she didn't wander away from the house or go too near the lake, it was fine. The housekeeper, Adriana, came once a week and cleaned up, delivering prepared meals in Tupperware, but most of the time both Lillian and Evelyn ate ramen noodles for dinner.

Life before Hayley's death held a different rhythm. Back then, Hayley would come over frequently to hang out and spend the night, escaping her mother's drug problems for a few precious hours. Those evenings became sacred rituals—Evelyn tucked safely in bed, the big house transformed into their private sanctuary.

Together, they'd explore the witchy practices they discovered online, debating which special powers they might cultivate. Candles would flicker as they danced in circles to haunting, rhythmic music. Most importantly, they created art together. Hayley directed their short films while Lillian assisted, learning from her friend's natural talent.

Hayley had the creative vision, the big ideas, the stories worth telling, the stories to tell. Lillian marveled at her friend's boundless imagination. Some films provoked laughter, others brought tears and some told stories that needed to be told, like her short film about Eddie March.

Now in the big, quiet house, Lillian connected her small projector to her phone, accessing the precious archive of Hayley's movies. This had become her therapy, her connection to what she'd lost. As Hayley's smiling face filled the blank living room wall, Lillian sat cross-legged on the floor, momentarily transported back to happier times.

She laughed as she watched the film called *Giving it Up*, about a girl determined to lose her virginity to her timid boyfriend. She recalled shooting those scenes with Manuel Heredia, and how embarrassed he had been, but Hayley helped him relax and act natural. The memory twisted into grief as she wondered if Hayley had managed to submit any of her work to the film festivals they'd researched together, before everything shattered.

Since Hayley's death, Lillian's world had become so small. Without her fearless best friend to defend her, Danny and Bella Granville, and their group, made school a nightmare. They targeted anyone who was different.

"Weak, stupid cowards," Hayley used to call them. Lillian clung to those words like an invisible armor.

There was a sudden knock at the door and Lillian froze. She feared it was the same kids who found every opportunity to mess with her. Afraid they would upset her grandma, she peeked through the side window and saw it was Emily Ray. She exhaled in relief, but she was still wary. She cracked open the door a few inches, blocking entry with her body.

"Hi! You disappeared earlier," Emily said, noting how Lillian kept one hand firmly on the doorframe, ready to close it at any second.

"Yeah, I had to get home," Lillian replied, her gaze fixed on a point somewhere over Emily's shoulder, refusing eye contact.

"I walked over to Papoose Lake to see the memorials left for Hayley," Emily offered gently.

Lillian's posture stiffened, her head snapping up. "How do you know Mrs. Granville?" she asked abruptly.

"I knew her when we were teenagers. I was going to introduce you but then I realized you probably know each other."

"Yeah, her daughter is in my grade at school. She's on the

junior cheer team. She's a bitch," Lillian said, defiantly, watching for a reaction.

Emily smiled and said, "Most of the girls on my high school cheer team were bitches, too."

Lillian leaned into the doorjamb, relaxing a bit.

"I thought you would've been the head cheerleader," she said.

"Don't let the blond hair fool you. I was a total outsider; I didn't fit in at all," Emily said, remembering how at Palos Verdes High School, she was like a strange zoo animal—the girl who had been held captive for years and had to be crazy. She never forgot the way the school moms stared from their Lexus SUVs in the pick-up line and looked away when she met their eyes.

"Huh. I guess you never can tell," Lillian said. They stood there for a moment, each wanting to say more.

"You want to tell me more about what was going on with Hayley?" Emily asked.

Lillian shrugged and asked, "Are you good friends with the Granvilles?"

Emily could see she was wary; her demeanor was stoic and inscrutable. Most teens wear their emotions like an LED light display, showing everything in high-definition color, moving fast and furious over the rough terrain of adolescence. Lillian was aloof, guarded. She reminded Emily of herself at that age.

"I'm not super close to them, I've never even met her husband. I just knew her years ago when I used to come up here in the summers with my dad. He's here but he's in mid-stage dementia so we have a local caregiver," Emily explained.

"My grandma might be getting something like that. Or she might just be old. She's kinda confused," Lillian said.

"Was that the lady I saw earlier on your deck?"

"Yeah. She likes to look at the water and I was feeding my crows," Lillian explained.

"You keep crows?" Emily asked, surprised and impressed.

"Yeah, it's pretty easy to train them," Lillian said. "You want a glass of water? Or a Coke?"

Emily recognized this small confidence from Lillian as an opening she couldn't afford to miss. "Sure, I'll have a Coke," she said with a gentle smile. "Can I come in?"

Lillian stepped away and Emily followed her into the house.

It looked like a page from a magazine. Expensive designer furniture and big art canvases. The house was clean but messy, with Lillian's clothes and books scattered about. On one wall, a collection of stunning photographs hung, all with mismatched, gilded frames. Hayley's video projected as if she were in the room with them.

"Is that Hayley?" Emily asked.

Lillian nodded. "Yeah. It's one of her films that we shot. I like to watch them sometimes." She muted the sound, which made Hayley's presence seem otherworldly, smiling and moving on the wall. Emily leaned in to look at the photos.

Lillian gestured to them nonchalantly. "Those are my parents' photos. They're photographers for *National Geographic*. They're in Africa right now," she said.

"Wow! These are incredible. How long have they been gone?" Emily asked.

"They'll be back soon. There's a lady who comes in every day to check up on us. Her name is Adriana, she cooks and cleans and does the grocery shopping, and the laundry," Lillian replied.

Emily could see that this was obviously a well-practiced response; Lillian didn't want people to know she was on her own with her elderly, impaired grandparent. But that kind of thing is hard to hide in a small town and Emily had seen her grocery purchases. It was clear that Lillian carried the adult responsibilities at home.

In one corner of the large living room, Emily noticed a small altar to Hayley. It was made of plywood, balanced on cinder blocks and covered with purple velvet. On it, Lillian had placed photos of them together, with crystals and candles, a red-tailed hawk feather, and other knick-knacks that held special meaning to her. On the coffee table, amid photography books, Emily saw paperbacks: *A Teenager's Book of Spells*, *An Introduction to Wicca*, *The Witch and Her Familiar*.

Emily picked up a photo of Lillian and Hayley dressed in black, flowing dresses with flower crowns in their hair.

"You two look like Stevie Nicks," she said.

Lillian looked at her blankly. "Who's that?"

Feeling about two hundred years old, Emily replied, "She's a rock star who has kind of a witchy persona on stage. I like your altar."

Lillian stared at her for a beat, caution and surprise colliding. "Really? Everyone else calls me a freak for having it."

"No, it's nice. It's good to have rituals when we lose someone or go through a big life change. It's easier to get through, somehow," Emily assured her.

Lillian's face lit up at this morsel of approval and she suddenly looked younger than fifteen. It hurt Emily to see how desperate she was for validation.

"Were you two doing a little witchcraft?" Emily asked, knowing that a lot of kids at that age had wish fulfillment fantasies of having special powers.

"Not seriously. It was just our thing, you know? We liked feeling different from the other kids. Nothing scary like black magic or anything. And sometimes Hayley played that role to get bullies to back off. She'd say she was gonna put the evil eye on them. We were just doing different stuff since everyone up here is a religious nut."

Emily's attention shifted to a state-of-the-art security system by the front door.

"Do you use this? Since you're alone a lot?" she asked.

Lillian shook her head. "No, my parents want me to, but it broke, so now I just skip it. Let me get your Coke."

Lillian disappeared into the kitchen and returned with a cold can of soda.

"You were talking about religious nuts. I've noticed there are a lot more churches now than when I used to visit," Emily said.

Lillian's expression soured. "That's a big thing in town. If you want to be in the cool group at school, you have to go to one of the hardcore churches. You've got to act all pure and take a pledge not to have sex or do drugs, even though they do all those things and lie about it. Hayley said it was like brainwashing from an early age. Everyone is super judgey and they treat you like trash if you're not part of it."

"And you and Hayley weren't part of it?"

"No way! My parents would freak out if they came home and found me at one of those church things. Hayley didn't go for it either. She was a good girl, so don't listen to what people say about her. Being into drugs and all that. She just got mixed up with some bad people."

"How do you mean?"

"She was shiny, you know? She had that spark that drew people to her. Even though her family was a clusterfuck, and they had no money or anything, she was special. We became best friends in third grade," Lillian said, wistfully.

"So, she was popular at school?"

"Yeah, everyone wanted to hang out with her or be like her until they got older and more jealous. The alpha girls, like Bella Granville and Maddie Marsden, the ones with dads who're cops or realtors."

"So, some of the girls were jealous of Hayley. And the boys?" Emily asked.

"The boys were a different problem..." Lillian replied, her voice faltering.

"Like the ones in the parking lot today?"

Lillian's cell phone rang, she looked at the screen anxiously, then slid it back into her pocket.

"Not just that..." she said, when her phone rang again. This time she looked at the screen, weighing whether to answer or not.

"Do you need to get that?"

"No, it's no one. The number is blocked, see? If it were someone in my contacts, their information would show. This is just one of those assholes from earlier."

"You mean that group of boys? The ones who looked drunk?"

"Yeah. They didn't just look drunk, they were. They call me all the time just to mess with me," Lillian said in frustration, trying to cover up her fear of them.

"Do they know where you live?"

"Sure, they do. Everyone knows everything here. They killed one of my crows and left it by the door."

"Did you report it to the police?"

She laughed. "To who? The cops? Danny Granville is the leader of that group and his dad's a deputy. You saw the cop in the parking lot at the market? He didn't do anything even though they were drunk off their butts. Some people in this town can get away with anything."

Suddenly, there was a loud banging on the front door. Lillian jumped and her grandmother, Evelyn, emerged from an upstairs bedroom in a pair of pajamas. She stood at the landing, looking over the rail.

"Is everything all right, Lilli?" she asked, nervously.

"It's fine, Grandma. This is my friend, Emily. She's staying next door in the fancy house."

Evelyn waved a bony hand at Emily. "Nice to meet you. Who's at the door?"

Lillian checked and saw a middle-aged woman.

"Lillian? Are you there?" she asked loudly, rapping her knuckles against the door.

Lillian rolled her eyes and said, "Ugh. It's Starhawk, she's a nutcase. I don't know why she's here!"

"Are you going to answer it?" Emily asked.

"I guess..."

Lillian opened the door but didn't move aside to welcome Starhawk. She stood in the doorway with her arms crossed. Starhawk was a heavyset, white woman who wore braided cornrows hanging down her back and multiple strands of turquoise, agate and other gemstones around her neck. She was dressed in a flowing tunic over paisley pajama pants.

"I just came by to see if you're going to the Artisan Faire this weekend, Lillian," she said, breathlessly.

"Hello, Mrs. Snyder," Lillian replied, with little enthusiasm.

"I'm Starhawk. I'm an energy worker," she said to Emily, extending her hand.

"Emily Ray."

"So, you two are hanging out?" Starhawk asked.

She stared at them, as if they owed her an explanation of what they were doing, standing too close, crossing the unspoken boundaries of personal space. She smelled of incense, marijuana and unwashed hair sebum. Emily took a step back.

"I'm visiting and Lillian is showing me around," she said.

"Really? Visiting from where?"

Lillian shifted uneasily under this questioning then said, abruptly, "She's from the city. Sorry but we're helping my grandma with something, okay?"

Starhawk smiled and stepped back. "Of course. Nice to see you. Give Evelyn my best!"

"Sure," Lillian said, shutting the door. "She's so weird, she doesn't even live over here."

"Is Starhawk her real name?"

Lillian rolled her eyes again. "What do you think? She's Sherry Snyder. Her daughter, Melora, grew up with us. Now, she calls herself Starhawk and she used to be kind of witchy, but now she says she's channeling the holy spirit, it's a Jesus thing. She's just a phony."

"In what way?"

"She takes in a bunch of foster kids, all with special needs so she doesn't have to work. She gets all this money for the kids, and she just sits around. We used to think she was cool, she gave us some crystals, but she turned out to be a big fake when Melora disappeared," she said bitterly.

"Her daughter disappeared?"

"Foster daughter," Lillian explained. "When Melora disappeared, Starhawk told the cops she ran away with some boyfriend, so they barely looked for her." She lowered her voice. "Melora had some developmental disabilities. She was really sweet, but she couldn't understand things sometimes and she didn't know how to interact socially very well. She definitely didn't have any boyfriend." Lillian shook her head in disgust. "Hayley and I knew Starhawk was lying. It was completely messed up. And guess what?"

"What?"

"She got a new foster kid right away to keep the cash coming in."

Before James Tibbs had taken her, Emily had cycled through multiple foster homes. She'd witnessed firsthand how many people entered the system solely for the monthly checks. A vulnerable teenager with intellectual disabilities and no strong family advocates made the perfect target—essentially invisible to the system designed to protect her.

"So, back to Hayley, you said the girls were jealous and the boys were what?"

"Hayley's mom, Dina, is a mess, right? She's a druggie. Her dad's not around. And the boys thought Hayley was... like, slutty or something, or she should be because of how her family is."

"That story is as old as time, unfortunately. When the boys are predatory—" Emily said, but Lillian cut her off.

"It wasn't just the boys, though..." Lillian began as Emily's cell phone rang. It was Lynne Smenck. Emily answered immediately.

"Hi, Emily, your dad is getting a little anxious. I wanted to know when you'll be back?" Lynne asked.

"I'll be right there, I'm just next door," Emily said, hanging up, turning back to Lillian. "But we should talk more about all of this. Maybe I can help you in some way," Emily offered.

"Really? I spoke to the deputy who came to our school after it happened, and he told me to get counseling and stop stirring up trouble," Lillian said.

"Will you be around later?"

"Sure. Here's my number, you can text me," Lillian said, taking Emily's phone and putting her number in.

Lillian stood on her deck, watching Emily hurry home through the trees. Their conversation replayed in her mind, bringing a knot of anxiety to her stomach. Had she revealed too much? Since Hayley's death, so many adults had told her to stop asking questions, to accept the official story, to keep quiet. Some had been gentle about it, others threatening. But the truth burned inside her like a hot coal she couldn't extinguish. It wasn't suicide. She knew it wasn't. And no matter how many times she was dismissed as a troublemaking teen, she would keep telling anyone who might listen—and even to those who refused to hear.

FIVE

Vannah Granville pulled the first batch of chocolate chip cookies from her oven, the delicious scent of freshly baked dough filling her big, sunny kitchen. She just had time to get the ground beef Tater Tot casserole for dinner prepared and put up before she paid a visit to Emily Ray and her dad at the Maison. She couldn't believe that they'd reconnected after so many years. As soon as she heard the name over the phone in the rental office that belonged to her mother-in-law, Dede Granville, Vannah remembered all the great times they'd had as teens during those lazy summer vacations. She'd spent an evening googling Emily Ray and sat stunned at her computer, scrolling through news articles about a decorated FBI agent who specialized in child abductions. The summer friend Vannah had described as "that nice girl from the city" had become something of a legend in law enforcement circles.

Back then, Emily had seemed like an exotic creature who'd flown in from another world. Now, she had a career as an FBI agent specializing in kidnappings and crimes against children. Just the thought of it made Vannah queasy. She knew it wasn't good for women to be involved in that type of demanding work.

It upset their feminine energy, throwing them out of balance. Her husband, Cody, said that a lot of those women had trouble having kids and had to go to specialists just to get pregnant, which is the easiest thing in the world for a woman to do, if her life was in balance with family, God and home.

Her circle of friends had known each other since childhood, attending church and school together, playing sports and eventually dating and marrying. They stayed in the same spot, the safe place where they knew everyone, and how everything worked. And their families were well respected, so most things were easy for them. Nothing ever happened that perturbed the calm, predictable waters of their lives. They married local boys, they worked for their parents or in-laws if they worked at all, since Pastor Jim Jenkins and their church looked down on that.

Every year the dogwoods bloomed at the same time; the boats came up the hill from storage down below to be loaded into their docks. The fireworks were set off from the same barge every Fourth of July, the Art and Wine Festival always featured the same artists, the Spring Home Tour rotated through the same selection of well-appointed houses. The first snow usually came by Thanksgiving; the local dance company staged *The Nutcracker* every Christmas, with the same costumes and cast, as the little girls who took lessons grew up and got bigger roles each year. Everyone knew what to expect. And everyone knew their place.

Except for the outsiders, the vacationers and the second-home buyers, who came from larger cities and expected the town to conform to their diverse and dangerous expectations. Vannah took a silicone spatula from a drawer and placed the warm cookies onto a cake plate. She didn't worry much about the visitors; they didn't have much impact on the town. But there were always some full-time families who just didn't fit in. Like Lillian Knox' s parents, whose lives were totally different from everyone else's. The fact that they traveled all the time and weren't involved in any church or school activities made it hard for them to fit in.

Not that they made much effort to. Vannah heard from the electrician who'd installed their security system that they had floor-to-ceiling shelves filled with books from every corner of the world and they had worked all over Africa and Europe as photographers. She couldn't even imagine how hard it would be to go to places where she didn't speak the language or know people to hang out with. She had no idea what type of food they ate in those distant places, but she knew she wouldn't like it.

And because her parents were so different, Lillian didn't really fit in with the other kids. She had been friends with Hayley Hope since elementary school and they were always misfits. Everyone knew Hayley's mom, Dina, since high school and she'd been into drugs as long as anyone could remember. Now she was just another mountain meth head, living in Crest Park and barely hanging on. It was little wonder that Hayley had run so wild.

Her mind flashed to Hayley Hope's smiling face, and she felt a shudder run up her spine. Her death had caused so much trouble—even Margery Miller, who ran the local newspaper, had held a meeting to discuss the impact Hayley's death could have on the town's image and real estate. No one wants to come to a place where a teenager drowned herself. But Margery didn't consider the bigger dangers that girls like Hayley and Lillian posed. All the furor over her death was starting to die down and Vannah was glad for it. The last thing Emily Ray needed on her vacation was to hear an earful from Lillian Knox about Hayley Hope.

Emily returned to the Maison and found Michael comfortably settled in front of the television while Lynne measured ingredients for brownies.

"I'm back," Emily called, hanging her jacket by the door. She studied her father's face, looking for signs of confusion or distress. "Everything okay, Dad?"

Lynne smiled as she mixed the sticky brownie batter. "He's better now. I think he was a little nervous without you here. He was telling me you work for the FBI? Is that true?"

"Yes, but I'm on leave from work right now," Emily replied.

"Do you solve murders like those shows on TV?"

"Occasionally, but the FBI is not how it seems on TV," Emily said with a laugh.

"It must be very stressful. How does your husband handle it?"

"Fine. He's an engineer, and quite busy with his work as well."

"That's lucky," Lynne remarked, her eyebrows lifting slightly. "I imagine it's not easy to find a man who can accept that type of thing in a wife."

"Well, I'm lucky. I found a good one," Emily said, keeping her tone neutral despite the outdated assumptions behind Lynne's comment.

She walked out onto the sunny patio and dialed Antonio. The call went straight to voicemail.

"Hey, it's me," she said, trying to sound casual. "Just checking in. Call me."

She stretched her arms and turned her face to the sun, letting the warmth seep into her skin. It felt indulgent to simply stand still, enjoying the moment without scanning for threats. She couldn't remember when she'd last existed without that constant vigilance—protecting her daughters, guarding her true identity, watching for the next crisis to upend her carefully constructed life.

Her therapist Lydia had spent years trying to help her dismantle this hyper-alert state. "You're carrying your past like armor," Lydia often said, "but armor gets heavy." Antonio had been pushing in the same direction, suggesting with increasing frequency that she reconsider her work with the FBI. "It's not healthy, Em," he'd said during their last argument. "You get too personally involved. Every case becomes about you, about what happened to you." Each time he brought it up, the tension between them thickened. That was partly what this vacation was about—space to evaluate what she truly wanted and whether she could become the person Antonio needed her to be.

Her phone pinged—it was a text from Vannah.

> I'm up the street, can I swing by and say hi to your dad?

> Sure, I'll buzz you in.

A few minutes later, Vannah was at the front door. Lynne had gone upstairs to prepare an afternoon bath for Michael who was still watching TV.

Vannah approached him and said, "I don't know if you remember me, Mr. Ray. I'm Savannah. Emily and I used to hang out when you came up in the summers."

"Savannah? You used to like to water ski," he said with a smile.

"That's me, although I stopped water skiing at baby number three. Are you both all settled in? Do you need anything?"

"No, we're fine," Emily said.

"Good. This area is very quiet, but there are a few oddballs, of course."

"You know Lillian Knox, right? I met her earlier today."

Vannah's face fell, and she shook her head. "I know Lillian Knox. She and Bella are in the same grade. She's a little crazy, makes up all kinds of wild stories, especially after her friend took her own life. She's been standing around town with these crazy signs, saying it was a cover-up. She lives in that big house all alone with her grandma. I don't think she has many friends."

Lillian hadn't mentioned any signs to Emily—it did sound a bit unhinged, and she could see why Lillian might be considered an oddball.

"Yeah, she mentioned that her best friend died recently. She drowned. Did you know Hayley Hope?" Emily asked.

"I knew her a little bit. She used to come to youth group at Church on the Hill with us sometimes. Not regular, she'd drop in for a few weeks, then we wouldn't see her.

"We tried to help her as much as we could through the group, but sometimes kids pull away. She and Lillian were into some scary stuff, it made people nervous. You know, witchcraft and things like that. And Lillian has all those animals that stick to her."

"She told me she trains crows," Emily said.

"Creepy, right? If there's a dog or cat out there, it finds Lillian Knox. She's kind of a weirdo!"

Emily thought of Lillian's altar with the crystals and hawk feathers, and the books about spells and witches.

Other people think I'm a freak for it...

"Lillian seemed lonely when I talked to her earlier. I gave her a ride home from the store, when some boys were bothering her," Emily said.

Vannah clucked her tongue in disapproval. "I'm sure she's lonely now. They were two peas in a pod but neither of them was involved in school or church or anything. They just kind of drifted, you know? I think that's how Hayley ended up on drugs."

Lillian's words hung in Emily's mind.

Hayley was a good girl, don't listen to what they say about her taking drugs and stuff...

"So, there's a big barbecue tomorrow right here at Peninsula Park, next to the marina. A whole bunch of people will be there, you and your dad should come. It'll be a great time," Vannah said brightly, changing the subject.

"That'd be nice, thank you. Did you hear that, Dad? We're going to a barbecue at the lake," Emily said. He smiled and nodded, then asked, "What can we bring?"

"Just yourselves," Vannah said, squeezing her arm. "I should go, I've got to pick Danny up from the skate park. Bella's at choir rehearsal, and the littles have a dentist appointment. I'm like an Uber driver!"

"I'll walk you out," Emily said.

As they headed toward the garages, Savannah slid an arm around Emily's shoulders. "This is gonna be just like old times. I'm so glad we reconnected!"

Emily nodded, returning Savannah's smile. Those fleeting summer friendships held a peculiar magic—brief connections forged outside the confines of regular life, preserved in memory with a golden glow that reality rarely matched. For a few weeks each summer, they'd created their own universe where they could reinvent themselves beneath the California sun. Emily thought of the long-ago revels at the Arrowhead beach clubs, the social distinctions that mattered so much to Savannah back then. She gathered that Hayley Hope, from the wrong side of the mountain, with the wrong type of parents and her oddball best friend, fell into that misfit group. The ones who didn't belong. The ones who were supposed to be easy and willing targets for the kids who held the carefully guarded social status. Some things were the same everywhere and they didn't change much over the years. The minefield of adolescence was one of them. She waved as Vannah pulled her big Chevy Suburban out of the driveway.

SIX

Emily fired up the barbecue on the deck as the sun went down, the silhouettes of the trees stark against the candy-colored sky. Michael looked out at the water, a few boats jetted back and forth, towing water skiers and wakeboarders. The steak and salmon sizzled on the grill, a platter of veggies roasting next to them. Lynne had gone home, the outside table was set, two cold Coronas were waiting in the ice chest. Emily walked to the edge of the dock and looked up to see Lillian on her deck, playing with a small black and white dog. Several crows perched on the railing, relaxed and watching.

Emily waved, calling out, "Lillian! Have you eaten dinner?"

Lillian nodded, and replied, "Thank you, but we're fine."

"Are you sure? We have steaks!" Emily offered, certain that a diet of ramen and Beefaroni left a lot to be desired. Lillian hesitated and then picked the little dog up under her arm. A few moments later, she was cutting across the walkway between their houses.

"Maybe I can come by for a little while..." Lillian said.

"Good. Does your grandma want to come?" Emily asked.

"She's asleep. She sleeps a lot lately," Lillian said.

"My dad does, too. Is that your dog?"

"I just found this little girl, running loose by the marina. She could get eaten by coyotes," she said.

"Come meet my dad and stay for dinner," Emily said, seeing the relief and expectation on the girl's face. When Michael saw the terrier, his face lit up.

"Look how cute she is! What's her name?" he asked, stroking her curly little head.

"The dog or the girl?" Emily asked, playfully.

"Both. I'm Michael Ray, Emily's father," he said, extending his hand to Lillian. Emily marveled how, in some moments, he could be so clear and focused, and in the next, confused and uncertain.

"I'm Lillian Knox," she said, "and I just found this dog. She doesn't have a name, yet."

"She looks like a Sammy to me. What do you think?" He turned to Emily, a huge grin spreading across his face.

She had considered getting him a small pet for company, they were allowed at El Sol. She'd been waiting for the right time but now it seemed the universe had made the decision for her.

"You're sure she doesn't belong to anyone in the area?" Emily asked. Michael now had Sammy seated on his lap.

"I've seen her for the past few days, running loose by the lake. No one has put up any signs or anything. I think she was dumped. That happens a lot up here," Lillian said.

"Do you want salmon or steak?" Emily asked. Lillian hesitated before answering. Emily sensed that she was afraid of asking for too much and realized she probably felt that way about a lot of things in life.

"I have plenty of both, we can't possibly eat them all," Emily said.

"Steak, please," she said.

"Watch the grill, I'll be right back."

Emily hurried up to the house as Lillian sat chatting with Michael, both fawning over the little dog. When she returned with the extra slab of rib eye, they were laughing easily together.

"Did you know Lillian is fifteen?" Michael asked.

"Yes, she told me," Emily replied.

He turned to Lillian. "You know, Emily came home when she was fifteen. She'd been gone for a long time and then she came back..."

His mind wandered and Lillian looked at Emily across the table, concerned.

"He's fine, just taking a trip down memory lane," Emily whispered.

"I read about you being kidnapped when you were little. I didn't want to say anything," Lillian said quietly.

"Don't worry about it. I'm fine, I survived," Emily said, immediately regretting her choice of words. Hayley Hope didn't survive.

Emily served the dinner and saw her father hesitate with his steak knife; small motor tasks were starting to confuse him. Lillian reached out and gently took the utensils from him.

"Would you like some help with that, Mr. Ray? This knife can be pretty tricky," she said.

"Thank you. You're quite a nice young lady. Your parents must be very proud of you," he said.

She looked embarrassed as she cut his steak into small pieces. "I guess so," she said with a shrug.

Michael grabbed the salt and began to shake it over his plate.

"Easy on the salt, Dad! You can't have too much, or you'll get a UTI, remember?" Emily warned. He'd battled recurring UTIs in recent months and his doctor had put him on a no salt diet.

"I just can't taste things like I used to," Michael complained. "Everything seems so bland."

"My grandma's exactly the same," Lillian said. "If I don't watch her, she dumps the entire saltshaker on her food."

The conversation flowed easily between them. Emily watched with quiet appreciation as Lillian guided Michael through dinner with intuitive patience, anticipating his needs without making him feel diminished. She carried herself with the steady calm of someone who'd shouldered adult responsibilities far too early.

As they finished their meal, Emily noticed a strange glow on the hillside above them. A moment later, Sammy began barking frantically, hackles raised. Through the trees, Emily spotted something rolling down the slope—something large and flaming.

"What the—" she began, rising from her chair.

A burning Coulter pinecone came crashing through the underbrush like a fiery meteorite, slamming into a nearby tree trunk and exploding into fragments. Sparks showered the dry vegetation around them, small flames immediately taking hold in the brushy undergrowth. "Grab the cooler!" Emily shouted, taking the pitcher of water and racing down the stairway to dump it onto the flames. Some of the sparks had caught the fallen branches; the fire was starting to spread.

"It's too heavy!" Lillian yelled as she struggled with the ice-filled cooler. Emily dashed back up the stairway to help her and together they carried the large cooler and poured its contents out onto the burning brush. They stomped the embers until everything was extinguished.

It had been a dry year, the trees and bushes creating perfect conditions for the flames to spread. Emily's heart pounded in her chest just imagining if it had turned into a real fire. Michael watched from the deck, clutching the little dog.

"What is it, Emily?" he shouted, nervously.

"It's nothing, don't worry, Dad. We've got it under control," she assured him.

She picked up a piece of the big, blackened cone and saw

gray fuzz tucked in between the scales. They were slippery, covered with some kind of greasy film.

"What the hell is this?" she asked.

"That's dryer lint, in the scales. It helps to ignite. And I think that's Vaseline on the outside of it," Lillian said. "You put them in your fireplace to make it burn quickly."

It hadn't fallen from a tree, packed with lint and Vaseline. Someone had lobbed it down the hillside, from the highway, intentionally. It had landed at the big cedar tree next to Lillian's house.

"This is really messed up. They haven't gone this far before," Lillian said, her voice shaking.

"You don't think it was intended for you?" Emily asked.

"Who else would it be for?" She looked nervously toward the road.

"It could be a firebug, they're always active in the summers. Let's not freak out. We'll finish cleaning up and figure it out," Emily said, to calm herself as well as Lillian.

She picked the cone up by a single scale to preserve any fingerprints, just in case, and put it gingerly inside the empty cooler. If the rowdy boys she saw earlier had tossed this incendiary device into a dry forest, this went beyond teen bullying. They ate dessert in the kitchen and Lynne's brownies and ice cream helped change the mood. When they had finished, Emily asked, "Daddy, will you be okay here for a few minutes? I'm going to walk Lillian home."

"I'll be fine, Sammy will keep me company. Take your time," he said. The little dog slept soundly in his lap. Emily saw that having her there helped him feel responsible and needed. He had lost those things since dementia had made his world so small.

They checked all the doors to the decks and the outside before leaving. Despite his assurances, Emily knew he might wander out and get lost at any moment. The moon had risen and there was a thin, orange ribbon of sunlight remaining on the horizon. The bats emerged from their roosts and began flitting like spirits across the sky as they walked toward Lillian's house.

"If you think that burning pinecone was intentional, you really should report it to the police," Emily said.

Lillian shook her head. "It will only make things worse than they already are."

"If the boys that harass you get cover from the police, it's still a good idea to have a report on file. It will show a pattern, a chain of incidents that they can't ignore if this continues."

Lillian stared at her, a look of defeat in her big, dark eyes, then said quietly, "You live in a big city, where people get in real trouble if they do bad things. It's not like that up here. If I say anything, it'll cause more trouble. But you could do it, right? If you ask questions, they can't just stonewall you, can they?"

Emily wanted to tell her that people do awful things in big cities all the time and get away with it. But Lillian had such faith in her ability to help, she didn't say anything.

"I think they know, that's what all of this is about. Coming by my house, the phone calls. They want to scare me," Lillian said quietly.

"Who are 'they'?" Emily asked again, sensing there was a whole range of things Lillian hadn't yet told her.

"I don't know exactly. But Hayley changed, she started hanging out with different people. She told me it was better if I didn't know who they were."

"Maybe an older boy? Did she have a new boyfriend?"

"No, she liked Manny Heredia since middle school. They dated a little, but Dina made it hard 'cause he's Mexican. Hayley would've told me if she had a real boyfriend. Whoever it was, something was off about it," Lillian insisted.

They arrived at the stairway that led up to Lillian's house and stood in the fading twilight for a moment, the crickets playing their nightly summer symphony.

After a beat, Emily said, "I lost my best friend when I was your age. She took her own life, and it was the hardest thing I ever went through. And I was never a popular kid at school. After my kidnapping, it was hard to fit in with any group. So, I know a bit about how you feel."

Lillian dug her hands into her pockets but said nothing. When she turned toward the moon, Emily saw that her eyes were filling with tears.

Emily continued, "I know you want to blame someone, but there may not be anyone to carry that load for you."

Her words hung in the darkness for a moment. In the distance, they heard the yipping of a coyote on the hunt. Lillian wiped her tears away and drew a beat-up Galaxy phone from her pocket and handed it to Emily.

"It's Hayley's. She hid it in her room, only I knew where it was. When they found her, I ran over there and got a box of her stuff 'cause I had a key. I haven't even looked at it, I was too afraid to. But she didn't kill herself. She kept everything on her phone, and they know that."

"How come you never gave this to the police?" Emily asked.

Lillian waited a moment before answering, gauging whether to reveal more. Without looking up she said, "Because I think they did something."

SEVEN

Danny Granville and his buddies drove too fast, making another loop around the lake. Billy Kupp handed him a joint and he took a hit before passing it to Billy's brother Clayton, who sat in the backseat. Danny loved days like these, the hot, lazy summer when he didn't have any pressures on him at all. No competitive sports with his dad shouting at the sidelines, no teachers giving too much homework. He could spend each day hanging with his buddies, smoking weed and getting someone's older brother to buy beer for them to drink on the docks.

Danny knew he could get away with practically anything on the mountain. His dad's position on the sheriff's force meant other deputies looked the other way when they caught him driving with a car full of other minors—technically illegal, but rules from "down the hill" didn't seem to apply up here above the clouds. The protective bubble extended to school, where Danny could fly a Confederate flag from his truck or wear clothing with messages that would get him suspended anywhere else. "You've got your rights," his father always reminded him. "Don't let anyone tell you different." When some kid had reported him to Principal McGannet last year, nothing came of it—which wasn't surprising considering she was married to his father's cousin.

They had just passed nutcase Lillian's house, and they'd tossed a lit-up widow-maker pinecone into her property, just to mess with her. He laughed to himself, thinking of her running around like an idiot, trying to put the flames out. His mom said it was no big deal to mess with her head, she was trouble for everyone. He hit the gas as they made the turn onto North Bay Road. The Rav4 fishtailed and crossed into the oncoming lane, barely missing a car. The other driver honked at him, but Danny flipped him off. He was probably a stupid flatlander anyway. He and his friends made fun of them, the city people who came up to the mountains and didn't understand how things worked. They walked at night, unaware that mountain lions roamed between houses or perched high in trees, weighing the difficulty of taking down a human being for dinner. Or that bears with cubs were to be avoided; they were not for snapping selfies with.

The Airbnb people were the worst, coming from Los Angeles or Palm Springs, expecting people to be okay with all kinds of crap like gay couples and Black guys married to white women. His grandma, Dede, had several vacation rentals and when she found out that the renters were Black or Asian, she'd cancel on them. It got on the news once and that caused a problem, so she had to pull her listings, but she put them back up a week later with a new name. From that point on, she and his mom were extra careful before they rented to anyone.

They passed Neveah Rylan's house; Billy Kupp had been hooking up with her at church for the past few weeks during Wednesday night Bible study. They met in the preschool building, telling the parents that they were cleaning it for the following day's classes, but they were doing it in the storage room. When Hayley Hope had been taking care of the littles on Wednesday nights, Danny hoped he could get her to do the same thing with him, but she refused. He'd even tried tricking her into doing it, but she figured it out.

Then she told his dad and that caused a whole shit storm of trouble. His dad had taken him to the basement and beat his ass with a belt, warning him to stay away from her. Hayley Hope was different from the other girls, everyone knew that. She didn't take any crap from anyone, and she stood up for the weirdos, like Lillian Knox and Eddie March. She even protected the retard, Melora Zane, when kids picked on her. But Hayley Hope was hot, all the guys knew it. She looked so cool in her boho hippie clothes, with that long, honey-blond hair spilling down her back. Danny thought her eyes were like green glass and her lashes were dark the way she wore that sexy makeup.

People said she was a witch, and she played along, for sure. Once, when they were messing with Melora, she told them she'd put the evil eye on them. They'd laughed but when he told his mom, she freaked out. Then Mark Miles slipped off that truck bed and was run over. The people at church said it was witchcraft, that Hayley did it. It was better that Hayley was gone; he didn't have to see her or feel the sting of her looking right through him every day at school. But he had seen and heard things the night she died, things that he preferred to forget. He started to have some bad dreams about it, but his mom said he just needed to pray about whatever was bothering him. When he did that, though, he felt worse, because he knew that what he'd seen wasn't stuff God would like. So, he had to keep secrets from everyone. Even God.

Emily sat watching a video on Hayley's phone. It was shot in semi-darkness; she recognized the big picture windows of Lillian's house. There were candles placed in a circle, the flickering light casting eerie shadows on the walls and the large photographs, whose images seemed to dance and shapeshift in the erratic illumination. Classical Baroque music played, and in the center of the circle, Hayley and Lillian danced.

Hayley wore a fitted, black velvet dress with long sleeves that extended over her fingers which were adorned with big silver rings. A red, transparent cloak fell from her slender shoulders as she moved and twirled in the candlelight. Lillian was in a dark sequined tunic worn over black leggings, her feet bare but decorated with silver chain anklets. Around her neck sat a jeweled snake choker; Emily had seen a similar one on Temu while looking for Halloween costumes for her girls the previous October.

Both girls wore heavy, dark smoky makeup and blood red lipstick; they had the sexy, provocative look of girls on the cusp of womanhood, who didn't yet realize the heady reaction they could elicit from boys and grown men. As the music played, they began to chant a spell of some sort, no doubt found in one of the books she had seen on Lillian's coffee table. The whole scene played like a home movie made for a high school class project; a blend of innocence and the universal antics of kids trying on different identities.

Then Emily discovered videos in an album Hayley had titled "insurance" which included her mother, Dina, having a drugged-out meltdown, hurling insults at her and smashing up the house as she spiraled out of control. In one, she was on an expletive filled rant, saying she'd call the cops to arrest Hayley for stealing or assault to teach her a lesson. There were also videos of Dina smoking methamphetamine, buying drugs from someone who came to the house, or passed out on the couch, a syringe on the coffee table. Emily assumed Hayley had recorded them as evidence to use if her mother ever got seriously out of control.

Emily was about to move on to Hayley's other social media accounts when she found a video that was clearly recorded surreptitiously. From the camera angle she could tell the phone was against Hayley's body, perhaps on a chain, half hidden by her shirt. Several adult men were drinking and smoking weed in some kind of lodge or clubhouse with a bar against one wall and an elevated stage area. The walls were made of tongue in groove knotty pine; the furniture looked like it belonged in a magazine ad from the sixties. Only the men's legs and lower bodies were visible and occasionally a hand would enter the frame to ply Hayley with beer, which she refused several times. It cut off abruptly and Emily had the clear sense that Hayley knew the vulnerable position she was in with this group; she seemed to be the only female present, which triggered all of Emily's internal alarms.

A teenage girl, alone with a group of men becoming increasingly impaired by alcohol and marijuana. How and why was she there?

Emily found Hayley's Snapchat account but there were no visible texts since the app deleted them within twenty-four hours. There was a privacy feature that a lot of kids used called For My Eyes Only, that saved special videos behind a password protected firewall. Emily had no way to breach it and see what might be stored there. There was a way to download all of Hayley's phone data onto a laptop and recover her chat history, but Emily had always relied on the FBI data analysts, Stephanie Leedom and Izzy Doqui, for that type of thing, and she couldn't contact them since she was under disciplinary review.

Emily felt the effects of the beer and altitude settling over her like a heavy blanket. Her eyelids grew heavier with each blink as she shut down the phone and secured it in the desk drawer.

She was heading for the bathroom when a furious barking erupted downstairs. Sammy's high-pitched yaps held an unmistakable note of alarm. Emily hurried down the stairs to find her father standing at one of the French doors, peering into the darkness.

"What's going on, Dad?" she asked, moving to his side while scanning the garden.

"The dog woke me," Michael said, his voice unsteady. "There was someone—I'm certain I saw someone at the window." His eyes darted around the unfamiliar room, confusion clouding his features.

Emily reached for the light switch, flooding the patio with bright light. Nothing moved in the illuminated space, but the stillness was unnerving. She stepped closer to her father, gently taking his trembling hands in hers.

"We're in Lake Arrowhead, remember?" she said softly. "This is the vacation house we rented. And this little dog joined us today—you named her Sammy."

Recognition slowly returned to his eyes. He relaxed slightly, bending to stroke the terrier's head.

"That's right. This is Sammy," he said, then looked back toward the window with surprising clarity. "She was protecting me. I know I saw someone out there, Emily. I'm not imagining it."

While Emily knew this could be true, he had also told her that a gray-haired woman was standing in his apartment when she'd visited recently, and they were alone. Still, she hurried to the bedroom and pulled out her duffel bag. Inside she had a locked gun case for her personal weapon, a snub nose thirty-eight revolver. She had other professional paraphernalia that she always brought when she traveled, just in case. She stuck the revolver in the waistband of her jeans and returned to Michael, before heading outside to check the perimeter.

"Don't worry, Dad. I'll go check it out. Can you go brush your teeth before going to bed in your room?"

He nodded and with Sammy, headed up the stairs. She turned off the light and slipped outside, onto the stone patio.

She scurried along the garden paths that led to the boathouse, but everything was quiet. Most likely, Sammy had barked at a raccoon or a skunk and Michael was mistaken. As she returned to the house, she heard something metal hitting the pavement, near the front entrance. She froze, then tiptoed behind a hedge of mountain laurel. There was no sign of anyone, just the deep shadows at the perimeter of the light thrown from the solar stakes and the outdoor floodlamps. A tiered metal planter was knocked over in the entryway; she heard someone or something running away into the woods. In the damp earth at the end of the driveway, there were shoeprints.

It could've been a prowler, or someone trying to break into a car. She walked the perimeter of the house and marked where the security cameras were placed, there were five of them visible. She'd call Vannah the next day and ask if she saw anything on them. There wasn't a lot of serious crime in the community, mostly petty drug offenses and burglaries. But it was also the place that James Tibbs had hidden successfully for years and murdered two people while everyone thought he was just a quiet solitary guy who wanted to live off the grid. Emily stood in the cool darkness, breathing in the fresh scent of the cedar and pine trees.

The video of Hayley with a group of grown men troubled her, even more that it was in a folder labeled "insurance." Insurance against what? She recalled Lillian's words.

Hayley changed; she started hanging out with different people...

Working with the FBI CARD team, Emily had dealt with cases of vulnerable young kids manipulated by adult predators who knew all the right things to say, the right gifts to give, and every small surrender and compromise that led to having complete power over a victim. She wondered if Hayley Hope had been lured into this type of liaison? Did she realize at some point that it was more dangerous than she had believed?

She said it was better if I didn't know...

And Melora, the throwaway foster kid who just disappeared one day, and no one cared to look for her? Emily had been that girl, before escaping captivity, before taking on the real Emily's identity. Before assuming her new identity, before escaping Tibbs, she had been ten-year-old Danica Hansen—another disposable child the system had failed to protect. Emily had hoped that reviewing Hayley's phone would put Lillian's suspicions to rest, help her move forward. Instead, it had only deepened the mystery.

As she walked back toward the house, the hairs on her neck prickled. The forest seemed to shift around her, branches whispering secrets just beyond her hearing. Somewhere among the shadows, watchful eyes tracked her movements—she was certain of it.

EIGHT

The sun broke, bright and promising. Emily moved around the kitchen, flipping pumpkin pancakes in the skillet while Michael sat brushing Sammy's fur. The methodical rhythm of mixing and flipping the batter helped quiet her mind, which had spun anxiously throughout the night. She'd gone to sleep wondering what other secrets Hayley's phone might hold, and after the search for a possible prowler, it had been hard to settle back into slumber. She glanced at her phone. She still hadn't heard back from Antonio. They had never gone a full twenty-four hours without speaking.

She slid a pancake onto the plate, with a faint smile of satisfaction at her small act of rebellion. For years she had eaten the same breakfast: oatmeal with precisely measured blueberries. She had worn a rubber band around her wrist to snap her mind out of catastrophizing spirals. These rituals kept her anchored and held emotional chaos at bay, but they had also imprisoned her. Now the rubber band was safely stored in her toiletries bag and today, she would indulge in fluffy, carb-filled pancakes.

"Dad, do you want maple syrup or jam with your

pancakes?" she asked, pulling her phone from her pocket to check once again for any missed calls.

"Jam, please," Michael said with a smile.

Emily looked at her plate of pancakes with a dollop of whipped butter and a waterfall of syrup slowly spreading out like a delicious puddle. Antonio would be proud of her, she knew. She took a photo of it and sent it to him with a thumbs-up emoji.

"Do you want to go see the hotel after breakfast? Where you and Mom honeymooned?" she asked Michael.

He smiled. "Yes, that's exactly what I want to do."

The front door opened, and Lynne shuffled in with grocery bags. She wasn't due to arrive for another two hours.

She smiled sheepishly. "I was at the store, and I got the fixings to make you a nice chicken casserole. They had a special on these beautiful carrot cakes, so I picked one up as well."

"Thank you, you didn't need to come in early."

"Oh, it's no trouble at all. So, you had a nice quiet evening?"

"Yes, we did."

"There was someone outside the house last night. Sammy barked," Michael said.

Lynne knelt down to pat Sammy. "Who's this little munchkin?"

"She was running loose, and we ended up with her, it seems," Emily said.

Lynne patted Sammy's curly fur. "Never seen her, poor little thing. Lots of people dump animals up here."

Michael nodded. "That's what the girl next door said."

"Did the Knox girl come by?" Lynne asked.

"Well, she dropped by with the dog," Emily explained.

"She needed an excuse to come over, I guess," Lynne said, shaking her head. "She's known to kind of stick to people, like gum on the street. But there was a prowler here?"

"I saw someone outside," Michael said.

"I went out to check, but I didn't see anyone. It might've been a shadow," Emily said.

Lynne got to work unpacking, and Emily was grateful that she had turned out to be such a calm and steady presence on the trip. So far, Michael had adjusted remarkably well to their temporary home. Not a single anxiety episode or moment of confusion since they'd arrived. Emily credited Lynne's steady presence and the calming effect of the familiar vacation spot.

After breakfast, they made their way to the Village and pulled into the Lake Arrowhead Resort, now owned by a corporate hotel chain. It had gone through several incarnations since its inception in 1923 as the luxurious Arlington Lodge. Michael nearly vibrated with anticipation as they crossed the parking lot toward the hotel entrance. His eyes brightened, scanning the grand lobby with its soaring ceilings and massive stone fireplace. His fingers tapped against his leg as he moved from spot to spot, recognizing features from decades past.

"The chandelier," he exclaimed, pointing upward. "It's the same one, Emily! Andie loved that chandelier!"

The lobby opened into the dining room, with birch wallpaper and rustic tables overlooking the water. The place had the feel of an elegantly appointed lodge, the air scented with pine and pumpkin.

"It looks so different now but still the same to me, somehow," Michael said, exploring the lobby. A couple of young female desk clerks worked the check-in area, while a stairway led down to the spa and out to the pool deck. Michael scurried down the stairs and outside, where he scanned the tops of a small cluster of tall trees.

"When we were here for our honeymoon, there were two bald eagles, a mated pair, that would nest in that tree. Andrea and I would sit here after dinner and watch for them to arrive. She was so beautiful, her face so full of expectation," he said wistfully. "And down there by the beach is where we had the firepit…"

Emily watched and followed him, as he relived one of his happiest moments. They walked out to the beach area of the hotel, which was deserted at this hour. The water in the lake was clear and quiet, a couple of ducks floated past. Michael kicked off his shoes and walked up to the water's edge, dipping a toe in.

"Too cold!" he said with a laugh. He turned in a circle, taking it all in, a smile spreading across his face.

"Do you know when she'll be back?" he asked suddenly.

"Who?" Emily replied, caught off guard.

"Andie, your mom. She went inside to get something, didn't she?"

These moments with her dad always brought her up short and she felt her heart turn over. He had lost the thread of reality and had forgotten that Andrea died years ago. He looked at her with such expectation, she had to turn away to hide the tears she felt rising behind her eyes, the pain of seeing how this cruel disease had taken so much from him.

"Andie's gone, Daddy. She's not coming back. She passed when I was away, remember?"

He stared at her in confusion and hurt for a moment, then turned toward the water, his eyes searching to find the woman he had lost years ago. Emily moved to him, taking his hand in hers.

"Remember when I was gone? When someone took me, and I didn't come back for a long time?"

He nodded silently, his expression somber. "It was that man; he took you from the park."

"That's right. And when you and Mommy were waiting for me to come home, she got sick."

His eyes lit up with recognition. "Yes. I remember now. She

got very sick, and I couldn't save her. She wanted to be there when you came home. She was waiting for you."

"I know. But you were there," Emily said.

He nodded. "Yes, I was. And she would've been so happy to have you back."

His mood had ricocheted like a pinball in just a few moments. He was happy now and Emily took advantage of that moment to loop her arm through his and lead him back into the hotel. While he looked at the vintage photos, she noticed two deputies were speaking in quiet voices to the desk clerk, a young Latina. She kept her eyes averted, looking down at the paperwork in front of her, but Emily could see from her body language that she was tense. Her shoulders were hunched, her torso contracted, as if she were trying to escape into herself and disappear.

Emily had seen the same stance on so many abused kids that it caught her attention. One of the deputies leaned in, his finger jabbing the reception desk for emphasis. Whatever he was saying, made the young woman recoil slightly. The other deputy rested his back and elbows against the counter in a way that was both proprietary and boorish, as if he were staking a claim.

When the hotel manager emerged from a back office, the young woman skirted away from the deputies, who then left. The way the girl refused to look at them struck Emily, as if she were afraid. Lillian's words again popped into Emily's head.

I think they did something...

She turned to her dad, but he had disappeared. She scanned the lobby for him, but he was gone. She felt a surge of panic, like losing a child in a public place, and hurried down a long corridor that led to conference and banquet rooms. She found him at the end of a hallway lined with photos of the resort over the years.

"See this one, Emily? This was taken the year we got

married—it looked just like this back then," he said, pointing to a black and white photo from the eighties.

Once her heart rate settled down, she said, "Daddy, you can't wander off away from me, okay? How about we head home for something to eat?"

"Don't worry, Emily. I'm never letting you get lost again," he said with a smile.

Back at the Maison, Emily got him settled in front of the television and found Lynne in the kitchen.

"There might have been someone here last night. I didn't want to discuss it with my dad since he can fixate on things and get anxious about them," Emily said, quietly.

"Did you see anyone? A man or a woman?"

"I didn't but there was a planter knocked over by the door. I heard something—or someone—running off. And there were fresh shoeprints in the dirt."

"This isn't good," Lynne replied, her voice dropping to a worried whisper. "Do you think it's safe for your father? With his condition, a prowler at night might be too much stress for him. And"—she hesitated, glancing toward Lillian's house—"it could be related to that Knox girl. You know the rumors about her."

Emily considered the possibilities. The mountain community had its share of petty crimes like thefts and break-ins. But not often in the gated, secure communities like Old North Shore. Still, she wasn't going to cut their vacation short over what might be nothing more than local teenagers causing mischief. Michael had been looking forward to this trip for months.

"We'll be fine," Emily said, with more confidence than she felt. "Dad decided to take a nap before Vannah's barbecue. I need to follow up with Lillian about something we found, and get my daily run in?"

She needed that run, desperately. Without it, she could feel the familiar gray fog creeping in at the edges of her consciousness. The low-grade depression that had become her unwelcome companion since Tibbs. Running was her medicine, the endorphins keeping the darkness at bay when nothing else could.

She changed into her workout clothes and headed out, swinging by Lillian's on her way to the highway. As she approached the door, Lillian opened it. She was dressed in a loose-fitting black tunic, a tangle of black beads around her neck.

"Did you find anything on the phone?" she asked.

"Yeah, I need your help with it," Emily replied.

"C'mon in."

Emily followed her inside and smelled burning sage and cloves. At her altar, Lillian had placed an array of spice jars from the kitchen and small glass bottles.

She knelt before it and said, "I'm just finishing a banishing spell to get rid of the people harassing me."

"Danny Granville and the others?"

"Yeah, I write their names on this piece of paper and then on the other side I write 'I bind you from harming me, now leave my life and let me be' and then I put it into one of these bottles. I add pepper for banishing and cloves for domination. And I seal it with black wax."

She took a long black taper and lit it; it spilled hot wax onto the cork stopper in the bottle.

"Then what?" Emily asked.

"I can toss it out to get rid of them or I can put it in the freezer to stop them in their tracks. You know, like freeze tag?" She went to the kitchen and placed the small bottle in the freezer.

"And where'd you get this spell?"

"TikTok," she said simply.

There was something about her innocence and belief in spells she found on TikTok that tugged at Emily's heart. Lillian was trying so hard to make a bad situation better, the only way she knew how.

"So, what'd you find on the phone?" Lillian asked.

"There are the usual videos that teenagers have and the witchy ones you two made. Her Instagram shorts are excellent."

Lillian beamed with pride. "Hayley was the best at every-thing. She wrote those and directed us. You should check them all out, they tell stories like episodes of a TV show."

"And I saw a few videos of her mom in a full meltdown."

"Yeah, she took those since Dina was always threatening to report her to the police—she said they'd put her in foster care."

"What a thing to threaten your kid with," Emily said, with disgust.

"Right? When she was the crazy one. Always high as a kite, causing confrontations. I don't know how Hayley didn't get into drinking like so many other kids up here."

"Is there a lot of teenage drinking?"

"Are you kidding? In middle school the kids start bringing vodka or gin in their water bottles. That's why the district doesn't allow them anymore. You have to drink from the foun-tains and most of them don't work."

The way Lillian described it, the local kids were bored and restless, which happens a lot in small towns. Too much time and nothing to do; it fueled the boom in small-town drug addiction in recent years.

"Do you know her Snapchat contacts? Take a look and see if anything jumps out as different or new," Emily said, handing her the phone. She scrolled through the app.

"No, these are all her regular friends. There's no one new."

"Do you know the password for the For My Eyes Only feature? There might be some data stored behind that firewall."

Lillian stared at Emily, her dark-rimmed eyes widening slightly. "You know about For My Eyes Only on Snap?" she asked, a newfound respect creeping into her voice. "Most adults don't even know Snapchat has hidden folders."

"I track down missing kids, I know a few things about where they hide the information they don't want their parents to see. Do you know the password?"

"Sure, I'll open it. She has a big file of important videos stored there," Lillian said confidently, attempting to open the folder, but she was blocked. She tried again with growing frustration.

"She must've changed the passwords. Why would she do that? We always knew how to get into each other's stuff," she cried, the anguish in her voice heartbreaking to hear.

"When was the last time you were able to log in to her social media accounts?"

"I don't know," Lillian replied, her fingers moving furiously over the phone screen. "Maybe a month ago? Or more?"

Emily watched her for a moment before asking gently, "Were you and Hayley drifting apart before her death? You say she had new friends, maybe she didn't have as much time for you any longer?" She kept her tone easy, non-accusatory.

Lillian froze, a flush creeping up her neck as she looked up, her eyes suddenly glassy with tears.

"No! We were the same as always!" The crack in her voice betrayed the lie. "We told each other everything, we were the same as always!" Her voice rose with each painful word. "You make it sound like I'm crazy, like they all do. You're just like the rest of them!"

Before Emily could respond, Lillian bolted up the stairs and slammed the door to her room. Emily heard the sound of the lock clicking shut and, through the door, Lillian's muffled sobs.

Emily recognized the reaction for what it was—Hayley changing her passwords cut deeper than Lillian would admit. It was tangible proof of what she feared most: she had been cut out of her best friend's life even before losing her completely. Emily waited for a few minutes, until Lillian's sobs calmed down, then slipped out and began her run, determined to shake off the emotional weight of the last twenty-four hours. Despite her plan to relax and escape the pressures of work on this trip, Lillian Knox had gotten under her skin. Emily was reminded of herself at that age; the odd girl who didn't fit in easily, wary, suspicious and easily hurt. Emily couldn't let this go. Years of working child abduction cases had taught her one undeniable truth: where there was one piece of suspicious evidence—like the video of Hayley with those men—there was always more. The sick feeling in her gut told her that Hayley Hope's story was far from over, that answering these questions mattered not just for Lillian's closure or justice for a dead teenager, but potentially for other young women at risk.

NINE

Emily ran hard down highway 173 into an area called Oak Lane Flats which was off the beaten path from the rest of the town. The streets were narrow and winding, the homes set at odd angles without any clear layout. It was more rural than other areas in Arrowhead; she saw goats in pens and several horses in corrals built on hillside lots. Like many residents in the mountains, the family names were displayed outside the houses.

In Oak Lane Flats there seemed to be a few family names that were prevalent: Kupp, Prentiss, Granville, Boone. Emily guessed that Vannah's husband must belong to the Granville clan, and there seemed to be a lot of them clustered in this neighborhood. She ran past several houses where the residents watched her but didn't offer any greeting, even when she made the first overture with a nod or a smile. She had the distinct feeling that she had wandered into an area where outsiders were unwelcome, where family ties and identity ran deep.

In Los Angeles, Emily moved through a world of constant reinvention. People shed identities like snakeskin, embracing the newer, better version of themselves.

Nobody cared which family you belonged to or how many

generations your ancestors had occupied the same zip code. But here in Oak Lane Flats, with its suspicious stares and hostile silence, she felt the weight of outsider status pressing down on her. The families who had rooted themselves in this soil generations ago regarded her like an invasive species, something to be monitored and contained.

The trees themselves seemed to stand guard over old secrets, their roots running deep beneath the surface, anchoring the status quo. These people, like the ancient pines, wouldn't bend easily—they would stand immovable until their final, crashing fall.

Emily quickened her pace toward the highway, lungs burning with effort and unease. Every instinct told her that Oak Lane Flats harbored dangers more significant than unfriendly neighbors. She needed to reconnect with Lillian as soon as possible, to unlock whatever secrets Hayley had stored away before time ran out.

Lillian had fallen asleep after a long crying jag left her exhausted. She wasn't sleeping well, her nerves frayed from worrying about what Danny and his jerk friends might try next. And Evelyn had a doctor's appointment coming up which was always difficult, now that she didn't want to leave the house. Lillian had to time it right, so Evelyn would be dressed and willing to go when the Uber driver arrived. There were only two drivers in town and if they weren't ready to go when he arrived, he'd take another call and they'd be stuck. If Lillian got Evelyn to the door and the car wasn't there, she might turn back and refuse to go.

She regretted the way she'd acted with Emily, but it hit a nerve. Lillian had been upset about Hayley drifting away from her in the weeks before she died. It was all so strange. She was busy doing other stuff; she said she was making extra money because she wanted to move out of Dina's house and start saving for college. Lillian had offered her house to Hayley many times. She had two extra bedrooms. But Hayley had said that she didn't want Lillian involved, whatever that meant. She knew Hayley wasn't hanging out with anyone from school and she wondered if she had met some older kids, maybe in their twenties. Even Eddie March didn't know who it could be, and they were in Media class together.

Lillian turned on the shower and left it cold; she stepped in for a quick jolt to her nervous system. She'd read somewhere that cold water could pull a person out of depression, and that heavy feeling came over her a lot lately. But she had to stay focused and strong if she was going to get anyone to investigate Hayley's death. She dried herself and got dressed then went into the living room to put Hayley's videos up on her projector. This was becoming a ritual for her, a way of keeping her friend alive. She knew people would say she was nuts, but she didn't care. They'd been saying that about her for years.

She synced her projector to her iPhone and pulled up one of the projects she had helped Hayley with, a comedic mock documentary about the history of Lake Arrowhead. Hayley kept cracking up when she was supposed to be serious, and they both dissolved into laughter on screen. Seeing those moments, projected onto the big white wall, made Lillian unbearably sad. Her grandmother came shuffling in, still in her pajamas.

"Lilli? Are you all right, dear? I thought I heard you crying," Evelyn asked, concerned.

"I'm okay, Grandma. I was just missing Hayley," she said.

Evelyn sat beside her on the couch. "I know she was a good friend to you, honey. But you'll find new friends now that she's moved away."

Lillian just stared at her grandmother's deep brown eyes. She had lied and told Evelyn that Hayley had moved, afraid that the truth would be too hard for her.

"That's right, Grandma. She's moved and maybe I can go visit her one day," Lillian said.

"Don't worry, you two will get together again. It's not that easy to lose a friend like Hayley. Would you like me to brush your hair?"

"Yeah, I'd like that," Lillian said, sitting down in front of the couch while Evelyn retrieved a hairbrush. She returned and sat behind Lillian, running a practiced, bony hand over her hair after each stroke.

"I used to do this when you were little, remember?"

"I wish I could go back to that time, and things could be the way they used to," Lillian said quietly.

"But then you'd never grow up and have all the wonderful adventures you're supposed to live," Evelyn said.

The adventures that Hayley will never have a chance to live, Lillian thought, the rhythm of the hairbrush calming her nervous system. On the wall of the living room, Hayley walked and talked and smiled, as if she were still alive, a beautiful ghost among them.

At two o'clock sharp, Emily called out, "Hey, Dad! You ready to go down to the barbecue?"

He emerged from his bedroom decked out in khaki shorts and a Hawaiian shirt with Sammy in tow.

"We're ready!" he said. "Are we taking the girl from next door?"

Lillian hadn't responded to Emily's texts. As they passed her house, Emily saw her on the deck, a murder of crows gathered on the railings. She and her grandma were eating sandwiches and drinking Cokes. Emily had to admit that the crows did look rather spooky if you didn't know Lillian had trained them with peanuts and treats. Lillian seemed recovered from her earlier upset, so perhaps she'd be willing to talk later. Emily and Michael followed the lake path past a small beach to Peninsula Park, a grass covered promontory with a wrought-iron fence and picnic tables. A low, rocky cliff led to the lake and a stairway to a fishing platform where a few men waited with their poles in the water.

A large group had gathered. Emily saw Starhawk chatting with a frumpy, older woman while kids climbed on the jungle gym, middle schoolers played frisbee and the teens huddled in small cliques, scrolling on their phones. A group of silver-haired seniors sat at a large picnic table, like an AARP advertisement. The whole scene looked like a Norman Rockwell painting.

Vannah stood by the jungle gym, surrounded by women Emily assumed to be part of her mom group; the tall, athletic man next to her appeared to be her husband, from the way he rested his palm protectively against her lower back. Cody Granville was handsome in an All-American quarterback kind of way. Fair, with close-cropped blond hair and pale eyes, he broke into a heartfelt laugh at someone's joke as Emily and Michael approached.

"Emily!" Savannah shouted, rushing to greet them. "I'm so glad you two made it!"

Cody had walked over and hovered behind her. She slipped an arm around his waist and beamed. "This is my husband, Cody."

He reached out and shook Emily's hand, then Michael's in a firm grip. His smile was easy and relaxed.

"Vannah's told me a lot about you and the wild times you two had up here years ago," he said, with a mischievous wink.

"Oh yeah, it was wild. Sneaking our own candy into the movies and catching a few too many trout," Emily said.

Sammy caught sight of a Yorkie and pulled at Michael.

"She's the boss now!" he said, letting Sammy lead the way toward the senior table. Emily followed with Vannah.

"I think your dad will have a good time. Let me introduce him to everyone," she said.

At the table, everyone rose politely to greet them. An imposing, attractive man with salt and pepper hair shook Michael's hand.

"Welcome, Mr. Ray! It's so nice to have you and your daughter here with us today. I'm Pastor Jim Jenkins of Church on the Hill. This is my wife, Mary."

Sammy had started wrestling vigorously with the Yorkie and Michael sat to join the group. Emily hovered, making sure her dad was relaxed and comfortable.

"Thanks for inviting us, Vannah. This is so good for him, to see new places, talk to new people," Emily whispered.

"Of course! Here, I want you to meet Caine March, he's our extra set of hands at church, always ready to help with anything, and his son, Eddie," she said, as a wiry man about sixty years old extended his hand enthusiastically. He had the roughhewn look of someone who worked outdoors. His son was tall and skinny, with the slouch of a kid trying to make himself smaller. Eddie March smiled self-consciously; Emily noticed that he hadn't joined the larger group of teens but stayed at his father's side. Vannah continued to guide her through the group, meeting people.

When they got to Starhawk and the frumpy woman, she said, "You know Starhawk already, but this is Glenda Kupp, she's our choir director and kind of like everyone's grandma."

"Heck, Vannah! I'm not that old!" Glenda protested in feigned offense.

Emily wondered how Vannah knew that she had met Starhawk the previous day but before she could ask, they had made their way back to Vannah's original group and she presented Emily with a flourish.

"This is my old friend, Emily Ray, from Los Angeles. She's taking a break from city life to just chill and relax up here in our little corner of paradise," she said. "This is Lacey, Amber, Kelly and Kristen. They're my ride-or-dies!"

The women were pretty in a wholesome, unglamorous way. Each sported a fat wedding and engagement ring set and wore the ubiquitous mom attire of skinny jeans with tunic-tee-shirts and tennis shoes. There was a small-town conformity about the whole thing, none of the eccentric individualism so common in a big city. But it was peaceful and predictable and that was what Emily had wanted.

"Are you enjoying the lake?" Kristen asked.

"Yes, it's beautiful. I took a run earlier and ended up in an area called Oak Lane Flats," Emily said.

They exchanged glances, as if she'd recently returned from a tour of landmines in North Korea.

"You didn't have any problems, did you?" Kelly asked.

"No, what kind of problems?"

"Nothing. Just the people out there are kind of... prickly," Kristen said.

The group tittered, and Vannah said, "Did you see how a lot of the same family members live in Oak Lane? Those families have been on the mountain forever."

Cody came over with two men, both with military style buzz cuts. The larger one extended his hand to Emily. She recognized them as the cops from the hotel lobby earlier, the ones who had been bothering the young desk clerk.

"Hi! I'm Roger Kupp. You've met my ball and chain, Amber," he said with a laugh.

Roger had dark brown hair and a broad, florid face. He was intoxicated; his eyes were glassy and he had a sheen of sweat on his brow. Amber had the pained look of a wife whose husband embarrasses her on a regular basis.

The second man shook Emily's hand and said, "Jackson Miles, we work with Cody. And we've known him since he was in diapers. Well, we were all in diapers back then!"

Miles had a baby face with dimples and was as skinny as a bean pole with a protruding Adam's apple. His nervous laugh, his eyes searching for approval from the group, told Emily that he was a follower, not a leader in this social circle. That role seemed a natural fit for Cody Granville.

Cody wrapped an arm over each man's shoulders. "We're just local boys who grew up playing sports and now we're all sheriffs together."

"But pretty different from being a big shot FBI agent, I bet! I mean, we're just small-timers compared to someone like you," Kupp said too loudly, a hint of veiled hostility seeping through his jovial attitude.

Emily just smiled; she'd been in many situations with men who couldn't handle a woman having a more powerful position than they did. Just looking at Kupp's gut hanging over his belt and his fleshy girth, she knew she could pin him in two moves, and he probably knew it, too.

"Are you enjoying your visit? Vannah told us you're staying in the Maison, the fancy French-style one, right?" Lacey asked.

"And she's next door to that weird Knox girl." Roger smirked, his eyes flicking to Emily's face to gauge her reaction. "The one who lives practically alone in that big house." Cody patted him on the back roughly, an obvious warning, but Roger was too inebriated to read the sign and continued, "We all heard about how you took that guy down up in Arrowbear, the kidnapper. But I bet there's stuff up here that would be more than you could handle, you know what I mean?"

Emily doubted there was anything that this sloppy drunk could handle better than she could but before she came up with a response, Cody cuffed him by the back of the neck and began moving him away.

"Why don't you go have a soda, Kupp, and shut up? You're embarrassing us and Vannah's friend," he said. "I'm sorry about him, Emily. Sometimes he gets like this, but he doesn't mean anything by it."

"No problem," Emily said. Cody led him toward the grill, out of earshot. Kupp stood still, like a child being reprimanded, his beer can resting limply in his hand.

Vannah laughed awkwardly and asked, "Is Lillian coming today? I hope you had a chance to invite her. I think it would help her to get out with people."

"No, I sent her a message, but she didn't reply," Emily said.

Vannah shouted to her daughter, "Bella! Go to Lillian's house and invite her to come down!"

Bella and her group of friends looked up, annoyed.

"But Mom..." she began to protest, but Vannah cut her off.

"I asked you to do something, so do it!"

"I'll go with them," Eddie March volunteered, which didn't seem to please Bella at all. She and her friends walked several paces ahead of Eddie, purposely not including him.

Vannah turned back to her friends with a smile. "Sometimes you have to get tough with kids. You can't be their BFF, you know?"

"Did you all grow up together?" Emily asked.

"Pretty much," Amber replied. "Though I hung out with a different crowd in high school."

Unlike the other women in the group, Amber had apparently stepped outside the rigid social boundaries before being pulled back into the fold.

"Yeah, that's when you were a wild child! Can you believe she's Pastor Jim's daughter? You won't believe the trouble she got up to in those days! The stories I could tell you!" Vannah said with a demure laugh. Amber responded with a stiff smile and looked away.

"But you found your way back to the flock," Kelly said. "Everybody has their 'come to Jesus' moment."

"Amen," Kristen agreed.

Lacey nodded. "He will tend to his flock like a shepherd, he will gather the lambs in his arms and that's exactly what he did for you when you strayed too far from the shore. Praise be to God."

"But you've got to be vigilant because every time you step out of the sanctified space of your home, Satan and his minions are waiting. We all must put on our spiritual armor every day. We are in a holy war," Vannah warned, with ominous sincerity. Only Amber Kupp seemed out of sync, fixing them with a dead-eyed stare.

For a moment, Emily thought they were being satirical—the whole conversation was like something out of *The Handmaid's Tale*—but when she saw how they all murmured in assent, she knew they were serious. Every woman spoke in the same soft, girlish tone, as if to make themselves smaller. Emily realized this wasn't just a barbecue, it was a church event, and they were evangelicals. No doubt Vannah hoped to draw her and Michael into the fold, which was never going to happen, but Emily smiled politely.

A group of kids ran past them toward the docks. Lacey shouted after them, "Jedidiah, keep an eye on the littles!" The kids waved her off and kept running.

"Is your family coming up? Vannah told us you have two littles," Kristen asked.

"Next week, yes, I have twin girls," Emily replied. She glanced at her phone, there was still no call from Antonio.

"We should all go out in the boat! The men can fish, and the kids can go wakeboarding," Kristen suggested.

"And we can feed everyone and clean up," Amber added. Emily sensed Amber's discomfort immediately. While the other wives spoke in demure, sunny tones, Amber's responses came with an undercurrent of resignation. Her posture—slightly withdrawn from the circle, arms crossed—contrasted with the enthusiasm of the others. Whatever had brought Amber into this group, Emily sensed it wasn't her preference.

A middle-aged Latino man approached tentatively from the marina adjacent to the park, a young woman walking behind him. It was the desk clerk from the hotel that Emily had seen earlier. The man didn't carry himself like a guest—he seemed out of place and uncomfortable. Jim Jenkins rose to go and meet him. The mood of the group shifted. Vannah waved Cody over and whispered, "Did you or Pastor Jim invite Ernesto and his daughter?"

He shook his head and walked over to where Ernesto hovered, holding a small black bag. Jenkins and Cody flanked him on either side as they spoke, Ernesto shaking his head and gesturing to his daughter. The girl looked at the guests, eyes darting from face to face. Vannah saw Emily watching the interaction and turned her away from it. Starhawk and Glenda had drawn closer as well.

"Sorry, it's a little awkward. Ernesto is the handyman at our church, but we didn't invite him today 'cause, you know, he's not really part of our group. He's an employee but I guess he heard about it and showed up," Vannah said.

The three men continued to talk quietly but Ernesto and his daughter didn't give off any sense that they wanted to attend the barbecue. They had come for something else. Ernesto pushed a black bag into Cody's hands. Emily caught Vannah's watchful glance and shifted her attention to Michael as she made her way to him. She checked the kids on the dock from the corner of her eye. The small ones were playing rough, too close to the edge, while the older kids ignored them, distracted by their phones. None of the adults were watching, their attention focused on the unexpected arrival of Ernesto.

The afternoon sun glinted off the lake as families lounged on beach towels and children splashed in the shallows. Emily kept one eye on Michael while chatting with Amber, noting the increasing restlessness of the unsupervised toddlers playing at the dock's edge.

"Maybe we should—" she began, just as one small boy leaned too far over the water, arms windmilling frantically.

Time seemed to slow. The boy's face registered a moment of surprise before he tumbled forward.

A splash. Then screams from the older children, who pointed and shouted but remained frozen in place.

"Dad, stay there!" Emily called out, already sprinting toward the dock as Sammy began barking frantically. Michael's confused shout faded behind her as she kicked off her shoes.

Without hesitation, she launched herself into the water, the cold shock taking her breath away for a moment. Opening her eyes underwater, she blinked against the murky darkness. Lake vegetation swayed like ghostly fingers around her ankles as she searched for movement, for any sign of the child.

The acrid taste of motor oil and algae filled her mouth. Lungs burning, she propelled herself toward the dock's underside, where shadow shifted unnaturally. Her hand brushed fabric—the child's T-shirt—and she grabbed it, pulling the small body toward her.

Breaking the surface, she hoisted the sputtering, terrified child upward where eager hands reached down from the dock. Through the chaos of voices and the crush of gathering adults, Emily caught sight of Michael at the fence. His face contorted with panic, he waved and shouted her name, clearly disoriented by the commotion.

Kristen pushed through the crowd, claiming the child with profuse thanks as Emily hauled herself up onto the dock, water streaming from her clothes.

"Thank you so much, Emily! I don't know how this happened!" Kristen cried.

"Emily! What was it? Why did you go in the water like that? Sammy ran off!" Michael cried.

"Don't worry, Dad, I'm fine. Sammy's right here." She pushed past the parents on the dock and made her way to Michael, sliding her arm around his shoulders.

Vannah approached, upset and apologetic. She looked like she was about to cry.

"I'm so sorry this all happened, Emily. I wanted this to be such a nice time for you and your dad!"

Emily waved her off. "It's fine, Vannah. Things like this happen. I need to get Dad home now. We'll talk tomorrow," she said, walking across the rocky beach with Sammy in tow. As Emily reached the path toward home, she looked back at the park. Ernesto and his daughter were gone.

TEN

Back at the house, it took Emily over an hour to get Michael settled. He was terrified by Sammy running off, the shouting and commotion. Everything about the afternoon had been too much for him. Finally, she gave him half a Hydroxyzine tablet, which his doctor had prescribed for both sleep and anxiety. Within fifteen minutes he was drifting off. She needed a hot shower to wash the lake residue off. The warm water felt heavenly, and she stood under the giant showerhead for several long minutes, feeling her nervous system settling down after the events at the barbecue.

She'd had a glimpse into Vannah's life, the clique of conservative, religious wives, the power balance among different church members. It was an insular world, so different from her own. But Emily knew her world was not for everyone, a lot more people lived in a world like Vannah Granville's. Emily and Antonio were not religious, but she made no judgments about people who were. Whatever helped people get through each day and stand up to face another one, was fine by her. Plenty of people would find her coping mechanisms strange.

Her phone rang as she was stepping out of the shower, and she was happy to see it was Antonio.

"Hey! I missed you yesterday. We had crappy cell service here," she said.

"Everything okay out there?" he asked.

"Yeah. Michael had a panic attack today, there was a lot of excitement at a beach barbecue. You've made it to Arizona safe and sound?"

"We're safely checked into Tia Yaya's guest room, there's *carne asada* on the grill and my cousins are teaching the girls how to play *loteria*."

She heard a woman's voice near the phone, laughing and saying, "*Toñito lindo*, come on, we're going to go get *helados!*"

Emily spoke decent Spanish; she knew that the word "lindo" meant beautiful. She had a momentary flash of wondering who the woman was that was calling her husband "beautiful Toñito".

Before she could ask, Antonio laughed and said, "That's my cousin, Angel. We're going to get ice cream for the kids."

Emily said, "They'll love that. By the way, Dad found a stray dog that I'm sure he's taking home. You'll meet her when you come."

She made a split-second decision to keep her investigation into Hayley Hope's death to herself. Antonio would only see it as proof that she couldn't let go, couldn't relax, couldn't step away from being an agent even for a family vacation. Her silence felt like another small betrayal.

"I'm happy you two are relaxing and taking it easy. It's kind of loud and busy here, lots of people, lots of chatter. I'll have the girls call before bedtime, okay?"

"Sure. Love you."

"Same."

They hung up and, with Michael asleep, Emily got dressed in a pair of sweatpants and a T-shirt and let Lynne know that she was going out to run an errand. She pulled out of the driveway and sent Lillian a text to meet her at the Old North Road turn-out hoping she would show up. When she got there, Lillian was waiting with Eddie March.

"Sorry about earlier," Lillian said. "I just got upset. I guess you met Eddie already. Can you give him a ride home? He lives over on Burnt Mill."

Emily was familiar with the area. It was upscale with custom homes and large wooded lots. Every house looked like it belonged on the cover of *Country Life* magazine.

"Sure, get in. Why didn't you come down to the barbecue? Bella and her friends came to get you," Emily said.

"So they can tell me how I'm gonna go to hell unless I join them? That church always does this, they act like it's a barbecue or a potluck and then it begins. Hayley and I went once because we were hungry, and they put us in a prayer circle," Lillian said. "And I never saw Bella Granville and her toxic Barbie clones. Eddie came to warn me after they ditched him."

"They didn't go to your house?"

Eddie chimed in, "No, they went to meet Jake Foster. He's Bella's part-time boyfriend but her parents don't know about it."

Lillian laughed. "He's like twenty-three or something. He's got a kid with some girl in Crestline, but we're supposed to believe that he respects Bella's purity ring!"

She spoke with a tough bravado, like a kid who'd seen it all. Emily knew it was a protective posture. She had done the same thing at her age.

"Did you find anything else on Hayley's phone? It's okay, Eddie knows I have it. He's cool with everything."

"Were you close with Hayley?" Emily asked him.

"I knew her since we were little. She was amazing, we were in Media class at Rim High together. She's a couple of years behind me," he said.

"Until his dad switched schools on him. Now he goes to the Christian school," Lillian said, bluntly.

"Why is that?" Emily asked. Eddie and Lillian exchanged a look.

"Because I'm gay," Eddie said quietly.

Emily wasn't sure what to say for a moment. She had several friends with gay children in Los Angeles, but she didn't know anyone whose response was to put their kids into a Christian school. It was clearly a different world in the mountains.

"How's that going for you?" Emily asked finally.

Eddie stared at his hands, interlocking his fingers nervously. When he looked up, there was a quiet defiance in his eyes despite the vulnerability in his voice.

"It's... okay. Not really, but I have to make the best of it until I can leave." He straightened slightly. "Hayley felt the same way, along with a couple of other kids. We called ourselves the Houdinis."

"Houdinis?"

"Yeah, like Harry Houdini, the escape artist. We were all planning to get away from the mountain," Lillian said. "But Hayley never made it."

"I found a video in a folder called Insurance on her phone. Maybe you have some idea where it was shot," Emily said, handing the phone to Lillian.

She began scrolling, with Eddie leaning over from the back seat to watch. She stopped to watch some of the Dina videos.

"Her mom is batshit crazy..." Lillian murmured.

"Wait, isn't that Glenda Kupp?" Eddie asked.

"Yeah, I hadn't noticed it before. It's her," Lillian said, handing the phone to Emily who pulled over to the side of the road to see it. The video showed Glenda Kupp at Dina's door, handing her a brown paper bag and taking something in return. Emily had seen enough drug deals to recognize one. She pulled onto the highway, handing the phone back to Lillian.

"I met her at the barbecue, today. She was like someone's grandma," Emily said.

"She used to be on yard duty at school," Lillian added.

"And she's the choir director at church," Eddie said.

"Wow! The church lady is a plug!" Lillian laughed sarcastically.

"Could she work at a pharmacy, making a delivery of a prescription?" Emily asked. Maybe there was an innocent explanation, but her instincts told her otherwise.

"She's on disability, she had back surgery and she can't hold a job anymore. But everybody up here has some story like that," Eddie said.

"And why would Hayley record it?" Lillian asked. "She knew who her mom bought from."

They scrolled more videos until they found the one of Hayley with the adult men.

"This is the only video that caught my eye. Everything else I saw was typical teenage stuff. See how it's recorded? She's trying to hide the phone; she doesn't want them to know. Do you have any idea why she would be in this place? It's like a clubhouse or something," Emily asked.

Lillian shook her head and handed the phone to Eddie. "Do you know where this is?"

"No," he said. "What's she doing with these guys? They're grown men."

"And they're trying to give her alcohol. Do you know who they are?" Emily asked.

Lillian shook her head, all teen bravado gone. "I can't tell from the voices. Can't you take this to the FBI?"

"No, it doesn't work that way. I'm on leave right now so I can't do anything officially. And even if I weren't, the local police have to ask us into the case. Is there anyone who might know the password for the Snapchat folder?"

"Maybe she told Manny Heredia, they were kind of close."

"Is he the boy in the prom photos?"

"Yeah. It was homecoming. He's in our grade. I can text him," Lillian offered.

"How about her mom, Dina?" Emily asked.

"She won't have the passcodes. Hayley didn't tell her anything," Eddie said.

"What if we just talk to her?" Emily pushed.

"You'd have to show up and hope to catch her at a good time. She never answers her phone," Lillian said.

They pulled up outside a large cedar cabin with a wrap-around deck at the entrance to Burnt Mill Canyon. Eddie looked from the house to Emily quickly, his embarrassment obvious.

"My grandma left me this house," he explained, one foot already out of the car. "Looks nice outside, but my dad's a hoarder, so it's kind of a mess inside." He hesitated, eyes darting toward the front door as if checking whether anyone was watching. "And about my dad—he's not a bad guy. I mean, with the Christian school thing and all." His voice dropped nearly to a whisper. "He's just... easily led, you know? I don't want you to think badly of him over the gay thing. He's just doing what they tell him to."

"Who's 'they'?" Emily pressed gently.

"Church on the Hill and Pastor Jim," Eddie replied, keeping his voice low. "They have a hand in everything up here. Everything."

Emily hesitated, processing this new information. All roads seemed to lead back to this church. A disturbing pattern was emerging, pieces clicking into place like a jigsaw puzzle revealing a darker picture than she'd anticipated.

"Are there any other girls who've gone missing or died under strange circumstances?" she asked, suddenly.

Eddie and Lillian exchanged a loaded glance. Emily saw that they shared some type of unspoken suspicion.

"Well," Lillian began slowly, "there was Melora who Starhawk said ran off with the made-up boyfriend. Melora has an older sister named Melanie who also disappeared one day, but I heard she left on her own."

Eddie nodded, stepping closer. "Remember Joannie Dietrich and Rachel Carson? How they just stopped showing up at school?"

"And Karlie Ann Smith," Lillian added. "She was in the grade above us."

"Did they have anything in common?" Emily asked, her pulse quickening. "Any connection between them?"

"They all went to Church on the Hill," Eddie said without hesitation.

"And they were foster kids," Lillian finished.

The implications hit Emily like a physical blow. If her suspicions were correct, this wasn't about a single tragic death. This was something far more insidious—a systematic targeting of the most vulnerable children in the community. The thought sickened her, even as her mind began methodically constructing a timeline and connection map, whose tentacles spread out like a malevolent shadow.

ELEVEN

Dina Hope lay on the threadbare couch, a thin blanket over her despite the warm summer day. She had the chills, and she was sweating, her body in a wild state of withdrawal. She didn't have anything to ease the struggle. She couldn't go back to the pain clinic, they'd turned down her request for a Norco refill and even the pill mill doctor in Crestline, Dr. Barret, couldn't give her anything now that his license had been suspended. She'd already driven down to the city center in San Bernardino at night, a few times, where drugs and prostitution were rampant. She'd even bought street heroin from a guy she didn't know and gotten really sick.

That night Hayley had taken her to the emergency room at Mountains Community Hospital where the doctors and nurses looked at her like she was just another mountain druggie. Behind the thin curtain that separated her from other ER patients, Dina had heard a young man telling them he hurt his back at a construction job and needed something for the pain, but she knew he was telling the same lie that all the addicts told. Once the opioids became restricted and the local doctors could no longer hand out prescriptions like candy canes at Christmas, the supply dried up. Several of those doctors had restrictions put on their medical license, some could only work in government facilities with heavy oversight, like prisons.

Now that Hayley was gone, Dina couldn't risk buying street drugs again. There was no one to watch out for her. Everything had gone to shit now that her daughter was dead. Sometimes she saw Hayley standing in the corner of the room, smiling her sweet smile. Maybe it was just a drug-induced hallucination or maybe Hayley's ghost was really there? Some days she woke up and went to her room forgetting how they'd pulled her body from Papoose Lake a few weeks earlier. Dina shook her head at the memory, trying to banish it. How did Hayley kill herself by drowning? Why would she leave?

She was a strong swimmer. She'd even been on a team down the hill back in middle school. In those days Dina was still functioning; she could drive Hayley to activities but that stopped when the drugs got worse. What was she supposed to do, all by herself with a teenager when her ex stopped paying child support? If she took him to court, they'd find out about the drugs, and they could've taken Hayley to foster care. Dina would've lost her food stamps for sure. All of it was just too much for her to deal with.

She felt sick to her stomach, and Hayley's face kept popping into her head, like she was trying to tell her something. She didn't drown herself, there was nothing that could convince Dina that was true. But she didn't know what else to believe, her brain was too messed up to even know what to do or who to ask. When those thoughts became too much for her, she'd smoke some meth or drop a few Vicodin so she could forget and figure it out another day.

The people from the church helped out; they gave her groceries and even a little something to get through the bad times. She'd known all of them since high school, back when she was Dina Fischer. Vannah Pratt and her friends were always bitches to her in those days; they thought they were better than the other kids. Then when Vannah got with Cody Granville, she really acted like her shit didn't stink. Dina would see her in the market and Vannah would act like she didn't know her. But suddenly they'd started coming around, asking if she needed any help. Vannah had gotten Hayley the job at the church and Dina hoped she'd get her hands on the money, but Hayley had kept it hidden.

Dina scowled, looking at her broken and dirty fingernails, her head bobbing as her mind ricocheted like a stray bullet. Hayley could be a little bitch, too. She kept that money when she should've given it to Dina. Said she was saving for college, like that was ever going to happen. Dina hadn't gone to college and neither had Hayley's dad, Ryan. Dina winced at the memory of the last night she saw Hayley—they'd fought over her job money and Dina had torn her room apart looking for it. Then Hayley left and she didn't come back, ever again. Dina's head felt heavy; she couldn't sit still but she had no strength to get up. She lay there, miserable and sick, wishing everything in her life were different but not having the will or a way to change it. She'd made a call about getting something to help her through; she hoped someone showed up soon.

Emily made a U-turn in Burnt Mill Canyon and Lillian navigated the route to Crest Park, where Dina lived. Crest Park was a small enclave of homes, near Highway 18. The residential streets were all access roads, which meant they weren't maintained by the county. They were narrow, with no sidewalks, so only one car could pass in one direction at a time. Many of the homes were ramshackle, with fencing made of old plywood and scrap metal. More than a few had cars with flat tires out front, with building material and other debris littered in piles, as if someone had brought it home with the intention of using it then just dropped it on the way in.

They passed a beat-up house that had two goats standing on a trampoline, a diapered toddler holding a bottle meandering alone in the road. An adult man shot past them at top speed on a mini motorbike, squealing in excitement, oblivious to the small child he almost hit. It looked more like a holler in West Virginia than Southern California. This hardscrabble neighborhood was a far cry from the glossy resort image the town presented.

At the end of the street, they stopped at a tiny, A-frame cottage on a cracked asphalt cul-de-sac. Beyond that, there were deep woods and looming rock formations. A clump of overgrown weeds spread across what would've been a front yard. Tin foil covered the first-floor windows. Everything about the house spoke of a person who had long ago given up any pretense of making a home. There were empty salt bags strewn by the front door, a snow shovel with a broken handle, left over from the previous winter. The front door had been splashed with bright purple paint that looked like vandalism rather than a decorative choice.

"This is it," Lillian said, climbing out of the car.

"What's up with the purple door?" Emily asked.

"Someone did that one night. It's a witch thing," Lillian replied.

"A witch thing?"

"Painting a front door purple was a way of marking a witch's house back in the day. We learned about it in U.S. History. You know, the Salem witch trials."

It had been many years since Emily had studied anything related to witch folklore and she could only recall some basic tenets of the persecution of suspected witches.

But she struggled to reconcile the photos and videos on Hayley's phone with this depressing place. The short vignettes Hayley had written and directed, her spooky videos with

Lillian, the girl whose charisma and talent provoked envy and admiration. It was heartbreaking for Emily, to imagine how hard Hayley had worked to rise above these sad circumstances.

The house next door was in similar condition and an elderly, imposing man with a thick shock of white hair stepped out.

Lillian whispered, "Don't worry, that's Roy. He's kind of out of it but he's harmless. We call him Crazy Roy."

He nodded at them in silent greeting and pretended to retrieve something from one of the old cars on his property. Emily had the clear sense that he was outside to keep an eye on them. Lillian rapped on Dina's door and after a few minutes, Dina Hope opened it. Emily was taken aback by how skinny and unhealthy she looked, with dark, purple shadows under her eyes and pale, washed-out skin. She was unsteady on her feet as she leaned against the doorjamb.

"Hey, Lillian, what's up?" Dina asked.

"This is my friend, Emily. I was telling her about how cool Hayley's videos were. So, I thought maybe I could show her Hayley's room?"

Dina stared at Emily, her bloodshot eyes narrowing with suspicion. Her fingers clutched the doorframe to steady herself as she swayed slightly.

"What d'you know about Hayley?" she asked, her voice a gravelly whisper.

"I'm a writer," Emily lied, "and Lillian showed me some of Hayley's videos. She was very talented."

"What kinda writer?" Dina probed, unmoving.

"I write... true crime books," Emily replied with the first thought that popped into her head.

Now Dina showed more interest. "I might have some good stories for you. There's a lot of bad shit that goes on up here."

"I'll leave my number, in case you think of something," Emily said quickly, hoping to gain a foothold with her.

"Cool, you can go to her room but I'm cleaning it out," Dina said, turning back to the television.

The house was dirty and disorganized, with McDonald's wrappers on the counter of the tiny kitchen and unwashed dishes in the sink. Empty soda cans spilled out of the trash and there was a strong smell of an uncleaned cat litter box. The beige carpet was stained and damp as they climbed the narrow stairway to Hayley's room.

A big, sequined "H" hung from her door and inside, Hayley's room was decorated in pinks and purples. Promotional posters for trendy bands Emily had never heard of adorned one wall and an elaborate altar made from a repurposed headboard stood at the foot of her bed. One side was upholstered with a paisley brocade, the wood side covered in a decoupaged print of a group of women in long white dresses, standing at the edge of a river under a full moon. The print was in neo-classical Maxfield Parish style. On a low shelf in front of it, photos were displayed, with beads, feathers and candles. In the center was a large pewter bowl filled with burnt bits of paper and dried plants. A small bookcase stood empty; the contents piled into a plastic crate.

"Isn't the headboard cool? We did the decoupage from a poster Hayley bought at a garage sale. We call it The Witch's River," Lillian said proudly.

"It's beautiful. Do you think she might have her passwords hidden in a diary or something?"

"Maybe. When I came and got her phone, it was inside the box spring. I got some other stuff, too. I'll show you later, but the phone was the main thing," Lillian said.

The drawers to her dresser were open and empty as well. Except for the altar, the room was in the process of being packed up, with cardboard boxes piled against one wall. The room was obviously a haven for Hayley, an escape from the chaos and disorder of her life with Dina. Lillian looked around, dismayed to see the vestiges of her friend's life being dismantled.

"She would hate this," she said sadly.

They dug around in Hayley's belongings for several minutes but there was no secret book or folder. Emily searched the shelves of her closet and under her mattress; if anything had been hidden there it was gone now. She ran her hands along the backs of the dresser drawers but found nothing. They heard a car pull up outside. Lillian moved to the window.

"It's Glenda Kupp!" she whispered.

Emily peered out and saw several teenage boys climb out of her SUV while Glenda fumbled in her purse.

"Who're the kids with her?" Emily asked.

"Her grandsons, Billy and Clay. They're tight with Danny Granville," Lillian replied.

Glenda extracted a key from her purse, and they heard the front door swing open downstairs. Lillian's eyes widened in alarm as she grabbed Emily's wrist, her fingers digging in with surprising strength.

"We can't be caught here," she whispered urgently, pulling Emily toward Dina's bedroom. "Especially not by Glenda."

Dina's room was a mess of strewn clothing, trash and plastic boxes half-filled with her belongings. It looked as if she was planning a move. They heard Glenda and the boys downstairs, Dina mumbling in conversation with them. The door to Dina's room wouldn't close properly so Emily pushed a plastic storage bin against it and turned the lights off. Lillian ducked into the closet, and Emily flattened her body against the wall behind the door. They heard heavy footsteps on the stairway and Glenda breathing hard as she ascended.

"She says the stuff is all packed up in her room. Whose car is that in the cul-de-sac?" Glenda asked as she passed the doorway.

"Maybe some hikers. Should we take all of it?" Billy Kupp asked. Emily recognized his voice from the beach barbecue.

"Yeah. They said it must be in her things, so we'll take it all back. Check the closets and under the bed. I'm gonna make sure Dina has her meds," Glenda said.

The boys carried the boxes from Hayley's room out to the SUV, making several trips. Finally, two of them navigated the headboard down the narrow stairway.

Clay asked, "Are we taking this, too?"

"Nah, just put that out with the trash where it belongs. We'll come back for the rest after we drop this off," Glenda said. Emily crept silently to the window and watched Glenda walk around her car, checking the license plate. Then she drove away with the boys.

"They're gone," Emily said.

"Let's get out of here!" Lillian whispered.

They hurried down the stairs and saw Dina, crashed out on the couch. She was so still; Emily checked her breathing. It was slow but steady, she was knocked out cold. Her skin felt normal to the touch, not clammy nor pale and blue. On the counter Emily saw a small brown bag that had not been there when they'd arrived. She opened it and found an unmarked bottle of pills and a small plastic envelope containing milky white crystals, with the telltale cat urine smell.

"Is it drugs?' Lillian whispered.

"It's methamphetamine," Emily said.

From Dina's blacked out stupor, Emily suspected a fast-working opioid, most likely mainlined into her bloodstream. She checked the trash and found a crumpled piece of foil with a white powdery residue on it and a fresh syringe next to the kitchen faucet. Emily checked Dina's breathing again. Though slow, it was regular and strong, her color still good despite her overall unhealthy appearance. The dose had been carefully calibrated—enough to keep her compliant and sedated but not enough to kill her. Whoever had supplied it knew exactly what they were doing. This wasn't Dina's typical self-medication; someone wanted her quiet but alive. Emily grabbed a paper towel and retrieved the foil, wrapping it carefully and slipping it into her bag.

"What's that?" Lillian asked.

"Harder stuff. That'll put you in jail for years," Emily replied.

They left Dina crashed out, certain she would not remember they had been there. As Emily started to pull the car away, Lillian jumped out to grab the headboard.

"Hayley loved this! I'm not gonna let them toss it out like trash!" she said. Emily helped her get it into the hatch of the Mercedes and started to back up when she saw the looming form of white-haired Roy standing directly behind her bumper.

Emily leaned out the window. "Excuse me, sir, we have to leave."

He just stared at her for a moment, his gaze as hard as flint beneath his prominent browbone.

"I do it for the children," he said hoarsely and stepped away. They drove back over the narrow, bumpy road and out of Crest Park. In the rearview mirror Emily saw Roy watching them leave, unmoving, like a scarecrow in a cornfield.

Roy watched the car with the strange woman drive off. He recognized the dark-haired girl with her. He'd seen her around town for years but could not recall her name. They'd been visiting Dina who used to have a loud house but now it was always so quiet. He used to call it that, the loud house. Because he could hear her voice, like a banshee screeching at her girl. The blond one, with the bright smile. He knew her by sight, but he couldn't remember her name. He had trouble with names. Despite his lanky, wiry body, he felt heavy. Everything in him felt heavy, his blood, his bones, his limbs, since he'd lost his girls. How he loved seeing them, even from afar.

When they told him he couldn't keep them, he used to hide outside and watch them, doing simple things. Raking the leaves or taking the trashcans in. He liked their smiles and the way their voices sounded. The bigger one was sharp, like a new blade. He knew she would manage but the younger one was different. She needed him to look out for her. She didn't know the right words to say when they talked fast and confused her. He knew that feeling, he'd been that way since he'd come back from the jungle a long time ago.

It had been hell in the jungle, fear was everywhere and sometimes, he felt he was right back there. The thick green trees, the air so heavy he could barely breathe, the wet rasping cough sucking at his lungs. The bugs. He couldn't forget the bugs. He'd never seen bugs so big and sometimes he felt that they were crawling all over him and he had to jump and shake them off. It was the bugs that made the lady in the suit take the girls. But he could still watch them until he couldn't anymore. They left and no one told him where they were. Some days he felt like his heart would break into tiny pieces, and others, he felt a white-hot rage come up inside him, like a dragon breathing fire. Some days he felt like burning everything down, the forest, the trees, the people with their fat, self-satisfied faces.

Roy stared into the darkness, his weathered hands curling into fists at his sides. They had taken his girls—both of them now—and the town conspired to hide the truth. The rage that had simmered for months threatened to boil over, burning away the fog of confusion that often clouded his mind.

One day, he would make them talk. One day, they would tell him where Melora was.

And if they wouldn't tell him—he'd make them pay.

TWELVE

Back at Lillian's, Emily helped her unload the headboard and place it in the living room. The decoupage was impressive, and it fit with the big dramatic ceilings of Lillian's house. Emily hadn't heard from Lynne and sent her a quick text to check in.

> Everything okay with dad?

> Yes he's fine. Still sleeping. Just took Sammy out for a bathroom break.

> Feel free to go, I'm just minutes away at Lillian's

> thx! your dad got up and ate a big serving of the casserole so he's good for the night

"I'm heading home, Lillian. Thanks for taking me to Hayley's," Emily said.

"Sure. I wish we'd found that password somewhere. I'll text you if I hear back from Manuel. Maybe he knows something."

Dusk was falling. Emily walked the path back toward the Maison and saw Lynne leaving. Emily waited behind a large cedar tree; she was too tired to make conversation. She slipped down to the dock and sat at the edge, dangling her feet just above the water. The lake looked like smoky green glass, with ripples making their way to the shore from a passing kayak. Emily felt like she was holding the shards of a broken vase in her hands, trying to fit the pieces together again. There could be a simple explanation for Glenda Kupp being at Dina's house. She was helping a member of the community in the aftermath of her daughter's suicide. But the bag of illegal drugs told a different story.

From what Lillian said, there had been no real investigation into Hayley's death, that a deputy told her not to stir up trouble. Emily would've liked to see the case files and the medical examiner's ruling on her autopsy, but she had no way of accessing that information. She had no standing to ask for it, especially based on the assertion of a fifteen-year-old girl she hadn't known forty-eight hours ago. But Lillian wasn't the only one who thought something was wrong. Eddie March agreed. While many adults were quick to dismiss teenagers as unreliable or overly dramatic, Emily knew better. Her years investigating cases had taught her that adolescents often noticed crucial details adults missed. They witnessed conversations not meant for their ears, picked up on subtle tensions and unspoken dynamics, and moved through spaces where adults couldn't follow. Teenagers lived in a liminal world between childhood and adulthood that gave them a unique perspective—one Emily had learned never to underestimate.

Emily felt there was something bigger, more sinister going on, but she was missing the connective pieces to put it all together. It was an instinct, a feeling that some people would ignore, but having survived James Tibbs, she knew that this organic warning system was rarely, if ever, wrong. She needed to dig into the histories of the girls Eddie and Lillian had mentioned: Joannie Dietrich, Rachel Carson and Karly Ann Smith.

Emily noticed a missed call notification from Vannah on her phone. When she tried returning the call, it failed to connect. The Maison apparently sat in one of the mountain's notorious dead zones—a technical quirk Vannah confirmed when she immediately responded to Emily's text message.

> I just feel so bad about today the whole thing was a huge mess!!

> No problem, things like this happen.

> How about coffee at my house tomorrow morning? I'm making cinnamon rolls!

> Great idea, thanks!

At the Maison, Emily found Michael sitting up in bed, watching a documentary about deep sea fishing in the Bering Sea. A large fishing boat was being tossed about on the screen like a child's bath toy.

"I don't think I would ever do this. Do you?" he asked.

"Nothing could get me to go out there," she said. "But it's kind of a stress release to see other people doing it."

"I don't know," he said, changing the channels. "I think I'll go to sleep; we had a big day."

He slid under the covers, and she left the nightlight on for him. She kept his door slightly ajar so she could hear him if he got up and roamed around. In her bedroom, she opened her laptop and did a search for the witch trials in the U.S. and Europe in the sixteenth and seventeenth centuries, to find any information about doors being marked with purple. She found numerous forums describing a purple door on a house being a sign that a witch lived there. She pulled up countless stories of people being targeted by neighbors and even family members. Although there were differences among countries and regions, there were some common threads.

The witches accused were overwhelmingly women, exposing the deep misogyny that characterized the era. Women who were older, single, unmarried, women who were natural healers who understood rudimentary, plant-based medicine. There were all manner of macabre tortures and tests that the women and girls were put through. She then searched for anything related to drowning and came upon a terrifying test called swimming the witch. A suspected witch would be bound and submerged in water to prove her innocence or guilt. Floating meant she was guilty, sinking meant she was innocent. Either way, the woman died.

In almost all the cases, regardless of the test, the women were found guilty in the end. They had to be guilty; they were the scapegoats for bigger issues. It wasn't about real witchcraft or magic; that was simply a name for the fear that gripped people who didn't know how to deal with a hostile environment, and it brought out the worst forms of violence and persecution against the easiest targets. They had to be gotten rid of. Some things hadn't changed, even with the passage of hundreds of years. Emily was beginning to believe that Hayley Hope, the beautiful, free-spirited girl who played at being a witch, posed a danger to someone and Lillian was right. It wasn't a suicide.

Online, Emily searched for any mention of Joannie Dietrich, Rachel Carson and Karlie Ann Smith, wondering how three teenaged girls could simply stop showing up at school and no one thought anything of it. But she knew very well how that could happen. It had happened to her when James Tibbs took her from Veteran's Park decades ago. It was weeks before anyone looked for her and by then, she was locked away in his bunker with the real Emily Ray, the girl whose name she took in an effort to keep her alive and escape her own sad reality. Vulnerable girls, throwaway girls were always the most at risk.

Since the girls had been in the foster care system, Emily couldn't access any information about them behind the county firewall in place to protect them. She sent a text to Izzy Doqui, one of the data analysts on her FBI team.

> Hi Iz, hope all is well need your advice regarding a firewall I need to get past

Izzy was a crack computer hacker; he could break through anything put up to safeguard information. They'd worked together on so many CARD cases, she knew she could trust him. And she was asking for advice and guidance, not for him to do the actual internet search. She knew that to investigate Hayley's case properly, she had to be reinstated with the FBI, even though she had promised her husband that she would take time off. She dialed Antonio's number, hoping they could discuss it, but it went straight to voicemail again. She guessed he was having a great time since he usually answered her calls right away.

She walked out onto the deck and looked up at Lillian's house, wondering how lonely she must've felt in the weeks since Hayley's death. That feeling, of being alone in the world, with no safety net, had haunted Emily her whole life. If there was a way to help one young girl escape that, she was willing to do it.

Vannah Granville looked at the mess of pantry staples strewn across her kitchen floor. A bag of flour split open; a broken jar of preserves smeared on the baseboards. Canned goods, bags of pasta and soda cans looked as if they'd been hit by a tornado. Her heart was pounding in her chest, and she felt short of breath. The destruction and disorder were her fault, she had done it in a fit of frustration and fury. She and Cody had fought, again. When she saw Ernesto and his daughter arrive at the barbecue, she knew why they'd come, and she was sure that the others knew as well. The black, plastic bag he held and pushed into Cody's hands was like a knife cutting through her. She knew what it meant, that her husband had been the one to give it. Just like the others.

They had prayed over their marriage; Pastor Jim had anointed them with oil, and they had knelt for hours asking for God's guidance. But it kept happening, Satan was triumphant over Cody's weak spirit and flesh. Vannah wiped the tears of rage from her face and began cleaning up. She cringed at the memory of how she had screamed at Cody when they returned home from the ill-fated barbecue. It was supposed to be a peaceful, idyllic afternoon for Emily to see how they lived, how close to God they were.

A picture-perfect contrast to Lillian's crazy life because they were all concerned about that connection. Emily had children of her own, so surely she saw that the Knox girl was like a train that had come off the track. Living in the big house with an old grandmother, indulging in dangerous behaviors, letting her mind run wild. The girl talked constantly, revealing details to strangers that certain powerful people in town preferred to keep buried. She should've been shut down by now, but nothing had gone according to plan.

Now stupid Kristen had left her kids unattended, and Emily was the one to pull little Shadrack from the water, making them look like irresponsible parents. And Amber hadn't helped with her snarky attitude. Ernesto arriving with that girl of his was the final straw. They were supposed to present a united front. None of them understood the importance of keeping Emily on their side or what was at risk.

Once Vannah found out she was coming up, knowing her background in the FBI, everything had been thrown into neutral, like a car idling at the race line. When Emily insisted on renting the Maison, next to blabbermouth Lillian Knox, Vannah knew they'd have to be vigilant. There was work to be done, chapters to be written and closed, for good. But that would have to wait now. It was hard enough to stay in this holding pattern, but Cody had provoked her. She looked up at the triptych of wedding photos she had blown up and placed prominently on the mantelpiece. They were poster-sized, placed there as if to remind everyone that they belonged together and they were happy. In the photos, she was only nineteen, just out of high school. She was tall and slender, she was beautiful.

She'd done everything she was supposed to do. Accepted her husband as the head of the family and her role as his servant. She'd been a faithful wife, birthed four children with two more on the way. She knew she had a duty to remain attractive and sexually desirable to her husband but after four children she was no longer the girl in the wedding photos. She had tried to get herself back into her high school size and shape, but motherhood made that impossible, combined with the relentless cycle of cooking, cleaning, childcare and church.

Pastor Jim would put the fault on her, that Cody strayed because of her failings as a woman. He'd already told her that the last time it happened. She'd taken his words like the lash of a whip, adding to her deep sense of failure and frustration. In her heart, she blamed Cody, though she knew it was a sin. She would have to make amends, do penance for the sin of anger and disobedience against her husband. She wondered what punishment Cody and Pastor Jim would decide on to break her of her pride and willfulness. She'd been forced to prostrate herself before them in the past; she'd lost her temper over Cody's attention to the young girls, and she'd paid for it.

She swept the broken glass into the dustpan and tossed it in the trash. She knelt and began gathering the pantry items to put them back in place. Anger was a sin; it did not lead to the righteousness of God. She had failed in her duty as a wife. She remembered the way she and Emily had run wild during those long-ago summer months, swimming in the lake after dark, drinking beers stolen from the fridge out on the docks of the empty houses. She could barely remember the girl she had been, the way she had looked and moved through the world. Before the Church on the Hill. Before Cody and making babies to be God's warriors. She prayed silently for God's forgiveness, for guidance to do His work.

Her knees ached, her bladder felt as if it would burst. She was exhausted. The spasms in her lower back always flared up in the final months of pregnancy and the weight of the babies felt unbearable. Cody suddenly came in and grabbed her hand, without a word, yanking her to her feet and pushing her ahead of him toward the bedroom. He had always been like this— angry confrontations meant silent, aggressive sex afterward, a show of his dominance and control, which she knew he was entitled to as the leader in their marriage. It was her duty to submit, to fulfill his needs in the way and at the time he desired. She fought back tears as he slammed the bedroom door shut behind them. She drew a deep breath, forced a smile and turned to him.

Danny Granville ran along Golden Rule Avenue, toward the lake and Tavern Bay. He reached the water and took the path toward the village, past the big lake houses. Many were empty and the path would be dark soon. He didn't care, he just wanted to get away. Away from his parents fighting again, his mother screaming and crying as his father shouted her down into submission, his voice like the air horn on a semi-truck. Then the sounds of things being tossed and broken, hurled across the kitchen and crashing against the walls. The sobs of his mother crying alone, surrounded by the mess she had created. When he was younger, he had helped her to clean up after one of these outbursts, but his father had beaten him with a belt for doing a woman's work, insisting that she had to show remorse for her willfulness and anger. He never helped her clean up again.

He ran until his lungs burned. He stopped and sat, listening to the sound of the lake, lapping against the docks as the patrol boat went by. His heart slowed, but his stomach remained in a tight knot. The cool, night air felt good on his skin, evaporating the sweat. He wished his parents would stop fighting, that they would act the way they did in public and at church when they were at home. Everyone at school thought he had the perfect life, his mom was always volunteering, bringing food to school events, the team mom for all his sports. They knew his dad was a deputy sheriff and the local cops would watch Danny's back, even when he got caught drinking at age thirteen behind the middle school or breaking into cars at the campground.

He could do whatever he wanted in town, but it didn't make him feel good, like everyone thought it did. He felt like crap, he felt weak. Like a baby who always had Mommy and Daddy taking care of him, never letting him stand on his own, like a man. He had to be everything that his parents expected of him. He knew he was supposed to hate Hayley Hope and Lillian Knox, but he didn't, even though he would never admit that to anyone. He went right along with harassing them, even instigating it to show everyone how he was a team player. But he liked Hayley, he thought she was the prettiest girl at school, and she was different from the others. Lillian was kind of weird, but she didn't bother anyone, especially now. She just kept talking about things that his parents insisted were nonsense. Everyone acted like she was crazy, even his grandma said that. At school, no one hung out with her except Eddie March.

They didn't bother him, but he knew he had to be against them, it was expected of him, and he was the leader of his friend group, just like his dad was. He had a role to play, shoes to fill and even if they didn't fit right or the load was too heavy, he couldn't shake it off. Sometimes he felt like he was drowning, he wondered what it would be like to go under the water and just open his lungs. The first moment would be bad but then it would be peaceful. Quiet.

He hoped it had been that way for Hayley, but he knew she didn't choose it. He knew things he wished he didn't and sometimes, running into the darkness of the night was the only thing that calmed him down and stilled the nagging whispers in his brain. He closed his eyes; it was dark now and the moon was rising. He wished he could stay there forever in silence, not moving forward or back, forgetting his name, his family, his life. And how Hayley Hope died.

THIRTEEN

The next morning, Emily found Lynne already bustling around the kitchen as she laced up her running shoes.

"I'm making some banana nut muffins for you both," Lynne announced, measuring flour into a mixing bowl. "You're not allergic, are you?"

"No, but I'm heading to Vannah's for coffee after my run. Dad's still asleep, but I'm sure he'll enjoy one."

Emily felt a flicker of guilt as she watched Lynne efficiently moving around the kitchen. This trip was supposed to be about quality time with her father, yet here she was, leaving him with a caregiver while she pursued both social obligations and her growing concerns about Hayley Hope. But Michael seemed content with Lynne's company, perhaps even more relaxed without Emily's watchful eyes constantly monitoring him for signs of confusion.

"I'm sorry that Knox girl next door is butting in on your trip," Lynne said, peevishly.

"She doesn't bother me at all. She's a smart kid, I like talking to her."

"Still, I think her parents should come back and give her

some guidance. From what I hear, she's got some screws loose," Lynne said.

Emily shrugged and ran out the door and made a loop along the highway, toward the Village. As she passed the marina, she saw several boats getting ready to launch. The sun was already shining brightly, and it was going to be a busy day on the water. Many of the homes had lawn flags with religious messages, one home had a gigantic wooden cross installed on the front lawn, with floodlights to illuminate it at night. She wondered how the neighbors liked it.

Forty-five minutes later, she was walking up the hill of Montrose Street to Vannah's house. It was at the end of a cul-de-sac, a white house with a front porch painted bright blue. A large wooden sign was set into the lawn on a stake. It read "God's Word Stands Forever." A collection of brass crosses hung by the front door. Emily knew that in the south, some people painted their homes or porches blue as protection from "haints" or evil spirits. It was as if Vannah's house were warding off some kind of evil, through the power of prayer, scripture and garden décor.

Before Emily could knock, Vannah opened the door with her hair pulled up into a messy bun and an apron tied around her protruding belly.

"C'mon in, Emily! I'm just pulling the cinnamon rolls from the oven," she said happily, a slight tremor in her voice.

Emily saw that Vannah's eyes were red and swollen. Vannah noticed her concern and fiddled with her ponytail.

"I know I look a mess! My allergies are really acting up this time of year," Vannah said, heading toward the kitchen.

She moved stiffly but Emily knew the final months of pregnancy with twins were physically hard. The house smelled delicious; it was decorated in white, beige and gray, with large throw pillows and kitschy metal signs hung on the walls. They all had religious messages or lines of scripture. An older woman emerged from a bedroom, holding twin toddlers by the hands.

"Emily, this is my mother-in-law, Dede Granville. She owns the property management company that handles your rental house," Vannah said, keeping her eyes down.

Dede Granville was a pretty woman but with a hardness that was common in many women who lived in backwoods counties and the rural middle America. She had an angular jaw, and her fair skin was dry and wrinkled beyond her years. She was probably in her early sixties, but she looked much older. She reminded Emily of a character from a film, set in the old west, a woman homesteader who would shoot a man dead from fifty feet away with a single bullet between the eyes. If Dirty Harry were a grandma, he would be Dede Granville. She extended a weathered hand; her grip was like a wrestler's.

"Hello, Emily, I'm Dede," she said, her voice a harsh rasp that suggested decades of cigarettes. The woman's hand grasped Emily's with surprising strength.

Emily felt an instant, visceral wariness. "Nice to meet you. I met Cody yesterday."

"I'm taking the kids over to Miss Amy's for the playgroup," Dede announced abruptly. "We'll be back for lunch." She ushered the twins toward the door, her movements efficient and authoritative.

"She's the best," Vannah chirped once Dede had left. "Always ready to help with the littles."

Emily settled onto a barstool, struck by the transformation in her former friend. The teenage Vannah she remembered had been bold and spirited, challenging boys to diving contests and flirting shamelessly with local lifeguards. Now she seemed diminished somehow, moving with the careful deference of someone accustomed to monitoring her every word and gesture. She pulled a tray of cinnamon rolls from the oven with practiced precision. A bowl of homemade frosting was waiting on the countertop.

"I just feel so bad about what happened yesterday," Vannah said, not quite meeting Emily's eyes. "It turned into such a mess, and your poor dad got so upset."

"He's recovered," Emily replied, watching Vannah's nervous movements. "He ate well last night. Today will be better."

At that moment, Cody Granville came down the stairs in his uniform, strapping his firearm into place in his gun belt. He kissed Vannah on the forehead.

"How's my babymaker this morning?" he asked, as she moved to pour him a steaming cup of coffee from a French press. She kept her eyes averted; her body language stiffened at his arrival. He settled onto a bar stool beside Emily.

"I was just telling Emily how bad I felt about yesterday," Vannah said, sliding his cup to him.

He looked at her expectantly and she quickly grabbed a small pitcher of milk and a sugar bowl, setting them next to him.

"It was unfortunate, for sure. We wished you all had been able to stay longer and really get to know everyone," he said with a tight smile.

"Maybe next time," Emily said.

"Yeah, Vannah said your husband and kids are coming up, right?"

"Yes, in a few days."

Vannah took a seat next to her; she was flanked by both of them.

"I just feel that... I don't know... maybe your vacation is being affected by the girl next door to you," Vannah said earnestly, placing her hand on Emily's arm.

"Lillian Knox? No, she's just a kid. She's not bothering me at all," Emily replied, reaching to pour herself a cup of coffee.

"Oh, I'm sorry! I should've done that! What kind of hostess

am I?" Vannah blurted out, quickly taking the French press and filling Emily's cup.

"Don't worry about it, this isn't the 1950s," Emily said.

On a stack of bills and other household paperwork, Emily saw the black bag that Ernesto had pushed on Cody and Jim Jenkins. She saw a logo for GoSmart Mobile, a brand of track phones that operate without a wireless carrier contract. A slim, white cell phone was sticking out of the bag; that was what Ernesto Garcia had returned to Cody.

"I know Lillian talks about all kinds of crazy things and I'm sure she's said some of that to you," Vannah said, looking to Cody for approval.

"Like what?" Emily asked.

"Like all that talk about her friend Hayley. How she didn't kill herself and all that. She's been saying that for weeks now, to anyone who will listen," Vannah said.

"I didn't take that seriously," Emily said.

Vannah looked nervously to Cody.

"You mean she said that to you?" she asked.

"Yeah, but she's a kid," Emily said.

They sat in awkward silence for a moment, then Cody said, "I need you to understand, Emily, this is a really small town. People have a different way of doing things up here. Some problems are just better dealt with in our own way."

"Like what?"

They looked at each other for a beat then Cody said, "Like the meth heads. There are people up here who get into these vacant houses, they cook meth, set up shop, and they sell it to the locals. Sometimes it's easier to just run them off, you know, scare the hell out of them than to go through all the legal steps, which may mean that they're out and back before you can blink an eye."

Emily nodded, keeping her expression neutral while her mind raced. The conversation had taken an alarming turn, and every instinct warned her that this seemingly casual friendship was connected to something far darker. She needed them to keep talking, to reveal more of what they were hiding.

Cody's casual dismissal of legal procedures sent a chill through her. This wasn't just small-town justice; it was a recipe for unchecked power and targeted abuse. A system where certain men decided who deserved punishment, free from oversight or accountability. Where a sheriff's deputy could designate someone as a problem and make them disappear. Where the vulnerable had no recourse against the powerful.

Vannah looked to Cody before speaking again. "I know you're here to relax, I just don't want you to get caught up in these little local dramas. Like with Lillian, I know you feel sorry for her. She's not normal, especially since Hayley died. They were both into creepy stuff, dangerous stuff."

"I think she's sad and upset. Her best friend just died," Emily said.

"Sure, but she makes up a lot of things for attention. She likes to stir the pot and cause trouble," Cody said.

"Like you said, Lillian's fixated on this wild conspiracy theory about Hayley," Vannah said, her fingers fidgeting nervously with her coffee cup. "But the truth is so much simpler." She glanced sideways at Cody, who gave a subtle nod of encouragement.

"Of course she killed herself," Vannah continued, her voice taking on a practiced, sympathetic tone. "The poor girl had serious problems—drugs, hanging around with a bad crowd. It's tragic, but not mysterious."

Emily noticed the choreographed quality of their exchange —how Vannah seemed to be reciting lines from a script they'd rehearsed, each statement validated by Cody's silent approval.

"Lillian doesn't like cops. We've been at her house a few times to check up on her since her parents are gone a lot and she's there alone with her grandmother, who isn't well. She's been going around telling everyone that Hayley's case was covered up, stuff like that," Cody said.

They looked at her with such intensity, Emily wondered why it mattered what she believed. She pondered her answer, taking time to respond. Sometimes silence was enough to push people to give away more than they plan to, and she was hoping that tactic would work here. A moment later, it did.

"I can arrange for you to talk to the detective who handled the case, Mike Prentiss, so you can see for yourself. Maybe that'll help Lillian to let go of her crazy ideas. We worry about her over there alone. She should use the security system, she'd be safer," Cody said.

Emily considered for a moment before answering. "Thanks for the offer regarding Prentiss. I might do that and you're right, if she feels that someone else checked it out, she may be able to move on." Emily stood up, signaling that the visit was over. "I have to get back to my dad."

Vannah leaned in to give her a hug. "Good. I don't want you to have any extra stress up here."

"With so many empty vacation homes here near you, I'll make sure you get some extra patrols in the area. Just so you know we're keeping an eye on you."

Emily smiled politely, wondering if that was a courtesy or a threat. She thanked them and left. They clearly didn't want her spending time with Lillian or listening to her suspicions about Hayley's death, so much that Cody offered up Mike Prentiss when she hadn't asked for it and had no jurisdiction. He was right, they had their own way of doing things up here that didn't follow law enforcement protocol. What else did that apply to?

As she crossed the highway back to the Maison, she wondered how Cody Granville knew that Lillian didn't use her alarm system. She guessed they had eyes on everything she did, since she kept talking about the things they wanted forgotten. Dede Granville managed the Maison du Lac, she had keys and knew the WIFI password. She had access to the video footage from the security cameras, which meant that Vannah and Cody could see everyone who came and went from the Maison. And they'd placed the illegal cameras inside. Emily realized that she had to disable the outside cameras, like she had inside the house. She couldn't trust Lynne to keep a secret either, she was too much of a town gossip.

Emily decided to take Cody up on his offer of access to Mike Prentiss, to see how it played out. Since Prentiss was another of the old family names in Oak Lane Flats, she had no confidence in him telling her anything other than what Cody wanted her to hear, but she would play along. She had good cell phone coverage on the highway, so she called Antonio to check in. The call went straight to voicemail again. She called Dolores, Antonio's aunt, who was with him on the family vacation in Arizona.

"Hi, mija! How's everything?"

"Fine. Very nice and relaxing," Emily replied, deciding not to tell her about Michael's meltdown the day before.

"The girls went to the water park with my sister, Inez, and her grandkids. They're just fine, eating and sleeping well. And getting very tan!" Dolores said.

"Good, they look extra pretty when they're nice and brown. I keep missing Toño, I have bad cell coverage at the lake. How's he doing?"

Dolores hesitated before answering, then said, "Toño's out with his cousins."

"Is everything okay?"

"Oh, yes. It's fine. He's been having fun."

"Tell him I'll call him later," Emily said.

On the way home, she passed the old UCLA Conference Center, an impressive lodge on a sprawling, multi-acre lot of forest land. It was bordered by a beautiful creek surrounded by wild birch trees. She stopped to take a photo when she got a text from Lillian.

> Got a hold of manuel heredia he said to meet him he's helping some friends move.

> When/where?

> Asap the address is in the villas he'll only talk if I come along

> Fifteen minutes in the Old North Road turning point

She picked up her pace and got back to find Michael eating a big omelet with cheese and peppers. Lynne had the TV tuned to a Cheers marathon.

"This is delicious!" Michael exclaimed, his eyes lighting up as he savored another bite of his omelet. "You should have one, honey. And look what Lynne found! My favorite show!"

Emily smiled, watching her father's simple delight. The brilliant businessman who once orchestrated international deals and commanded boardrooms now found his greatest joy in food and old television reruns. His world had contracted, but there was a strange peace in his forgetting. The sharp edges of past trauma and regret had softened for him.

Unlike those whose lives ended before they'd truly begun— before they could outrun their demons or reconcile with their pasts. The real Emily Ray. Hayley Hope. They would forever remain frozen in their final moments, denied even the bitter-sweet mercy of memory's decay.

Half an hour later, Emily and Lillian pulled up at a house perched on a hillside in the Arrowhead Villas. A pickup truck with a U-Haul trailer attached was sitting out front. Two young men were securing a tarp over the load in the bed of the pickup.

The taller one waved, and shouted, "Just let me finish up here so they can leave."

"That's Manuel," Lillian said.

He went inside. Emily put the car in idle. They were high on a winding street called Halstead Court that overlooked the San Bernardino valley down below. The woods were dense, with a wild feel not found in the more curated neighborhoods of Arrowhead Woods. In the Villas it seemed like they were in the middle of a vast forest from an old fairy tale and strange, mythical creatures might be hiding around each thick tree trunk. A young buck moved silently in a small meadow, stopping to stare at them with his velvety rack of antlers. Several black crows flew over and perched on the tall branches of a cedar tree as if they were listening in on them. Lillian took some peanuts from her pocket and tossed them to the ground. A moment later the crows swooped down and grabbed them.

"Do you think every crow on the mountain knows you?" Emily asked.

Lillian smiled. "Maybe."

Manuel emerged and introduced himself. Emily stepped out to meet him.

"What exactly do you want to know about Hayley?" Manuel asked, shifting his weight from one foot to the other. His dark eyes darted past Emily to scan the street behind her. "Lillian said you're looking into what happened?"

"She's in the FBI," Lillian interjected, a hint of pride in her voice.

Manuel tensed visibly, taking a half-step back.

"I'm not investigating in any official capacity," Emily clarified quickly, employing the measured tone she'd perfected over years of interviews. "Lillian's shared some things that don't quite add up. I'm just trying to get a clearer picture of Hayley's life by talking to people who knew her."

Manuel's shoulders remained rigid. He glanced toward his house before lowering his voice. "My parents can't know about this conversation. They already told me not to talk to anyone when the cops came by after it happened."

"The cops talked to you after she drowned?" Lillian asked, surprised.

"Yeah, Hayley and I had a fight about a week before that and they kept wanting to make it seem like I was involved. I wasn't even on the mountain when it happened, I was at my uncle's house in Riverside, but they kept pushing until my dad told them to leave."

Before Emily could ask another question, the young woman from the hotel desk came out carrying a small suitcase. She saw Emily and froze for a moment, then she hurried back inside.

"Who is that girl?" Emily asked.

"That's Daila, my friend's sister. They're moving back to Mexico. There's some family emergency or something."

A moment later, Ernesto hurried out with a knapsack, followed by a woman carrying a small dog. They got into the cab of the pickup, then Daila scurried into the backseat, her eyes glued to the ground. Everything about their departure looked rushed, anxious and sudden. There were still boxes and some furniture in the driveway.

"Do you think I could talk to them before they leave?" Emily asked Manuel.

"I'll check," he said but as he approached the truck, Ernesto waved him off, started up the engine and drove his family away, without a glance back. They were running from something. Emily watched in dismay as his taillights disappeared around the next curve in the road. The buck sniffed the air and made a sharp rutting sound before he bolted off into the woods.

FOURTEEN

They drove through the winding, narrow streets of the Villas, and Emily explained what she had seen at the hotel and the barbecue with Ernesto and Daila.

"Something happened. Ernesto had just gotten a new job with a landscaping company and Daila was starting junior college in the fall. The Gomez family lived here for years. There's no way they would've just left like that. Those people did something," Manuel said.

"I told you," Lillian said from the backseat.

"They think they can do whatever they want, all the ones that go to that big church. They act like they run the whole town," Manuel said, shaking his head.

"But what's the Hayley connection? She wasn't part of that religious scene, was she?" Emily asked.

"No, but she got a job watching the kids on their Wednesday night prayer meetings. She was saving to get out and away from Dina," he said.

"Like the other Houdinis," Emily said.

"Yeah, I'm one, too. I don't want to stay up here. It's a bunch of racist bullshit, all the time," he said. "Some of these kids I've known my whole life, come up to me at school and tell me to go back to my own country. I was born in San Bernardino!" He laughed bitterly.

Lillian was strangely quiet; Emily checked her in the rearview mirror. She was averting her gaze out the window, clearly upset.

"Did Hayley change after she started that job?" Emily asked.

"Sometimes she would disappear on the weekends, just go silent. And she stopped making and posting her little movies to Instagram," he said.

"What d'you guys fight about?"

"One day she had a new phone, one of those GoMobile track phones that can't be traced. I thought it was weird, and she wouldn't say where she got it. We had a fight over that, and we didn't speak for a week or so. I thought we'd make up, I thought I'd have time..." His voice broke. "They called it a suicide because they didn't want to look into her death. The cops wanted it to go away, they didn't dig into it to see what they could find."

They drove in silence for a few minutes. Emily remembered the black GoMobile bag she had seen at Vannah's house. It was what Ernesto had pushed into Cody's hands at the beach barbecue. Emily knew from her years with CARD that gifting a secret phone was one of the first tactics that predators used with vulnerable youth, supplying them with a private line of communication. She wondered if the police didn't want to investigate Hayley's death because they already knew all the answers. They dropped Manuel off near his house and Lillian got into the front seat, still strangely quiet.

"The most important thing we need to do is find that phone, the one she and Manuel fought about. Daila Gomez had a similar phone, and her dad gave it back to Cody Granville. I saw it at their house," Emily said. Lillian remained silent. They drove for a few blocks without speaking.

"There were so many things I didn't know. Like she got that job at Church on the Hill, or she had a new phone. She never told me any of that. I guess you were right, we were drifting apart..." Lillian said, her voice so small it was barely a whisper.

"Sometimes we have to reframe the way we think about things that hurt us. We jump to the most painful conclusion but maybe you should think of it in a different way," Emily said.

"Like what?"

"Like maybe Hayley knew she had gotten involved in something bad. That video shows that she was being careful, trying to record what was going on. And she didn't tell you about any of it to protect you. She didn't want you involved so you wouldn't get hurt, too. I think she was keeping you safe."

Lillian wiped the tears that threatened to spill out. "You're right. I'll look at it that way, so it doesn't hurt so much." The fight against her tears was a losing battle and she began to cry uncontrollably. "Everything just hurts so much..."

Emily pulled over and drew Lillian into her arms. The girl resisted for just a moment before collapsing against her, thin shoulders shaking with sobs that seemed torn from somewhere deep inside. Emily held her, understanding all too well the crushing weight of isolation at that age—when grief feels endless, and adults dismiss your suffering.

As Lillian's tears soaked through her shirt, Emily felt a deep stirring of her conviction. In this girl's desperate fight to be heard, in Hayley Hope's struggle to escape, Emily saw reflections of herself—the terrified child she had been, the vigilant survivor she had become. These weren't just cases to solve or victims to rescue. They were extensions of her own story, battles she would never stop fighting.

No matter how many times Antonio suggested she step back, find balance, disentangle herself from these painful echoes of her past—she couldn't. More importantly, she realized with sudden clarity, she didn't want to. This was who she was, who she needed to be.

Half an hour later, Emily pulled up to the sheriff's station. It was a squat, drab building sandwiched between a tiny Masonic Lodge and a community senior center. The parking lot was almost empty; it was a typical sleepy, small-town police station. She entered and saw wildlife displays of taxidermy coyotes and bobcats, with faded brochures advertising the search and rescue team program and other scant social services. In the tiny outer office, she approached the receptionist's window and asked for Detective Mike Prentiss.

The desk clerk was like a robot, going through her tasks. She barely looked at Emily, as if denying her existence would make her go away. She kept her eyes averted as she buzzed the detective's desk. A tall, pretty woman in her forties passed by holding some paperwork, obviously eyeing Emily. She noticed several other people who cruised by the receptionist's window to get a look at her. She felt like a strange zoo animal on display. Emily figured the whole sheriff's department knew she would be coming by and why; they were most likely circling the wagons to protect each other. Prentiss emerged. He was a short, stocky man with a bull neck squeezed into a dress shirt and blazer. His eyes were close set, and his teeth were abnormally white. He'd gone way overboard on the Crest Strips. He wore a "Don't Tread on Me" pin on his lapel, featuring the coiled snake of political, self-determination movements.

"I'm Detective Prentiss," he said, extending a pudgy hand. His grip felt clammy, and Emily fought the urge to pull her hand back and wipe it on her pants.

"Emily Ray, thank you for meeting with me," she said, with a smile.

They left the tiny, cramped waiting room and walked out into the bright sunlight. Across the street was a cabin rental accommodation called Mountain Lilac Cabins. They sat on one of the roughhewn, redwood tables outside, the sweet scent of the purple lilac filling the air. Prentiss held a single sheet of paper.

"Cody told me you'd been hearing these crazy rumors that Hayley Hope's death wasn't a suicide, but we ran a tight investigation. Talked to her family, the guy she was dating. It seems she'd gotten into drugs, you know, like a lot of troubled kids up here. Her mom's a meth head, the dad used to cook up here until we ran him off," he said.

His explanation was built on the premise that kids from unstable families were pre-destined to get into drugs, to adopt anti-social behaviors, and when bad things happened to them, it was to be expected, or worse, they deserved it. He looked at Emily with the self-assurance of a man who thought all he had to do was offer up a hollow, baseless explanation of Hayley's life, and she would accept it.

But she wasn't there to learn about what happened to Hayley—she knew she was not going to get the truth from Mike Prentiss. She was there to learn how far Cody and Vannah would go to convince her that Lillian Knox was a liar. So far, they were willing to trot out Prentiss, a police detective, in this dog and pony show. She played along as he slid the piece of paper across the table to her. It was a list of names and phone numbers of the people they'd spoken with regarding Hayley's death. There were minimal notes related to those conversations. It was a simple Microsoft Word document, anyone could've written anything on it.

"How long had that been going on? Lillian Knox said she was a good student; she didn't do drugs. So, maybe she fell in with a bad crowd?"

Prentiss hocked up a gob of saliva and spit it into the dirt.

"Those two girls were into witchcraft, okay? They were opening portals to all kinds of evil. It just wasn't what kids do," he said.

"But who really takes that seriously? Tons of kids read Harry Potter and bought magic wands at Target."

"My kids sure didn't read any of that stuff," he blustered. "But the Knox kid lives in that big house with just her grandma. That place had to cost a fortune, her parents are always gone. She can buy anything she wants. She's been going around talking about Hayley's death since it happened. She even stood out there on the highway with a big ass sign about it! A lot of people are tired of it. But I can assure you, as a detective, there was no cover up. Hayley was a poor kid who fell victim to her own bad choices. The whole community was upset when she died. It hit us hard."

Mike Prentiss might as well have been shouting into a bull-horn to let her know all of his petty resentments and prejudices. He resented that Lillian's parents had the money to buy a big lake house. She had expendable income. He didn't like that she and Hayley didn't conform and follow the acceptable trends of other girls in town. It was clear that everything about Hayley and Lillian pushed this jarhead's buttons. She was certain he was not alone in that.

She stood to leave and extended her hand. "I appreciate your time and insight, Mr. Prentiss. And you did go through all her social media on her phone?"

He shook his head. "We couldn't find her track phone."

"How do you know it was a track phone?" she asked. His surprise registered before he could cover it.

"We don't. Could've been a Galaxy or a Google phone. We never found it, but we checked her computer and there was nothing of any importance on it."

"Thank you for your time. It may help Lillian Knox to know

that all due diligence was done on Hayley's case. I think she's just a kid going through a tough time."

He looked pleased with himself as he gave her hand a vigorous shake and said, "I hope so. I'd hate to see something happen to Lillian. She's just a kid."

She stopped, his hand still in hers. "Like what?"

"Sometimes suicides come in clusters. Kids do copycats, you know? I'd hate for her to go the same way Hayley did."

She held his gaze for a beat. The smug look in his porcine eyes, the barely veiled threat to Lillian hit all of her emotional triggers. She felt it in her gut, like a leopard being released from a cage. She would find out what really happened to Hayley Hope. Until she did, Lillian would never be safe in this town.

FIFTEEN

Back at the Maison, Emily caught a glimpse of Lillian on her deck, a single crow taking food from her hand. A clowder of young cats she had not seen before rubbed against her legs. She wanted to warn her about the threat from Prentiss, but she had to couch it in a way that wouldn't scare her. She could easily spend the whole day working the Hayley Hope case, but she felt guilty. This trip was to relax and spend time with Michael. She heard her husband's voice in her head, telling her that she had to step back, not lose perspective.

She saw that Izzy Doqui had replied to her text.

> Sure, whatever you need. Give me a call

Emily slipped into the bedroom and dialed Izzy. He answered in one ring.

"What's up, boss?" he asked.

"I need to find out some information on three girls who went missing from the mountains up in San Bernardino. And I need to get into a Snapchat account that's password protected," she said.

"Aren't you on vacation?"

"Yes, but I kind of... stumbled into this situation," she explained.

Izzy chuckled. "I know you, Emily. You don't know the meaning of downtime. You have one setting and it's go-go-go! That's why you're the head of the team."

"How's everyone doing?" she asked.

"Fine. Leedom's on vacation, hiking somewhere in the Himalayas, you know how young people are. Diaz is good and the cop from the Josie Vance case, Detective Ryan, applied to join the bureau and he got in."

"I'd heard that. He said he was going to Quantico. How's Grice?"

Izzy sighed. "Grice is the same as always. Not the head of the CARD team, like he thought he'd be. Not after that fiasco of having us out in the desert, chasing the wrong guy. They put Agent Doans in as the interim head. I think they're holding that spot for you."

"Say hi to everyone for me. The names of the girls are Joannie Dietrich, Rachel Carson and Karlie Ann Smith. They were in foster care, and they went missing. I think there's a link to a girl who died a few weeks ago. I don't know how to hack into the system to get more information on them. I thought maybe you could tell me how to do it," she said.

"I could tell you, but it'll take you a long time to figure it out. It can't be done from an official bureau computer, but someone might be able to do it from their personal laptop, if they had the skills."

"I see. *Someone* might be able to?"

"That's right. *Someone*. Why don't you check back with me a little later this evening? On my landline at home? And text me the Snapchat account you need to get into," he said, before hanging up.

Emily knew he'd get whatever information he could, off the

books. Like her, Izzy was willing to go a little rogue when it meant helping at-risk kids. His words echoed in her head.

I know you, Emily. You have one setting, go-go-go...

He was right. She would never be able to step back and disengage the way Antonio wanted. This wasn't just a job, she couldn't put it away like a file left on a desk until the next day. Once an investigation began, she lived in it until it was resolved. There was no way to be "less involved" or "less intense" as Antonio suggested. The unsettling thing was, she hadn't changed; she had always been this way. He was the one who wanted a shift that she didn't know if she could accommodate. They needed to have a real conversation. Soon.

She found Michael in the kitchen, happily sharing a slice of cheesecake with Lynne, peaceful and unaware of the growing mystery swirling around his daughter.

"Dad, do you remember going on the Arrowhead Queen with Mom?" Emily asked.

"The Arrowhead Queen?" he looked at her, uncertainty in his eyes.

"The boat in the Village. It takes you all over the lake and they give you the history of the town," Emily said.

"Oh, it is special! The guide shows you all the homes of famous celebrities, like Sammy Hagar and Jay Leno," Lynne added.

Michael looked at them, confused, and asked, "Are they friends of yours?"

An hour later, Emily and Michael were boarding the boat outside the Lakeside Art Gallery. It was an old-fashioned paddleboat, painted white with a wobbly gangplank.

"I remember this! Your mother and I took this boat ride! It goes around the lake, it's a tour!" Michael said, with excitement. He seemed to get the most pleasure from revisiting the moments he spent with Andrea. Emily resolved to take him back to the hotel, perhaps for dinner so he could relive more happy memories.

There were a few other guests, mostly from a tour bus that brought people up from various assisted living facilities in the Inland Empire. A handful of senior ladies boarded with them, and Emily was surprised to see that the attendant was Amber Kupp. She recognized her from the barbecue.

"Over on this side of the boat is better," she said, guiding them to a seat. "It doesn't tilt as much. Is your dad feeling better?"

"Yes, thank you. He's recovered," Emily replied.

"Kristen never keeps an eye on her kids. They're always having accidents that are avoidable, always lots of drama," she said.

"Have you worked here a long time?" Emily asked.

Amber smiled ruefully. "Only since tenth grade. My family runs the boat attraction. My brother is the captain 'cause he didn't want to go into the church like my dad. I just started helping one day and never stopped."

Captain Glenn, her older brother, began preparing to leave as the final guests got settled. Michael smiled and nodded at several senior ladies in sun hats. Amber took the open seat next to them. Of everyone Emily had met in Vannah's friend group, she felt Amber was the most authentic. Vannah and the others all had the perpetually happy, unflappable demeanor so common in Christian housewives. They spoke in quiet, child-like voices as if they were afraid to take up any space or breathe too much air. Amber had the disillusioned look of a woman who had been sold a bag of faulty merchandise with no way to return it. *The Queen* moved away from the dock and Captain Glenn began his narration with a corny enthusiasm.

"Lake Arrowhead was founded in nineteen-twenty by a group of investors that bought Little Bear Lake, the original name given by the Native Americans known as Yuhaaviatam, later called the Serrano Indians by the Spanish. Now, they have that big casino and they're sitting pretty while I ride this boat around every day!" He laughed loudly.

Amber shifted uncomfortably. "I wish he wouldn't say that anymore."

Michael's laugh startled them, and Emily saw that he was sharing a bag of peppermints with the sun hat ladies.

"My late wife and I came here on our honeymoon..." he said, and the ladies smiled approvingly.

"Your dad's got game," Amber said.

"Evidently."

The boat made a wide turn, approaching an area called Shelter Cove. Glenn was pointing out the house that belonged to pop icon, Barry Manilow.

"Do you ever wish you could wake up one day and start your whole life over?" Amber asked suddenly. Emily wasn't sure how to respond.

"Sure, sometimes."

"I guess being in the FBI is exciting, your life must be great. Very different from living here."

"Everyone up here seems to know that I work with the FBI."

"That's Vannah. When you guys connected again, she googled you and found out everything about you. And she has a big mouth, so she told everyone."

"So I gathered."

"They wanted you to rent a different house, over near John Muir Drive. They didn't want you being so close to..." She stopped suddenly, catching herself.

Emily waited, then asked, "So close to what?"

"I mean, there are so many empty houses near where you are. On John Muir there are more full-timers so it's not so quiet. You must do a lot of exciting things living in L.A. I mean, there's nothing here. You just get married and have kids and go to church and have more kids... and that's all," she said, wistfully.

Captain Glenn rang the gong, signaling that they were stopping.

"If any of you want to get a photo, that house up there used to belong to Liberace!" he said loudly. Luckily the passengers were old enough to know who Liberace was.

Emily sensed that Amber wanted to talk, that something was stirring beneath the surface of her secure, small-town life.

"I imagine it's nice growing up here with a group of friends that you have for life," Emily said.

Amber shrugged. "I guess. Sometimes it feels kind of... stifling. Like you have to do all the same things as everyone else. You have to follow the leader."

"Who's that?"

"Cody and Vannah, they're the alpha couple of our group. He leads, of course, she follows him, and we wives follow her example."

Emily thought back to the barbecue, how Cody cuffed Roger by the neck, the nervous look on Miles' face. The way the wives deferred to Vannah as an extension of his authority. How she kept looking to him for approval during the odd coffee date at their house, his cool air of control over her.

"Amber! I need your help up here!" Glenn shouted suddenly. Amber gave Emily a small nod and left to join him. He whispered something in her ear and had her steer the boat for the rest of the trip.

"We rented a boat and went fishing but I dropped my line into the lake..." Michael was regaling the ladies with another honeymoon story.

Emily walked to the back of the boat and looked out at the wake left behind the paddle as it pushed across the water. She was beginning to get a clear idea of the power balance within Vannah's church and in the social culture of the town.

Cody and Vannah are the alphas... he leads, she follows and so do we...

On the return to the dock, Emily got a text from her daughters looking like cute, drenched rats, eating lunch at the water park with Antonio's aunt Inez. He wasn't in the photo, but Emily figured he was probably shooting down the vertical slide the girls were not allowed on. She was happy to see them having a good time and it was nice to get an update, but she missed talking to her husband. After extended goodbyes with the ladies from the boat, Michael and Emily headed back to the car, parked in the Village lot.

"That was a lot of fun, Emily. I think I've still got it!" he said with a wicked smile.

When they arrived at the car, Emily saw that a note had been slipped under the wiper blades. It was handwritten on a torn piece of lined paper.

If you want to know about Hayley Hope, talk to deputy Jamie Dougherty. His brother works at the Cedar Glen Canteen.

SIXTEEN

Lillian had slept for two hours after they met with Manuel Heredia and now, she lay in her bed, ruminating about all the things she had learned. She was trying hard to take Emily's advice and reframe how she felt about the changes Hayley had been going through; the secrets she'd kept from her. She pulled up the file on her phone that held Hayley's videos. She wondered if maybe she had left a clue in there or some kind of warning, anything.

Lillian scrolled through the videos, recognizing all of them. Most were teen coming of age type stories, a few were spooky thrillers, one was about a ghost living in an old, abandoned cabin in the Villas. Hayley shot that one when they stumbled upon a small, beat-up cabin with peeling green paint that was still full of old furniture and items from the nineteen thirties. After that, the green cabin became their hiding place, like a secret fort from childhood.

At the end of the ghost video, Lillian noticed something strange. The final scene showed Hayley pouring tea and sitting by the window, watching for the spectral visitor. But instead of ending there or transitioning to the next film, the footage continued unexpectedly.

The picture stuttered and jumped—clearly spliced in afterward. Suddenly Hayley appeared in completely different surroundings, running through dense woods. The camera bounced wildly, capturing glimpses of the forest floor, tree trunks flashing past, branches snapping underfoot. Hayley's labored breathing provided a frantic soundtrack.

The image whirled as she flipped the camera to film herself. Her face filled the frame—flushed, sweating, eyes wide with unmistakable fear. Unlike her carefully composed film persona, this Hayley was raw, unscripted terror.

"I told him and he lost it," she gasped between ragged breaths, her voice trembling. "Grabbed my wrist and I ran... but he's coming..."

The clip ended abruptly in blackness—as if the phone had been dropped or the recording forcibly stopped.

Lillian stared at the screen, disoriented by what she'd just witnessed. This wasn't one of their creative projects. Hayley had always made Lillian her collaborator—assistant director, prop manager, special effects helper. They'd worked on all her films together, but this... Lillian had never seen this footage before.

The technical quality matched their other projects—the framing, the lighting choices—but the fear in Hayley's eyes had been horrifyingly authentic. Had her friend hidden this from her deliberately? Had she been in genuine danger?

Lillian's heart pounded as she forwarded the clip to Emily and reached for her phone to call Eddie. Maybe he knew something from their Media class that would clarify this. Maybe there was an innocent explanation.

But a cold certainty was already settling in her stomach as she rose from the bed. This wasn't fiction. This was Hayley documenting something real—something dangerous.

Lillian moved to the door, it was time to make her grandma's lunch. The house felt too quiet. Evelyn wasn't in the living room where her half-finished puzzle waited, nor in the den where her favorite shows usually played on Pluto TV.

"Grandma?" Lillian called, her voice rising with each empty room. "Grandma?"

She knocked softly on Evelyn's bedroom door, praying to hear a sleepy response from the other side.

"Grandma? It's time to eat," she said, pushing the door open. The room was empty. Evelyn was gone.

Emily hurried home with Michael, whose energy was flagging from the boat ride. Holding forth with a group of strangers was exhausting for her and she didn't suffer from dementia. She knew he needed a nap, so she got him into bed and waved to Lynne who was preparing dinner for that evening. She drove to Cedar Glen with the note in her pocket, to find Jamie Dougherty.

Cedar Glen was a small neighborhood in Arrowhead, with a commercial corner that featured a thrift store, laundromat, a few trendy home décor shops and the Cedar Glen Canteen. It was a quaint, rustic restaurant, all knotty pine and big booths, a Mr. Coffee Machine on the counter. She stepped into the sweet, intoxicating aroma of pancakes on a griddle, fresh coffee and hash browns toasting on a skillet. This was a place that served breakfast all day, every day. She pulled the note out.

The hostess smiled and said, "Can I get you a table, honey?"

"No, thank you. I'm looking for someone named Dougherty?"

"You mean Jeff? Sure, he's back there." She gestured to the kitchen and shouted, "Jeff! You got someone to see you!"

A tall, slender man in his early thirties whipped off a cook's cap and came out, wiping his hands on a towel.

"What can I do for you, ma'am?"

Emily hesitated, then showed him the note. "Someone left this on my car in the Village today."

"Let's go outside," Jeff suggested, his eyes darting nervously around the diner. Emily followed him into a narrow alleyway behind the Canteen. Jeff scanned the area, as if afraid that something would jump out and corner them.

"Are you a cop?" he demanded, anger and fear mingling in his voice.

Emily considered her response carefully. The note on her car had been deliberately placed there after her visit to the sheriff's station. Either someone had followed her, or the station had a leak. Either way, this connection felt both promising and dangerous.

"No," she replied, keeping her demeanor calm and steady. "I'm just looking into what happened to Hayley Hope for a friend. I spoke with a detective today, and an hour later, I found this note on my car."

"You were at the sheriff's station?"

"Yes, mid-morning."

"I'll give Jamie your number and have him call you. I'll tell you the truth, I hope he doesn't. I've told him again and again to let it all go, forget about it, but he can't," he said. "If he calls you, fine. But don't ever come back here again asking for me."

Emily wrote her number on his order slip, and he jammed it into his pocket. Then he hurried back inside.

On the way back, she decided to pay a visit to Church on the Hill. It was located on Willow Road, across the highway from the marina, not far from Papoose Lake. She circled a few times—all was quiet, the big parking lot empty. It was a large, modern structure, with several extensions attached to the main building. There was a play area for small children, the church preschool, a fence decorated with handmade signs that read:

Apart from the Lord Jesus, there is no Savior" and *"One faith, our journey begins."*

She tried the door of the office and found it locked. She peered into the windows; it was dark and empty. She walked around the back and found a dried, abandoned garden area surrounded by a chain-link fence with a gate secured by a heavy padlock. With no sign of anyone, she walked back to the parking lot and as she rounded the corner of the building, she ran into Roy. He was dressed in baggy pants and a dirty button-down shirt. He carried a large metal shovel and planted himself in front of her.

"I do it for the children," Roy repeated, his vacant stare and monotone voice setting off alarm bells in Emily's mind. Behind the apparent mental confusion, she sensed something sharper— a focused intent that drew him to that place.

"That's good," she replied cautiously, subtly shifting her weight to ensure a clear path to her car. "Helping children is important work."

"I'm looking for the girl," he said, tapping the shovel against the pavement, menacingly.

"Which girl?" Emily asked, watching Roy's face closely. "The one from the lake?"

He shook his head vigorously, agitation rippling through his gaunt frame. "The other one."

"Which other one?" Emily pressed gently.

"My girl's girl," he said, his voice suddenly clearer. "The younger one. I think she's here. I think they're keeping her here."

The man's weathered face held a desperation that was different than mere confusion. Behind his disjointed words, Emily sensed a genuine anguish—not delusions, but perhaps a truth he couldn't quite articulate.

When she tried to leave, his hand shot out with surprising

speed, fingers digging into her arm. "Have you seen her?" he demanded. "My girl's girl? Have you seen her?"

"I haven't," Emily said softly, working to extricate herself without escalating his distress. "But if I do, I'll make sure to tell you."

She pulled away and walked briskly to her car, resisting the urge to break into a run. Something about Roy's insistence nagged at her—less like the ramblings of someone disconnected from reality and more like someone struggling to communicate a terrible truth.

Lynne looked out the big window in the kitchen, toward the water. In the distance, along the lake path, she saw Evelyn Knox walking unsteadily. She was drawing near to the part where the path narrowed and the drop to the water was dangerous. There were rocks below and one wrong step could plunge a person into the cold, bracing water. It was only four feet deep, but it would be risky for someone to fall in and suffer an injury. People drowned in shallow water all the time.

It had been easy to lure Evelyn outside while the girl slept. Evelyn liked going on the deck and often forgot to lock the door behind her. She loved custard tarts and Lynne had heated some up and put them on a pretty china plate to offer her. She knew Evelyn liked pretty things, back from the days when she was involved in all the activities at the senior center. While Emily and her father were out riding the Arrowhead *Queen*, she had slipped across the path to the Knox house and let herself inside. The girl was asleep, and Evelyn was in the den watching television, the same old shows from years ago, like Michael Ray. They all liked those programs, once their minds started to go. All she had to say was that the girl was lost and that was enough to get Evelyn out the door.

Evelyn and Michael were the lucky ones, they had nice

places to live and didn't have to work any longer so what did it matter if they forgot who they were? They had money and a soft place to land, not like Lynne who had to work all day and then take care of her aging husband, Rufus, who was a quarrelsome old coot. She wished she'd never married him after her first divorce but now he was her burden. God gave every woman her cross to bear and Rufus Smenck was hers. All day taking care of rich geezers who didn't know what day it was and then a full workload at home since Rufus made a mess every single day, in the kitchen, the bathroom and everywhere. She thought some days that he did it on purpose.

But being so close to people, inside their homes, came with opportunities also. Like the baubles that people wouldn't ever miss from the jewelry box, those old people weren't getting dressed up and going out any longer. A gold tie clip, a ruby brooch. And she learned a lot, too. People forgot the caregiver was there, like a lamp on a dresser, she overheard many things. Lynne smiled to herself as she watched Evelyn walk unsteadily toward the water. The old woman wouldn't remember how she'd gotten outside or why she was wandering toward the dangerous drop-off point. Perfect. A tragic accident involving a confused elderly woman would redirect Lillian's attention, give her something to occupy her mind besides Hayley Hope and her wild conspiracy theories. The girl talked too much, asked too many questions in a town where questions were dangerous.

A text came through from Emily,

Just checking in, how's my dad?

Lynne smiled and replied:

Everything here is fine. He's still asleep I just took Sammy out for a potty break

She looked out the window and saw Evelyn, peering out at

the water, anxious and distressed. Then she closed the window shade.

Emily was on her way home when she got Lillian's text.

my grandma is missing!!!!

Emily's heart dropped. The terror of losing an elderly, impaired person was one of her worst nightmares. She could only imagine how Lillian felt. She texted back:

Where are you now?

Searching the woods near the house with Eddie

I'll be there in a few minutes don't panic we'll find her

Emily hurried home and rushed out toward the docks. She scanned the lakefront; it was deserted. She waved down a passing kayaker.

"Have you seen an elderly lady out here? She may have wandered away from home," Emily shouted.

"No, but I came from the village side of the lake. Try going around that curve, toward Shelter Cove. There's a lot of wooded areas you can't see from here," he shouted back.

Emily ran along the lake's edge, where the path twisted and dipped, and the ground was rocky in some places. She feared Evelyn might've fallen into the cold water but as she came around a bend, she saw her, standing in a shallow puddle of brackish water. It was a small inlet, filled with debris from trees and bushes, a few ducks paddling peacefully. The standing water was rank and foul smelling, Evelyn was up to her ankles in it.

"Evelyn!" she called out.

Evelyn turned to her, frightened. "I'm looking for Lillian! They said she was lost!" she said, in anguish. Emily texted Lillian.

> Found her. Bring new shoes and socks, she got wet she's safe!

Lillian sent back a string of hearts and thumbs up emojis.

Emily led Evelyn out of the inlet and to the dry dirt of the path. Her slippers were soaked with dirty water, and pond weed tangled around her ankles.

"It's okay, now. Lillian is on her way right now. How did you come out here?" Emily asked gently.

"The lady told me Lilli was lost! That she'd wandered off! I had to find her..."

"She's fine, she's not lost. She's been looking for you. Who told you she was lost?" Emily asked, wondering who would play such a terrifying prank on an old woman.

"It was the lady, I don't know her name."

She began leading Evelyn back toward home when Lillian and Eddie came running toward them.

"Grandma!" Lillian cried, tears of relief streaming down her face as she ran toward Evelyn. She threw her arms around the confused woman, who stood trembling in her soaked slippers.

Eddie quickly draped his jacket over Evelyn's thin shoulders while Lillian knelt to replace the wet footwear with dry socks and sneakers she'd grabbed from the house. As they began the slow walk home, Lillian murmured reassurances to her grandmother, who clutched her hand like a lifeline.

Eddie hung back with Emily, his face taut with anger. "This crosses every line," he whispered fiercely. "They deliberately put a confused elderly woman in danger! They have to be stopped!"

"You're right," Emily agreed, keeping her voice low. "This

was no accident. Evelyn told me someone specific—a woman—told her Lillian was missing."

Eddie's expression darkened. "They're all connected in this. All of them. The church, the sheriff's department, the 'good Christian families.'" His voice dripped with disgust at the last words. "It's one big web."

Once they got Evelyn settled back at home, Lillian drew the curtains and set up her mini projector to show Hayley's movies on the wall. Suddenly, Hayley's smiling face was filling the space, as if she were there with them.

"Where d'you get that cool projector? My kids would love it," Emily asked.

"TikTok," Lillian said.

The first video was about a deaf child who was a math savant and used numbers to communicate. Eddie starred in the next one, about getting bullied at school for being gay. Emily guessed it wasn't far from his own experience.

"She was going to enter this one in a film festival competition for teens. I bet she would've won," he said.

"She was serious about it. She had a bunch of festivals she was going to submit to. She was on her way to something big," Lillian added sadly.

Seeing the movies, with Hayley's clear perspective and style, brought her to life for Emily. She felt like she knew her, understood her dreams and longing, the things taken from her so young.

"Look at this one, it's the one I sent to your phone. It's spliced in at the end of the ghost movie. See? I think this might be real and she hid it at the end of the other movie," Lillian said.

Emily watched with a growing sense of dread as Hayley ran through the woods with someone in pursuit. When it cut out suddenly, she was taken aback.

"And that's it? There's no more explanation?" Emily asked.

"Yeah, it just ends abruptly. We weren't doing anything like this in Media class," Eddie said.

"I think it's real, it's a record of something like the other video with the three men," Lillian said.

"Go through all her video and film clips, every single movie, and look for any more of these false endings. She might be trying to tell you something," Emily said. "I spoke to Mike Prentiss about Hayley. He tried to convince me that they did a proper investigation. He mentioned the missing track phone."

"Prentiss? He's one of the worst. He's the one who told me to shut up and stop causing trouble," Lillian said.

"You need to be careful with him. I think he's dangerous," Emily warned her. "And then I got a note on my car, telling me to speak to a deputy named Jamie Dougherty if I want to find out about Hayley. Did either of you talk to him after her death?"

"I only talked to Prentiss and Cody Granville," Lillian said. "And they kept asking me when Hayley started taking drugs and I told them she didn't, and they got pissed."

"I never spoke to any cops. Just Pastor Jim. He had youth counseling sessions with all the kids who knew Hayley," Eddie said.

"He spoke to each of you privately?" Emily asked.

"Yeah, and he taped the interviews, but he tapes everything. He's, like, obsessed with taping everything."

"What did he say about her death?"

"It wasn't counseling, he never asked how I felt. He kept insisting that she was a troubled girl, that she had strayed from the path, that she was on drugs and a sinner. It was like he wanted everyone to agree with the police version of it. I pretended I did just to get out of there," Eddie said.

"What do you guys know about Roy? Hayley's neighbor? I ran into him at Church on the Hill a little while ago."

"You went over there?" Lillian asked. "Did they see you?"

"No, it was closed."

"They saw you, they have cameras everywhere. They see everything and everyone who comes on the church property," Eddie said.

"I wanted to see what paying them a visit might shake loose," Emily said. "I ran into Roy who kept asking about his girl's girl, said he was looking for her."

"He used to attend Church on the Hill regularly," Eddie explained. "Then, about a year and a half ago, he just stopped coming."

"Do you know his last name?" Emily asked, trying to place the man in the broader picture she was assembling.

"Bishop, I think. Or maybe Bingman?" Lillian frowned, trying to remember.

Before Emily could press further, her phone rang—an unknown local number. She hesitated before answering, her guard instantly up.

"Is this Emily Ray?" A man's voice came through, traffic sounds humming in the background.

"Yes. Who's calling?" Her tone was professionally neutral, giving nothing away.

"Jamie Dougherty." The name from the note. "What exactly do you want with Hayley Hope?" His voice was tense, suspicious. "Who are you really, and why are you asking questions?"

SEVENTEEN

Emily walked outside to take the call. He sounded hostile and she wasn't sure how much she could tell him. Perhaps the note was meant to throw her off track or put her into a dangerous position with someone who had a lot to lose. Maybe it was meant to remove her from the situation entirely.

"Mr. Dougherty, I'm on vacation, the girl next door is Hayley's best friend and she's been telling me that she thinks something is wrong, that Hayley didn't kill herself like the police say she did." Emily waited a beat, then added, "I'm with the FBI but not officially on this case."

"Could you get the FBI involved?" Dougherty asked bluntly.

"Maybe, if I get solid information."

There was a long pause. She thought he had hung up, then he said, "I can meet you tonight after eleven p.m. But it can't be in town. There's an American Legion Hall in Sugar Pines Park, outside of Crestline. It's not used anymore. We can meet behind it. Stay in your car, I'll be in a black Tacoma truck."

"Okay, see you—"

He hung up before she could say goodbye. She went back inside to Lillian and Eddie.

"You guys know where Sugar Pines Park is?" she asked.

"It's way the hell out there, past Crestline. There's a big Christian camp nearby," Lillian said.

"Yeah, they sent me there for a weekend retreat to try and make me not gay," Eddie said. "It didn't work," he added with a little laugh.

"You went to a conversion camp? That's been illegal in California since 2018. It's illegal in about sixteen states," Emily said.

"Do you think they care? Up here everyone acts like the laws don't apply to them," Eddie said.

Cody Granville had told her they did things their own way up in the mountains.

"Are you going out to Sugar Pines Park?" Lillian asked.

"Jamie Dougherty wants me to meet him out there tonight, outside of town. At eleven p.m.," Emily said.

"I can stay with your dad, if the caretaker leaves before that," Lillian offered. "My grandma takes medication to help her sleep and she's always out cold by nine o'clock. Today she'll be exhausted from all the excitement."

Emily considered. She was counting on Lynne Smenck being gone for the evening; she had something to take care of away from her prying eyes.

"Okay, but make sure you lock your doors before you leave to come over," Emily said.

"My grandma has this old flip phone she never uses," Lillian said. "I'll slip it into her pajama pocket before I leave. If she wakes up and wanders around, I can track her location."

She paused, glancing up at Emily with naked worry in her eyes. "There's absolutely nothing out in Sugar Pines Park except trees and darkness. What if this is some kind of trap? What if they know you're asking questions?"

Emily had been weighing the same possibility. Jamie Dougherty could be legitimate—another person with suspicions about Hayley's death. Or this could be an elaborate setup to isolate her miles from help, with no witnesses. The fact that she couldn't dismiss either scenario spoke volumes about how dangerous this situation had become.

Back at the Maison, Lynne had left for the evening. Emily and Michael ate an early dinner and watched *To Kill a Mockingbird* on Turner Classic Movies. It was one of his favorite films, he loved Gregory Peck as Atticus Finch. Michael leaned forward in rapt attention, quietly saying the lines of dialogue in the courtroom scenes; he had seen the film so many times that he knew them by heart. Emily watched him, remembering the first time they watched it together, when she'd escaped from Tibbs and was slowly constructing new family memories with Michael. She had placed a bowl of popcorn between them on the big couch in the den, and they'd reached for a handful at the same time, bumping their fingers together and sharing a laugh. She knew how precious these moments were now. She had no idea how many more they would have together.

After he went to bed, Emily walked around the back of the house with her small headlamp and a multi-purpose Leatherman tool to locate the electrical panel. The Maison also had a large Generac backup generator that plugged into a special panel next to the main box. She unplugged the Generac, which she knew would come on automatically when the power went off. She flipped the main switch to the house and the whole property went black. She had already noted the location of the outside security cameras; she collected them and went back into the darkened house.

In the kitchen, with the light from the headlamp, she expertly opened the backs of each camera and used the

Leatherman to detach the cables connecting them. Then she unscrewed the IR boards in each camera holding the small lens, which she removed before reattaching everything. The cameras looked exactly as they had previously but now, they couldn't record any video. She stored the lenses in a plastic bag in her duffle bag and went outside to put the cameras back in place. The whole process took less than twenty minutes, and she flipped the power back on. Dede, Cody and Vannah Granville would now be in the dark about any activities at Maison Du Lac. She texted Lillian to come over in an hour.

Her phone rang; it was Izzy Doqui.

"What's up, Iz?"

"Okay, all the girls were put in foster care, first in San Bernardino and then up in Crestline. Their parents were in and out of rehab, lots of drug problems. They ended up with the same social worker, Alice Boone, who lives in Lake Arrowhead. She put Joannie and Rachel with the same foster parent, Sherry Snyder. Karlie went to a different household. I'll forward you Alice Boone's information. Joannie and Rachel had a history of running away from care, so they bounced around a lot. There's been no update on them at all—as far as the system knows, they're with Sherry Snyder and Alice Boone is doing the check-ins. If they're not there, then Boone is lying and reporting that everything is fine."

Emily wasn't surprised, despite her hopes that the situation would prove to be a simple mistake or miscommunication. If Boone was covering up their disappearance and Starhawk was still pocketing the monthly foster care payments, it suggested something much darker.

"Any luck with the Snapchat firewall?"

"It's blank. Been totally wiped. Whoever had that phone, they were damn good at protecting what was on it."

"It was a fifteen-year-old girl," Emily said.

"Then she's pretty tech savvy. She should study computer science and take my job!" He laughed.

"She's dead, Iz. That's what I'm looking into," Emily said solemnly.

There was a long silence on the phone, then he said, "Whoever they are, you'll get them, Emily. But you have to get Powers to reinstate you. This review is all for show and they know it!"

They hung up and Emily sat on the big living room couch with the windows open, letting the cool evening breeze in. On her laptop, she ran a background search on Roy Bishop; there were thousands of men with that name. She narrowed the search parameters and found one that was the approximate age and matched the address in Crest Park.

He was a Vietnam veteran who had done two tours and had been part of an Agent Orange lawsuit against the government. Roy Bishop had been in and out of the Veteran's Hospital in Loma Linda for psychiatric disorders in the past two decades. He had been married twice, with two children. His son, Arthur, died in 2012 with no descendants. His daughter, Carlene, died in 2016 leaving two daughters behind, Melanie and Melora Zane. Their father was a man named Tom Zane; he'd died of Covid in early 2020.

Emily stopped cold when she saw the name: Melora. It was so unique, she doubted there were many others with that name. She would be about Lillian's age. Her parents died, possibly leaving her a ward of the state. She would've entered the foster care system, perhaps near her only adult relative, her grandfather, who was too impaired to care for her.

I'm looking for my girl's girl, the younger one... they told me she's here...

Melora Zane, the missing teenager, had an older sister, who might still be alive. She texted Izzy Doqui.

> can you get me contact information on a melanie zane, roughly nineteen years old, from the Arrowhead/San Bernardino area
> ASAP!! THX

All Emily had now were loose threads and theories. Jamie's revelations would be challenged by other corrupt cops and without hard evidence, it would be impossible to arrest anyone, let alone prove a case in court. She needed to find the missing piece that tied it all together. Despite the late hour, she texted Special Agent Kristen Griffith in Riverside. Griffith had been one of the first agents to arrive in Arrowbear after Emily's final confrontation with James Tibbs. The city of Riverside was only twenty minutes from San Bernardino at the foot of the mountain, but it was a bigger, more prosperous city. The FBI offices there had greater resources, and Emily had kept in touch with the young agent.

> Special Agent Emily Ray here. need your input and help on a new case. call anytime. Urgent!

She looked at the words she'd written, calling her suspicions a "new case." That's what it was now, and she needed to get back to work, officially, before anything happened to Lillian or anyone else.

Cody, Roger Kupp, Miles and Prentiss huddled around the stone fireplace at Church on the Hill, their voices low and tense. Pastor Jenkins had summoned them for an emergency meeting—damage control after Hayley's death had drawn unwanted attention from people with influence. The Chamber of Commerce was pressuring the sheriff's office, worried about the impact on tourism. Local business owners were asking uncomfortable questions. The carefully cultivated image of their peaceful mountain community was at risk, and with it, their entire operation. They didn't want that type of scandal and put a ton of pressure on the local sheriffs to solve the case quickly. The realtors were stressing, too—how were they going to sell a three-million-dollar house near the marina if a dead teenager was found in Papoose Lake? Luckily the two local papers hadn't run more than a brief mention of it. A resort town must sell a particular image, and it cannot be marred by violence, suicide, racism or the other unsavory things that might make someone consider Idyllwild, Ojai or Palm Springs instead.

Cody and the other sheriffs promised they'd have it wrapped up right away but the plan to pin it on Manuel Heredia hadn't panned out. He had been in Riverside for days before Hayley died and he had an airtight alibi. Her mother Dina couldn't remember what she had for breakfast, she spent most of the day fighting withdrawal or nodding off. She couldn't have managed to get her healthy, strong, teenaged daughter into a locked, fenced private lake to drown her.

The only other option was suicide, and they'd made a pact to stick with that story, no matter what happened. Luckily, Cody and Kupp had taken care of things when they discovered her body. But it didn't help that Lillian Knox kept pushing the newspaper people and even stood out on the highway by Papoose Lake with a big, handmade sign. When they ran her off, she showed up in the Village which infuriated the Chamber. She even did it at the entrance to the hotel parking lot. That time, they'd threatened to arrest her, but she knew her rights and didn't back down. Miles had been on duty that day and he was pissed that none of his tactics worked. She was too smart, and her parents had money. If they made trouble for her, Mr. and Mrs. Knox would bring in a Los Angeles attorney and wipe the floor with them. Lillian Knox was trouble and there was nothing they could do about it just yet.

Jenkins wiped a tissue across his forehead and said, "We're in this mess 'cause of you, Cody. You knew you had to be careful, stay under the radar, but you let things get out of hand. And you can't control your wife too well, either. It's the sin of pride, boy. Thinking you're the one in charge!"

"Everything is fine, you're the one panicking. We can deal with Lillian Knox once things calm down. It will be easy," Cody replied, his anger simmering.

"You cast your net too wide, boy. Too wide. You weren't satisfied with what you could handle, and it went too far, all of it. Lots of people come here from other places, big cities that see things differently. Professionals, lawyers... even those internet people, the pondcasters? They're always looking for stories, true crime, digging around!"

"They're called podcasters, not pond," Kupp said.

"I don't give a rat's ass what they're called, idiot! They talk, they put things online, they investigate. I don't know what I'm gonna do with all of you. I don't know how you expect me to handle this!" Jenkins bellowed.

Miles was too frightened to speak, and Prentiss just stared at his feet. He hadn't been the one to set everything up, it was Cody Granville. The rest of them just went along, like they did in high school. Kupp was fiddling with a pop top to calm his nerves, and Jenkins was sweating as if he were in a sauna. Cody was the only one unbowed by Jenkins' outburst. The old man needed to get himself under control or he'd become part of the problem.

"Why don't you leave everything to me, Jim? I've always handled it. Vannah and I talked to Emily at our house; she's not that interested in any of this. She said Lillian is just an unhappy kid. She spoke to Prentiss, too. I suggested it and it worked," Cody said calmly.

"Yeah, she came to the station, and we talked. She seemed cool with all of it. Said maybe the Knox kid just needed to feel like someone listened to her," Prentiss added.

"So, forget about it, okay, Jim? Just let it be and let me

handle everything," Cody said, in a tone that was more of a warning than reassurance.

"Well, you better be right. That's all I got to say!" Jenkins snapped.

Cody looked at him coldly, not a hint of fear or regard in his dead blue eyes.

"Or what?" he asked.

Cody, Kupp and the others left. Jim Jenkins watched them huddle together in the parking lot to talk. He wondered what they were saying and kept an eye on them until they dispersed. He wiped his brow again and wondered if he might be sick. He'd had Covid four times, and it always started like this. His heart was going too fast, but he knew that was anxiety. Ever since the Hope girl had been found in Papoose Lake, he'd not gotten a good night's sleep. He knew it wasn't what they were saying it was. He had eyes and ears, he knew what the church women thought of her. And he'd seen the way Cody had looked at her, like she was a tender piece of chicken, how he'd been grooming her. Just like the others.

He stood before the big wooden cross that hung over the fireplace. He bowed his head and prayed. He knew he'd been tempted, that he had strayed, but he didn't deserve this. He had built so much in the community, helped so many people. Shouldn't a sin of weakness be forgiven? Women were the carriers of the original sin, and they all had the temptress inside them. It was a mark of their own evil, and the frailty of their spirit as well, that they made bad, reckless decisions. He was above this sordid mess, despite his part in it. None of it should touch him. He should remain blameless in the eyes of the Lord and of man. And he would, no matter the cost.

. . .

Roy Bishop sat in his truck, parked up the block from Church on the Hill. He watched as Cody, Kupp, Miles and Prentiss got into their cars and drove away. They didn't see him. They never did. He took a drag on an unfiltered Camel cigarette, slowly exhaling the smoke into the cab of his beat-up Tacoma. It rose like a halo around him. He knew they were up to something, and he knew it was no good. They were a cancer, like the one they found in his lungs, slowly eating away at everything alive and good in town. He remembered when it had been like a dream, living in the forest, among the giant trees and the wildlife. Everyone doing their best, helping each other out. Then it started to change when people like Jim Jenkins showed up. The bad things started happening, like with his girls.

As if on cue, Jenkins scurried out of the church. He moved like a nervous rodent. Roy kept his eyes trained on him, the way he had in the jungle. He'd been a sniper, he knew how to be patient. Jenkins drove away and after a few beats, Roy followed. He had no particular place to be. He knew where all of them lived. He would keep watch. He liked keeping watch.

EIGHTEEN

Promptly at ten o'clock, Lillian knocked on Emily's door with Eddie in tow. Emily assumed he would be keeping Lillian company, but he announced, "I'm following you to Sugar Pines Park. It's too dangerous to go by yourself."

"I can't let you do that, Eddie," Emily said.

"I just turned eighteen a week ago, Ms. Ray, so not to be rude, you can't do anything to stop me."

"You need backup. These people are nuts, they could do anything. Look what happened to Hayley," Lillian said.

Emily was nervous about going to a remote, unfamiliar area late at night on her own. She was used to working with the whole CARD team and other agents as backup. Even when she took down Tibbs, she had two detectives with her initially. She'd never even been to Sugar Pines Park. She had no idea what the landscape was like. She would bring a firearm but even so, the situation could turn deadly, with no witnesses and no one to fall back on. While she would never have asked two teenagers to help, she looked at Lillian and Eddie in the doorway, their faces so hopeful and open, and she was humbled by their courage. They were just two kids living in a place that made them feel unwelcome and wrong, and they were ready to step up in ways that many adults were afraid to.

She checked her thirty-eight and stashed it in her fanny pack. She tried to GPS the directions to the American Legion Hall, but Eddie said, "GPS doesn't work up here. It will take you to the wrong place. You can follow me and then before we get there, we'll switch, and I'll hang back. There are a lot of wooded areas where I can hide the car with the lights off."

Emily found herself impressed by Eddie's strategic thinking. For a teenager facing genuine danger, he showed remarkable foresight—thinking several steps ahead rather than simply reacting.

"You mountain kids are tough," she said.

"You have to be up here. Snowstorms, ice storms, wildfires, sometimes no power, no water, and if you can't figure out what to do on your own, you're screwed," Eddie said.

They were about to leave when Antonio called. It felt strange not to have spoken to him for a few days, but this wasn't the moment. She saw his number and realized she hesitated because she would have to hide what she was doing, investigating Hayley Hope's death. She could imagine his words, letting her know that it was all too much. Her drive, her intensity, her commitment to her work. She dreaded hearing the disappointment in his voice when she told him the truth, and she couldn't deal with that distraction now. She had compartmentalized her life for so long; it was easy to do when there was work to be done.

They left in tandem, Emily following Eddie who drove a big, older Suburban. The streets of the town were quiet—everything was closed at that hour and people were safely at home, fast asleep. They followed the Rim of the World Highway to the Crestline cut off and then traveled west toward Sugar Pines Park. The area was dense with trees, the houses were spread out, with large lots adding to the sense of isolation. Eddie called

Emily to tell her they were getting close and to drive on past him. He pulled over to let her pass and then followed, cutting his headlights. Despite the late summer weather, the area was deep in fog that had blown in, surrounding the hills, like a scene from *The Legend of Sleepy Hollow*.

Emily came upon one street with a handful of small businesses, an indie convenience store called Johnny's Jumpstart, a run-down auto repair shop and the American Legion Hall, the destination for her meeting with Jamie Dougherty.

In the window of the American Legion Hall, with its retro plastic signage, a hand-lettered piece of poster board that read "Taco Tuesdays" hung limply in the window. It was an old structure, pinned in time, harkening back to a day when the hall probably held dances and other social events. Now it was battered by the extreme mountain weather, neglected and out of step with the modern world. A faded For Sale sign was staked to the ground out front.

Emily checked the rearview mirror; Eddie was nowhere to be seen but she knew he had to be back there, hidden in among the trees and obscured by the fog. She tried to text him, but her phone had no signal. She was glad he was nearby—at that hour Sugar Pines Park looked like a killing ground from a movie thriller.

She drove behind the Hall. It was a few minutes before eleven and she saw the black Tacoma. He flashed his headlights at her, and she pulled in next to him, rolling down her window. She reached for her thirty-eight and stashed it on her seat, beneath her thigh.

"Jamie Dougherty?" she asked, fully expecting Cody Granville or Roger Kupp to emerge from the shadows.

"Yes. We should get in one car, easier to talk that way."

She wasn't getting into his car, and he knew it. He got out and came to her passenger door which she unlocked, and he climbed in. Now that he was no longer in shadow, she could see his face clearly. Jamie Dougherty was handsome, in a rugged, unpretentious way. Slender and lanky, he had a light stubble on his chin and his pale eyes were weary. He wore a faded blue ball cap.

"We should drive further up the road, where no one will look," he said.

She could feel her revolver, hard and metal against her inner thigh, and she kept one hand loose and ready on the steering wheel. She drove down a quiet street with a few scattered homes; only one had a light on.

"Here's fine," he said, pointing to a clearing, surrounded by thick trees. She pulled in and cut the engine.

He pulled a pack of cigarettes from his pocket and asked, "You mind?"

"No problem," she said, rolling down the window. He lit up, the orange ember from the cigarette tip the only light in the darkness.

"You've spoken to Lillian Knox, I think?" he asked.

"I'm renting the vacation house next to her and we became friendly," Emily said, filling him in on her dealings with Lillian to that point.

"She's a nice kid but she talks a lot, and she's put herself in danger," he said.

"From whom? I've done some digging; I get the sense there is something bigger going on here."

"It's big. Extortion, blackmail, trafficking. It's RICO," he said, referring to the statutes used against organized crime syndicates.

"How's it tied to Hayley Hope?"

"It's those assholes, Granville, Kupp and the rest of them. They're all from Deer Lane, they think they're the OG families up here and they live in their own world. It's everything bad, white supremacy, vigilantism, racism, sexual exploitation. And Jenkins is at the center of it," he said with disgust.

"Pastor Jim?"

"He used to be in the Baptist church, hardcore but like a regular, established church. Then he broke off a few years ago and bought that big building and started his own group, Church on the Hill. And he got more extremist, which got the attention of wackos like Kupp and Cody and the rest. They formed an inner circle, and the thug stuff started small. They'd see a business doing well and they'd hit them up for money. If the owner refused, something would happen. A car firebombed, a pet goes missing and they'd find it dead in the driveway. All that old school intimidation to scare people. And it worked, since Cody, Kupp and the others were in the sheriff's office."

"So, people don't feel they can go to the sheriff because these guys will know and retaliate?"

"Yeah, and the police down the hill are pretty hands off. San Bernardino is a clusterfuck on a good day, so they just let this stuff up here go. They let the mountain rednecks figure it out for themselves. Or kill each other in the process."

"And it escalated?"

"It was the girls. Cody Granville is a sick fuck. He's into young girls but so is Kupp and the rest. They're like dogs, the younger the better, even more if they're throwaway kids, you know? When Jenkins set up his church, they used the youth group to get to them. And they always focused on the kids in foster care, the ones with shitty families, or the ones with no one looking out for them."

"Like Hayley?"

"And Melora Zane. Her sister Melanie got away, she just took off one day. They would go after Lillian, but her folks have money; they're scared of that. They give the kids gifts, stuff they can't afford, stuff they keep hidden from the foster parents. Suddenly the girls who never had much, have new clothes, a new phone, maybe some AirPods."

"It's page one of the predator handbook," Emily said.

"There's a social worker up here who's in on it. Alice Boone. She puts the problem kids with people like Sherry Snyder. They're in on the whole thing. Snyder used to live in her van, now she's living in a nice place in the Villas, owned by Dede Granville. She's got all these foster kids, taking in a bunch of money. They set her up to do that, the paperwork and all."

"I looked into Joannie Dietrich and Rachel Carson. They were part of it, Alice Boone put them with Sherry Snyder. And the other girl, Karlie Ann Smith. Lillian told me they just stopped showing up at school and no one even cared. And Melora Zane went missing, too," Emily said.

"It's a ring of people who traffic minors and use threats and intimidation to keep everyone in line."

They heard a crackling sound outside the car. Both reached for their firearms and froze. A moment later a brown bear lumbered out of the brush, snapping twigs and branches as he sniffed and scavenged the ground in front of the car. He was huge, his claws able to decapitate a person in one swipe. Emily didn't move but Jamie relaxed and laid his gun on his lap. The bear looked at them in the car, uninterested.

"I see we both came armed," he said, with a chuckle.

"Hell, yes. I'm not meeting a strange man, deep in the woods in a town I don't know, without protection," Emily said.

"They're afraid of you, that's what's going on."

"Of me? What do I have to do with it?" she asked, incredulous.

"This shit with Hayley just went down a few weeks ago. She's found in Papoose Lake, the whole town freaks out. It's too much this time. She didn't just disappear quietly like the Zane girls. They say she killed herself, she was on drugs like her mom. You know the drill, blame the victim. But it won't go away because Lillian Knox won't stop talking about a cover-up. And she's right," Jamie said, with growing frustration and anger.

"I figured that. Mike Prentiss made a threat against her earlier today when I spoke with him," Emily said.

"When Vannah did your vacation rental, she wanted you as far away from Lillian Knox as possible because the kid won't shut up. And she finds out you're this big FBI investigator, crimes against children and all that... and their worst nightmare comes true when you meet Lillian Knox. Then you're asking questions, and now it's getting out of hand for them."

"But does Vannah know about it? That her husband is involved with young girls? She seems like the perfect Christian wife. I can't imagine she's okay with it."

He paused, knowing it would be hard for her to hear. Then he said, "She has to defer to him in all things, that's their doctrine. She can't challenge him; she can't divorce him. So, she helps him, she's the one who gets the girls into the youth group, she hires them to watch the kids at prayer meetings. She seems safe, she's a wife and mom, and she puts those girls in the path of Cody and the others. She's in it up to her neck. But when the girls know too much or they push back, they have to go."

Emily felt sick. "Go where?"

"Anywhere that they can't talk about what happened to them. Melanie Zane took off on her own when she was about eighteen. Melora just disappeared. They like them young, easier to intimidate, easier to mold into whatever they want them to be. Everyone knows it's going on. They whisper about it but they're afraid to go after them."

Emily thought of Ernesto, fleeing with his family from one day to the next, leaving a life they had built for years in a place they thought they would be safe, where they could put down roots. Until Cody and the others took an interest in Daila.

"Hayley was different. Her family's a mess and she might've been impressed at first with the gifts and such, but everyone knew she would get off this mountain. Maybe she wanted out, maybe she said she'd tell someone. Or maybe Vannah got jealous of her. But something got out of hand," Jamie said.

He took a long drag on his cigarette, blowing the smoke out his open passenger window.

Then he said, "I grew up here, I've known these people all my life. Cody, Miles and the others were bullies in school. Kupp raped a girl in high school and his family covered it up. No one wants trouble. And a lot of the retired people, they have no idea. They want to drink white wine on their boats and believe that this is some kind of paradise, free from all the shit down the hill."

The bear suddenly rose on its hind legs, its massive form silhouetted against the night sky. Its nostrils flared as it sampled the air, small eyes narrowing as it swiveled its head toward the dense forest behind them. Emily and Jamie turned instinctively, straining to see what he was alerting to. Nothing visible—just a heavy, pulsing blackness.

Without warning, the bear dropped to all fours and crashed away through the underbrush, moving with surprising speed for its bulk. Emily's hand moved to her weapon. Bears didn't flee without reason. Something—or someone—was out there, watching them from the shadows. She sat perfectly still, ears straining for any sound, eyes scanning the tree line for movement. The forest remained unnervingly silent, as if holding its breath. "So, how do you know all of this?" she asked.

"My cousin, Kathy Warne, works in the sheriff's office with us. She's been in a thing with Cody for the past few years. It's a typical fucked-up relationship, he has women all over this mountain. But he likes to drink when he's at her place and when he drinks, he talks. A lot."

"Why not go higher up the chain of command?"

"I've got nothing concrete I could take to my superiors," Jamie admitted, his eyes weary. "Just whispered rumors, patterns I've noticed, things that don't add up. And Kathy's testimony, which they'd discredit in a heartbeat. They'd paint her as a scorned lover trying to get revenge against a married man."

He rubbed his temple, clearly troubled. "Everyone in this town has heard pieces of the story—which girls to keep away from certain men, why certain families suddenly move away in the middle of the night. But it's all carefully contained, just disconnected fragments that never form a complete picture. It's a small town and you can't keep this stuff secret forever. I'm done at the end of the month, I'm moving. I want to take them down before I go, if I can. And maybe you can help."

"How? I'm on leave, under review from the FBI."

"But you could get it to someone? If I can get you the proof, you can take it to them?"

The things he was talking about, the extortion, the trafficking of minors among multiple adult offenders, was indeed something for the FBI to investigate. Emily would have to get hard proof and then take it to her unit chief and SAC in Los Angeles. If she got it to Kristen Griffith, she might be able to work with it until Emily was reinstated.

"What proof can you get?" Emily asked, watching Jamie closely.

He leaned back, some of the tension leaving his face. "Kathy's done with Cody for good. She's leaving for her father's ranch in Wyoming, and I'm joining her there next month. Getting as far from this place as possible." His voice dropped. "But before she goes, she says she's got something solid—something they can't explain away."

A piercing screech cut through the darkness, followed by a heavy thump against the car's rear wheel. Emily was out of the vehicle in one fluid motion, weapon drawn and ready, her heart hammering as she scanned the darkness. Jamie mirrored her movements on the opposite side, both crouched in defensive positions.

"Get in!" he hissed urgently. "Now!"

They dove back into the car simultaneously, doors barely closed when a mountain lion materialized from the shadows. The massive predator padded past their headlights, its muscular body sleek and powerful under the moonlight. Between its jaws hung the limp form of a raccoon, blood glinting black in the darkness.

Emily watched, barely breathing, as the cat disappeared into the tree line, its long tail swishing with each deliberate step. Her pulse gradually slowed as the immediate danger passed, but the night's oppressive weight remained.

"Kathy told me," Jamie continued, as if there had been no interruption, "that when they found Hayley's body, Cody tampered with everything. They pulled her from the water before the forensic team arrived from San Bernardino. They manipulated evidence, falsified the police report." He met Emily's eyes directly. "And Kathy knows exactly where they hid the proof."

"How does she know?" Emily asked.

"Because Cody told her to do it for him. She was part of it and she's willing to face charges. But I told her, she might avoid prosecution if she turns state's witness. She was planning to wait until she got to Wyoming but with you here, she wants to get it to you before she goes."

A false police report, intimidating a county employee to destroy evidence, tampering with a body to cover a crime. Emily knew if they could get that type of evidence against Cody Granville and the others, they would go down hard. Lillian would be safe. Hayley Hope would have justice.

The smoke from Jamie's cigarette hung in the air. The forest was deadly silent but for the faint chirping of the crickets. It felt as if they were the only two people on earth.

"Let's do it," Emily said.

NINETEEN

Emily drove back toward home, meeting up with Eddie then following his taillights in the dense fog. Jamie promised that his cousin Kathy would call her in the morning to set up a time to meet and retrieve the evidence of Cody's crimes. Back at the Maison they found Lillian watching old episodes of *Stranger Things* and eating ice cream.

"How'd it go?" she asked.

"Deputy Dougherty confirmed that there is a lot of criminal activity, centered around the church and several deputies are involved. It involves underage girls, intimidation, extortion. It's big."

"I knew it! They all said I'm crazy, but I knew it!" Lillian exclaimed. "Was it spooky out there?"

"It was fire! I sat out there in the shadows, I could see the back of your car. I was ready, I even had my dad's Smith and Wesson M & P Shield under the driver's seat!" Eddie said, pumping his fist in the air.

Emily blanched. "You had a gun with you?"

"Yeah, I've been shooting cans in the forest since I was about nine years old."

"What if something had happened? You could've been hurt or killed!" she admonished him.

"No, I'm really good with a gun. I wouldn't have gotten shot, but I might've taken the other guy out!"

She sank into a chair, imagining the horrible outcomes that could've occurred. Then she asked, "Did you know that Roy Bishop is Melora's grandfather?"

They both stared at her in utter surprise.

"Roy? Crazy Roy? He's Melora and Melanie's grandpa?" Lillian asked.

"You know Melanie, too?"

"Yeah, she's a few years older than Melora but she just took off one day. No one's seen her since," Lillian said.

"Maybe that's why he shows up at church, he's always looking for someone," Eddie said.

"How's my dad? Did he wake up?" Emily asked.

"Your dad was fine, he just got up to pee a bunch of times. Said he felt a pressure in his lower back. Sounded like a UTI, my grandma gets them a lot," Lillian said.

Emily was dismayed at the news; Michael had been prone to urinary tract infections of late and they made his life miserable.

"You should get back home to her," Emily said.

"I've been checking her location on the phone. She's still in her room, hasn't moved," Lillian said.

"I'll walk back with her, Mrs. Ray. Can I stay over, Lillian? I don't feel like going home," Eddie asked.

"Cool. We can watch movies," Lillian agreed. "And, Emily, I have to show you some things of Hayley's that I took when I got the phone. She had all this awesome camera stuff for her movies."

"Good, we'll do it tomorrow. One more thing, I want you to stop talking about what happened to Hayley, about the cover-up and the rest. Deputy Dougherty and I are handling it from here on. No more signs, no more calling the local paper, okay?" Emily said.

"Okay, I guess the FBI is better at this than I am. Sleep tight!" she said, taking Eddie in tow, heading for the door. "Oh, also, that caregiver lady can't cook for shit. I was hungry and I ate some of the mac and cheese. It tasted like ass!"

"You probably got my dad's portion. The caregiver puts everything in separate containers since he can't eat too much salt," Emily said.

"No salt? It had so much salt I thought my tongue would shrivel up!" Lillian said, walking off into the darkness with Eddie.

"Text me when you get home, let me know it's all safe and sound," Emily said.

She watched them disappear into the shadows, swallowed by gnarled branches of ancient trees that loomed over the path like sentinels from some dark fairy tale.

Emily's head was spinning with all the information Jamie had shared. She had dealt with fringe groups before, people colluding in crime for money, sexual gratification or power. She had confronted the worst of the worst child predators. She had saved kids; she had lost kids. She'd been there in time, and she had arrived too late.

But this was different—painfully personal. The smiling teenage girl she'd once known during carefree summer vacations had transformed into something unrecognizable. The Vannah she remembered had become entangled in a web of exploitation, apparently willing to sacrifice vulnerable children to satisfy her husband's depravity and maintain her position in their twisted social hierarchy.

She was about to step into a hot shower when her phone buzzed; the screen showed 1:15 in the morning. It was Antonio.

"Hey, babe!" he whispered, sounding a bit intoxicated.

"Hey, how's the family?" she asked.

"It's great, all great. Having a lot of fun. The girls are loving it." He was definitely intoxicated, which was rare for him, but she was glad he was unwinding and cutting loose with his family.

"I'm hoping they're asleep at this hour?" she asked.

"Yeah, they're at a sleepover, so I'm just chilling, and I missed you."

"Whose house are they sleeping over at?" she asked, concerned.

They had a hard and fast rule of no sleepovers for their daughters. With what Emily knew about child predators, they were not allowed to stay at anyone's house, ever.

"Don't worry. They're at Tito's and Dolores is with them," he assured her.

Emily had met his cousin Tito and his wife many times and Dolores's presence reassured Emily somewhat. Antonio had been gently pushing her for years to loosen her protective instincts, to trust people and situations more readily. "Not everyone is a potential threat, Em," he'd say whenever she insisted on personally vetting every playdate, every babysitter. Perhaps this was an opportunity to practice what he preached— to accept that sometimes, normal family visits were just that, with no hidden dangers lurking.

"How's the fishing up there?" Antonio asked, changing the subject. "Catch anything yet?"

"Not yet. Dad is fine, having a good time. It's very peaceful and quiet," she said.

She knew she couldn't tell him the truth of what was going on with Hayley Hope and all the things that she had discovered in the last few days. But she wished that she could. In the past, she would have called him immediately, laying out the suspicious patterns, the troubling connections, the mounting evidence of something sinister operating beneath the town's picturesque surface. He had always been her sounding board, providing perspective when she became too immersed.

He wanted so much for her to shift her work away from dealing with young victims, he would've gotten upset if he knew the truth. His gentle suggestions that she consider a different career path had evolved into more pointed discussions about how her work affected their family.

If she told him about Hayley Hope now, it would only confirm his belief that she couldn't disconnect, couldn't prioritize family over work, even on vacation. With him already sounding slightly intoxicated, this was definitely not the time to have that particular conversation.

They hung up and she took a quick shower to wash off the day and relax her muscles. On her way to her bedroom, she heard Michael talking aloud. She stuck her head in and found him sitting up in bed, talking with someone who wasn't there.

"I'm not going to do that, Martine. We're not going to add any more footage to Model A..." he insisted, agitated. Martine was an architect who had worked with him on a number of building projects.

Emily sat on his bed, and he jumped, startled. "I didn't see you come in. Is everything okay, Emily? Do you need me to take you to school?"

"No, Dad. I'm fine. You need to go back to sleep," she said gently.

"I can't. Not at this stage. Martine is changing the plans, and I have to make sure they are finalized before they pour foundations. And we may need new permits!"

His frustration was growing, and she knew it had to be a UTI. In older people, a urinary tract infection could cause a kind of disconnect with reality, which he had from time to time anyway with his dementia. But this type of agitated lapse had happened before. She hoped to get him back to sleep so she could take him into the local ER in the morning to get him started on antibiotics and fluids. He pushed the comforter back and climbed out of his bed.

"I have to use the restroom, I just feel that I have to go all the time," he said, disappearing into the bathroom. Urination was painful with a UTI and there would be no waiting until morning. She pulled his sweatpants and a shirt from the drawer and waited for him to finish. It had been an emotionally exhausting day, she could barely stand up, but he had to go in.

A half hour later, they walked into the Mountains Community Hospital's emergency department. It was a small hospital perched high above the Lake Arrowhead Marina. There were medical offices and a long-term care facility on the grounds; it was just across the highway from the Maison. She texted Lillian to let her know that she had brought Michael in. It was quiet and well organized, a far cry from any emergency department in the city, which would've meant a six-hour wait at least.

A nurse took them in, and they saw a doctor who suggested that given his mental state with the UTI, Michael should be admitted to the hospital for observation over the next day by the medical staff.

"What if he gets more confused? His anxiety spikes sometimes when he's surprised by changes he isn't prepared for," Emily asked, worried.

"Don't worry. We've given him a mild sedative and we'll get him started on antibiotics and fluids to help support his system as he flushes it out. I feel better knowing that we're here with him in case anything worsens," the doctor assured her.

She hated leaving Michael there, but the sedative had taken effect; he drifted peacefully in a state between wakefulness and sleep as she said goodbye. His features were relaxed, unburdened by the confusion and anxiety that had gripped him earlier.

Perhaps Lynne had been right about the trip being too taxing for him. Though Michael had seemed to enjoy their activities until the UTI struck, any disruption to his routine carried risks. Emily made a mental note to consult with his neurologist about strategies for future outings.

She drove across the highway and into the gates of Old North Shore Road. Sammy ran to greet her, and they went outside for the little dog to do her business. Emily sat down, looking at the stars scattered across the sky. She closed her eyes, hoping to calm her racing mind. There was a rustling in the bushes and Sammy began to bark furiously. Emily scooped her up, afraid it might be a coyote but, in the shadows, she saw the form of a young man, hovering.

"Who's there?' she called out. "Who are you?"

A moment later, Danny Granville stepped out and stood a few feet away from her, trembling. He had a large bruise on his face and held his arm as if it might be broken.

"Danny? What're you doing here?" she asked.

"I don't know... I just... came here... I don't know where to go," he stammered.

Knowing his history with Lillian, she was suspicious, but she could plainly see that he was traumatized, and she moved closer to him, cautiously.

"Do you want to sit down?"

He nodded and sat quickly on a patio chair. Despite the warm night, he was shaking. She was afraid he might go into shock.

"I'm going to get you a blanket and a glass of water, okay?" she said calmly, and he nodded. She took Sammy in and returned a moment later, wrapping Danny in a plushy throw.

"What happened, Danny?"

He kept his eyes down; his voice was barely a whisper.

"I don't know... my mom and dad were fighting again... and I just snapped. I yelled at him to stop and then he came at me. My mom tried to stop him, and he pushed her. She fell and then I ran... but he caught me..."

"Does this happen a lot?"

"Sometimes, lately a lot. Things are bad at home and... I don't know what to do..."

He gulped the water down and pulled the blanket around his shoulders. She couldn't call the local police; they would hand him right back to Cody.

"Do you want to stay here to sleep? It's late to try and go to a friend's house. Is your head okay? Did your dad hit you in the head at all?"

"No, I slipped and hit the door with my chin when he punched me in the stomach and my back. But nothing feels broken."

"Let's just sit here quietly while you calm down. Can I check your arm? Then you can go into one of the guest rooms and we'll figure it out tomorrow."

He nodded and she gingerly examined his arm, which he held stiffly against his body. He winced with pain, but he could move it. He sat back in the chair, closing his eyes. Emily watched him, stunned at his injuries and the story he told. Despite knowing him as the teen bully, she saw that he was a victim as much as Lillian was. Looking at him now, all she saw was a terrified child caught in a dangerous and volatile situation. And he needed help.

After getting Danny settled into the guest room with an ice pack and ibuprofen, Emily retreated to the kitchen. She didn't trust him entirely, but she couldn't leave him on his own, distraught and injured. She hadn't eaten in hours and opened the refrigerator, grabbing one of the Tupperware containers that Lynne had prepared. She spooned chicken casserole onto a plate and heated it in the microwave. She took a bite and immediately recoiled at the level of salt, spitting it into a napkin. She checked the container and saw it was marked with her father's name. Lynne had marked all the containers to keep them separate.

She remembered the dinner on the dock when he kept adding salt to his food and said he couldn't taste anything any longer. He must not have noticed how salty the casserole was, and she knew he had eaten several servings with Lynne. And Lillian had commented on it as well. Emily threw it down the garbage disposal; she would speak to Lynne about it the next time she came over. She washed up and was preparing for a quick shower when her phone pinged with a text.

> Melanie Zane, nineteen years old. Lives in Eureka CA at 4325 Oakdale Avenue. Phone is 707-342-8972. This girl was impossible to find, took a lot of digging even for me. Whatever she's hiding from has to be bad. Keep me posted!

Emily read the text message, a jolt of gratitude momentarily overriding her exhaustion. Izzy Doqui had come through for her once again, proving why he was the most valuable analyst on her team. If anyone could penetrate the bureaucratic shields protecting information about those missing girls, it was Izzy.

TWENTY

Dawn had not yet broken, and the mountain sky was a marbled gray, with a lavender hue pushing through at the edges of the horizon. Eddie hadn't slept at all. He'd stayed at Lillian's to keep an eye on her and Evelyn. They'd watched movies and Lillian had shown him a box of Hayley's cameras. One was in a watch face that could be worn on a chain or a wristband. One looked like a Bluetooth earpiece. They were for recording secretly and Eddie could guess why she'd bought them. She didn't use them in her Instagram movies, they were for something altogether different. When Lillian went to sleep, he stayed awake to keep watch.

He was at Church on the Hill a lot. His dad, Caine, was the church handyman and there was always something to be done, especially since Pastor Jim acted like Caine's services were a donation. They took advantage of him but when Eddie mentioned it, his dad shut him down. But Eddie saw a lot of things. He saw when Vannah brought Joannie Dietrich and Rachel Hogan around to the youth group. Glenda Kupp brought Karlie Ann to the youth Bible study. The girls had always been at the edges of the high school hierarchy, those invisible girls that just faded into the background. Suddenly they were involved in all kinds of activities.

He knew them from school. They never had new clothes, and they brought a can of Coke and Cheetos for lunch when they lived with Starhawk. No money for the school lunch or any after-school activities, like a lot of the foster kids. People like Starhawk were only interested in free things, she wasn't going to spend a penny of that county money on anyone. And Church on the Hill was all about free things for the kids. That was how they roped in young parents who were on a budget, having them bring their toddlers for arts and crafts while they preached fire and brimstone to the adults. Or Awanas, where parents could get a childfree evening by dropping their kids off at church and five-year-olds could earn badges for learning Bible verses. But it was different when they started bringing the teenage girls around. The tone of everything shifted, there was a tension among the adults and a sense of secrecy.

Now, Eddie stood on Lillian's deck, forming a plan. He had a way of getting evidence of what was happening at the church, something Emily could use to take to the FBI. He couldn't tell her; she'd dissuade him or stop him from following through with it. And he was done staying quiet, not fighting back. He'd had enough of the bullies and the intimidation. He wanted to know what really happened to Hayley and the others.

The sun was shifting the color of the sky from gray to a gold drenched shimmer, as it broke over the eastern ridge. He looked toward the Maison and saw movement by the side door of the house. He doubted Emily was up yet and bolted down the stairs, ready to confront whoever might be sneaking around. He came around a corner and crashed into Danny Granville, grabbing him by the collar and shoving him against the wall. Danny winced in pain and surprise. Eddie held him there and leaned in close to Danny's face.

"What're you doing here, Granville? Stirring up shit again? Trying to scare people?" Eddie said.

Danny didn't even resist. "No, man. I'm just going home. I came here last night, and Emily let me stay..." he replied.

"Bullshit! She'd never let an asshole like you come over here. She knows who you are and what you do. What are you really doing here?" Eddie demanded, giving him a rough jerk.

"Nothing, Eddie. I swear," Danny protested, near tears. Eddie was taken aback to see Danny on the verge of breaking down. He loosened his grip and Danny exhaled.

"I came here 'cause I didn't know where to go. There's stuff I wanted to tell her..." he said.

"What do you know?" Eddie asked.

At that moment Emily emerged from the house with Sammy.

"What's going on?" she asked, looking from one boy to the other.

"He said he came here, and you let him stay," Eddie said.

"That's right. He was beaten up and afraid to go home," Emily said.

Eddie looked at Danny, shocked. Like everyone, he thought the Granvilles were the perfect family.

"I gotta go, they're going to be looking for me," Danny said, weakly.

"What were you going to tell her?" Eddie asked.

Danny looked to Emily and said, "I gotta go... but... let Lillian know she and her grandma aren't safe in that house, okay? Just tell them," he said, before jogging off toward the highway, his gait uneven and clumsy as he pushed through the pain of his injuries, like a broken marionette.

Emily led Eddie inside and he asked, "Did you really let him stay here? He's one of the bad ones!"

"I know but he was in trouble. He still is, I'm sure. But his warning was serious. I'm going to make reservations at the resort for Lillian and her grandma, I need your help. I'll put it under a different name, since we don't know who's with Cody and the rest of them. Is there a way to get inside without passing the front desk?" she asked.

"Yeah, you go through the Burnt Mill beach club and there's a path to the hotel pool deck. You can catch an elevator there and no one can see you."

"Okay, go help Lillian and Evelyn pack an overnight bag, okay? And I'll let you know when to take them over. Do you feel safe at home? I can book a room for you, too," she offered.

"No, my dad is fine. I'll go get them started. And, Mrs. Ray, that was nice of you, with Danny," he said, slipping out the door.

Emily sent a text to Lynne to let her know not to come, since Michael was in the hospital. She replied immediately.

Oh, the poor dear! It's all too much for him!

Next, she dialed Kristen Griffith, who answered in one ring.

"Agent Ray! It's a pleasure to hear from you! What's going on?"

Emily briefed her on what she had uncovered in Arrowhead, with Church on the Hill being central to all the criminal activity, as well as possible widespread corruption in the sheriff's office.

"Wow! Who would've thought it? We used to go there in the summers. We thought it was high class and where the rich people lived," Griffith said.

"If I get hard evidence today from Kathy Warne, I may need to hand it off to you. If I'm not yet reinstated, I need to get it some place safe. Do you think you could get your office to launch an investigation?"

"We'd need a formal statement from Deputy Dougherty and from Mrs. Warne."

"Okay, I'll get that today. And I am hoping to speak to a young woman whose sister is one of the missing girls," Emily said.

"Okay, I'm here. Get back to me," Griffith said.

Emily then called the resort to book two rooms, to be safe. She couldn't use her own name, in case someone in Cody's circle worked there. When the clerk asked for a name, Emily paused and decided to use a name she hadn't heard or claimed since the day she escaped from James Tibbs.

"Please book it under Danica Hansen," she said.

The sun streamed into Vannah's kitchen where she stood with Dede, staring at the screen of her laptop. Amber Kupp sat at the counter, drinking a cup of coffee, wishing she were anyplace else. But her mother-in-law, Glenda, had dragged her over; they wanted to know about her conversation with Emily on the boat.

"They're not working—maybe the power is off?" Vannah asked.

"I don't think so. The rental agency gets an update from Edison if the power is out and it seems fine. Maybe they malfunctioned or the wiring is damaged on the main unit," Dede suggested.

They had discovered that the outside security cameras were not working at the Maison du Lac. The interior cameras hadn't worked since Emily's arrival and there was no way to go in and reset them since they were illegal. But now the outside cameras weren't showing anything. Up to this point, Vannah, Dede and Cody had been able to see who was coming and going from the house. They had seen Lillian come over and Emily walking across the path to her house several times in the past few days. With no idea what was going on, Vannah began to imagine every worst-case scenario.

"What if she took them down herself? Because she knows?" Vannah said with growing hysteria.

"But why would she do that? Most places have exterior security, there's nothing suspect about it," Dede replied coolly. Someone had to stay calm, since, according to Cody, Vannah had been a basket case lately. She'd started losing control when Hayley Hope came into their lives, working at the church.

"I know. But why were they working just fine and now they're not? I think something happened to them," Vannah said.

"It could've been an electrical short. It's probably nothing. I'll send Caine March over there later to reset them. You need to get a grip, Vannah," Dede cautioned her.

"I just want this over and for Emily Ray to leave the mountain. I don't want to be on pins and needles like this!" Vannah cried.

"You put yourself in this position, don't forget that. You couldn't leave things alone and follow your husband's commands. You are the one who committed the trespass," Dede berated Vannah. "What did you talk about with her, Amber?"

At that moment Danny Granville walked in, covering his limp. Vannah hadn't told anyone that he'd run off the previous evening; now she went to him with a big smile.

"Hi, honey! How was the sleepover?" she asked.

He nodded, familiar with this game. They always had to put on a show for company or church friends, pretending that everything was great.

"It was fun. We played Call of Duty all night. I'm going to shower, excuse me," he said, heading toward his bedroom.

Vannah and Dede turned back to Amber.

"Did she say anything?" Vannah asked.

"No. I think you're all overreacting. She's on vacation, she just asked about the celebrity homes and stuff like that," Amber lied.

Dede's laser-focused stare would have intimidated most

people. Amber felt it burning into her, but kept her gaze fixed on the Costco advertisement in her hands, idly stirring her coffee. She had years of practice appearing submissive while harboring a rebellious heart.

The boat ride earlier had been a rare moment of freedom—a brief escape from the suffocating role she'd been trapped in since high school. Back then, she'd been the wild one—drinking, dating boys, sneaking behind the church to smoke joints with friends. Things had changed abruptly after her mother's breakdown, when her father clamped down with rigid control over every aspect of her life.

No more dating. No more friends outside church circles. When Roger Kupp showed interest, the match was presented as a foregone conclusion—his family owned half the mountain, their influence extending into every corner of local life.

She'd never actually liked Roger—he was dull-witted and emotionally stunted, content to follow Cody Granville like an eager puppy. But she'd walked down the aisle anyway, taken vows to serve and obey, become the "traditional wife" they expected. Four children and countless casseroles later, she found herself hollowed out, depression lurking behind every forced smile. Unlike Vannah, who seemed to have fully surrendered her identity, Amber couldn't make herself believe this was God's plan for her life.

"I think Amber's right," Glenda interjected with artificial cheerfulness. "We should keep calm and carry on. Everything will work out just fine."

Dede silenced her with a withering look that could have stripped paint.

"Those cameras need to be up and running again today!" Vannah insisted, her voice shrill.

"Don't worry, they will be. I'll take care of it," Dede said.

She fixed her daughter-in-law with a dead-eyed stare, as if she were appraising an animal at a livestock auction. If Vannah couldn't keep a cool head, they might have to send her away for a while, the way they did with Mary Jenkins. After the day she broke down and began screaming obscenities at Pastor Jim, she came back from Angel Voices Christian Rehabilitation Center calm and submissive. Perhaps Vannah needed the same thing. Dede would keep a close eye on her, for Cody's sake.

Kathy Warne put her final suitcase by the front door. She would be picked up late that evening for a red-eye flight to Wyoming. She had the house rented and a moving company was coming first thing in the morning. She'd already closed her bank account and transferred her money to a small credit union in Casper, not far from her dad's ranch. She'd also shut down her social media accounts. She was ready to disappear, to a place where Cody Granville could never find her again.

She looked around the big house where she had raised her three children, reflecting on how her life had arrived at this point, where she was fleeing and covering her tracks. She had gotten the part-time job at the sheriff's station to fill her time after her divorce. Then she met Cody, who was ten years younger than she was. How surprised she'd been when he flirted with her. She was a pretty woman, tall and athletic with thick blond hair and clear, green eyes. The affair started easily, and it was uncomplicated for a time. She had no expectation that he would leave his wife, and she didn't want him to. She simply liked the attention to ease her loneliness.

But then he became demanding and demeaning. His moods shifted with no warning and she was left walking on eggshells, trying to win his favor again. Which he withheld until she capitulated to whatever perverse request he made of her. It was a power play, to see how much control he had. Every time it happened, it chipped away another sliver of her self-esteem, until she was an anxious, unhappy shadow of who she used to be. And she knew he had women all over the mountain, up in Running Springs and Arrowbear, careful to keep them away from his social circle of church and home.

But everything changed when he met Hayley Hope. He became reckless. She saw it was an obsession—he had to control the young girl, to have her for himself. When she heard that Hayley had drowned, she never believed it was a suicide. She knew Cody had something to do with it. He'd been short-tempered for several weeks prior and then, the day they found her body, he came by her house with bindings he'd taken from her body when they pulled her from the lake. He even admitted what they were, so sure of Kathy's loyalty and allegiance to him.

"Get rid of them today," he ordered her, before leaving, knowing she would do it and implicate herself in his crime. He wanted leverage to hold over her.

But he was mistaken. She had already made her secret plan to get away from him. She wasn't covering for him, whatever he did to Hayley's body that awful day. That plastic bag with the wet rope bindings, greenish gray from the lake water, were stored in the back of her refrigerator, as insurance. And now she had a person who might know just what to do with them. She dialed the number Jamie had given her as she pulled her car out of the driveway. She checked her rearview mirror repeatedly, watching for any sign of someone following her. She hadn't answered any of Cody's calls in the past two days.

"Hello, this is Emily Ray."

"Hello, I'm Kathy Warne, Jamie's cousin. I have something I think you would be interested in," she said, tentatively.

"Good. I'm available whenever you are and wherever you choose," Emily said.

"Cody doesn't know I'm leaving. I only mentioned it to a close friend from work."

"Can you tell me what it is that you have in your possession?"

Kathy paused. "It's several lengths of rope. When Cody gave them to me, they were wet and dirty, and there were some smears of blood on them," she said, her voice shaking.

"He gave them to you?"

"Yes. It was in the evening of the day they found Hayley's body. He and Roger Kupp were the first on the scene and they'd removed them from her ankles and wrists. That's what he said. They were trying to give her CPR and they took them off," she explained. "Then he asked me to get rid of them."

Emily knew that no law enforcement officer would take key evidence from a possible crime scene, let alone try to hide it. Unless he was protecting himself or someone else. The bindings might have trace DNA on them, and there could be other forensic evidence as well. She needed to get them as soon as possible.

Kathy continued, "I think he falsified the police reports as well. We had two different copies, and he submitted the wrong one. He told me to shred the other, but I didn't. I have three copies of it, just in case. I have them here in my car. I just want to be rid of them and give them to someone who can do something!" she said, her voice shaking.

"When and where do you want to meet?" Emily asked.

"I'm running down to my storage unit right now to get a couple of things. I don't like having this stuff with me, I wish there was a safe place to leave them, but I'll be back within the hour. I can't risk running into Cody before I get out."

"Do you think he'll try to stop you?"

"He'd do anything to protect himself," Kathy whispered, her voice thin with fear. "He's a true psychopath—charming on the surface, but completely empty beneath. He told me to destroy that evidence, and he assumed I would. I always did what he wanted."

Her voice dropped even lower. "If he finds out I'm leaving—

that I kept those items—he wouldn't hesitate. He'd kill me without a second thought."

"Where exactly is your storage unit?" Emily asked. "Maybe I could meet you there directly."

"It's on Fortieth Street, a CubeSmart facility. I need about an hour to get there and back," Kathy said. "I'll text you when I'm heading back up the mountain. We can meet somewhere public but discreet."

"I'll be waiting for your message," Emily promised. "Drive carefully."

After hanging up, Emily stared at her phone, acutely aware of what was at stake. The evidence Kathy possessed wasn't just material for a court case—it was a live explosive capable of bringing down the powerful men who had terrorized this community for years. Kathy was essentially carrying a grenade with the pin pulled, praying she could hold it long enough to hand it off safely.

Emily only hoped Kathy would survive to make the exchange.

TWENTY-ONE

Cody had been calling Kathy Warne since last night, while he was out looking for Danny after he bolted from the house. Nothing was going right; his universe had been tightly ordered, and it functioned the way he needed it to. But lately, since Hayley's death, it was like a planet spinning off its axis. He'd deal with his son and his insubordination later; right now, he needed to find Kathy and be sure that she had disposed of the items he gave her. He kicked himself for playing those stupid games, pushing to prove his power over her. Jenkins was right, even if he hated to admit it. It was reckless but that was part of the thrill and Cody needed the adrenalin rush of danger more and more. And he'd talked too much, about too many things, when he was with her. He liked talking to Kathy, she knew a lot about life.

It wasn't like talking to Vannah, who might as well have been a parrot, just repeating what he said, no thoughts of her own. All Vannah did was smile and cook and clean, waiting on him like a maid, showing him the new cake recipe she made or some other boring-as-bread bullshit. Of course he needed other women to keep his fire stoked. Vannah was good for making babies, she was like a solid, reliable workhorse, but that wasn't what lit his spark any longer. And he liked variety. Kathy usually called him back right away; he had her in his hip pocket. He'd driven by her house and knocked on the door but there was no answer. He rapped on the windows, but no response. He didn't know what the fuck was going on, but he would find out.

At the station, he didn't see her. She hadn't called in sick, she just hadn't shown up. He looked to Janine Waters, another office clerk who he knew was friendly with Kathy. She was a frumpy woman in her late thirties, with thin, stringy hair and bad acne-scarred skin. She had a habit of oversharing about her disastrous online dating life to everyone within earshot. Cody went out to the lobby and got a frothy cappuccino from the new coffee machine and returned, sidling up to Janine's desk, sitting on the edge of it.

"Hey, Janine! I got you a coffee. I figured you liked these sweet cappuccino drinks, right?"

Janine blushed. "Thanks, Officer Granville."

"Officer? C'mon, we know each other a lot better than that. It's Cody!"

"Thanks, Cody," she said with a grin.

"Is everything going okay for you here? Is there anything you need?"

Janine shook her head. "No, it's all fine. But I do get some carpal tunnel from using the keyboard, sometimes."

"You need one of those little pillows, right? They're to protect your wrists. I'll make sure you get one today."

Janine blushed again. "Thank you."

Cody shifted his weight to lean in closer to her.

"What's up with Kathy? I heard she didn't call in today. Is she sick?" he asked.

Janine shook her head, taking a loud slurp from the coffee. "No, she's probably packing."

"Packing?"

"Yeah, she's moving to Wyoming. Don't tell anyone, she said it's a secret but she's leaving. She said she's done with everything here and she's got good insurance," she whispered with a giggle.

Cody's gut tightened at the word "insurance."

"When is she going?"

"She might be gone already. I said goodbye to her yesterday."

"Thanks, Janine," he said, with a wink, running his hand along her shoulders. He dialed Kupp who was out on patrol.

"Hey, Cody. What's up?" Kupp answered.

"I need you to find Kathy Warne today, I have to check to make sure the stuff we got from Hayley Hope's body is gone."

"I thought you took care of that?" Kupp asked.

"I did! I gave it to Kathy Warne to get rid of it. But she's leaving town, and I can't have her out there in the world, knowing what she knows," he said.

There was a long silence.

"What d'you want me to do?' Kupp asked.

"Find her. And make sure she can't talk to anyone about anything."

Emily knocked on Lillian's door to find her and Evelyn ready with their bags packed and Sammy on a leash. Eddie was going through the house checking windows and doors.

"Ready to go?" Emily asked.

"Yeah, but why? Eddie said we can't stay here?" Lillian asked.

"It's just a precaution. Danny Granville said it wasn't safe for you to be in the house," Emily said.

"And since when do we trust Danny Granville?" Lillian asked.

"Just trust me, okay? The hotel is nice, you can order room service. But you have to go with Eddie to avoid the front desk. And no roaming around, no swimming in the pool. We're hiding you, right?" Emily said.

"Kind of like a spy movie," Lillian said, a spark of excitement breaking through her anxiety. For perhaps the first time since Emily had met her, she looked like what she was—a fifteen-year-old girl, momentarily distracted from trauma by the promise of adventure.

"Exactly," Emily replied. "I'm reaching out to the FBI office in L.A. today with everything we've discovered. Between that and what Deputy Dougherty has provided, we're building a solid case." She placed a gentle hand on Lillian's shoulder. "Once I'm reinstated, I'll bring the full force of the FBI to deal with this. But until then, you and your grandmother need to stay safely out of sight."

Evelyn smiled vaguely from her chair, patting Sammy's head. "This is quite exciting, isn't it? Like in those television programs."

They drove to the resort and Emily checked in while Eddie brought Lillian and Evelyn through the pool area to avoid being seen. They met outside Room 315 and Emily handed out the room keys.

"Keep it locked, don't answer to anyone except me."

Lillian grinned. "You know Eddie's going to help you," she said cryptically.

"What do you mean?" Emily asked.

"Shut up, Lillian! It's nothing," Eddie said.

"Really, he's got a genius plan to get you the evidence you need. He's brilliant!" Lillian said.

"Shut up! Jesus, can't you keep quiet about anything?" Eddie said.

"I don't want you doing anything reckless, Eddie. Leave this to the grown-ups at this point, okay?" Emily warned him.

"Yes, got it," Eddie agreed with a warning look to Lillian.

Emily left and checked to be sure the door locked behind her. Eddie turned to Lillian and gave her a small kick.

"Blabber mouth. I'm never telling you anything again," he said. Lillian smirked and went to explore the minibar for in-room sodas and snacks.

Eddie felt his heart beating hard in his chest. He had lied; he wasn't going to leave anything to the adults. They were outsiders who didn't know how this town worked or where the secrets were hidden. But he did and he was going to get them.

Emily arrived at Mountains Community Hospital and found her dad's room. He was sitting up in bed, his eyes clear, eating a bowl of cereal. A fluid bag hung beside his bed, attached to an IV in his hand.

"Hi, honey! I feel much better. These doctors know what they're doing," he said.

"You were a little nutty last night," she said, sitting on the bed, taking his hand.

"This damn UTI! I get them too much these days," he grumbled.

A doctor came in and checked Michael's chart. "We're going to keep him a little longer, Ms. Ray. The UTI is clearing up well, but I just want to be sure there's nothing else going on."

"How much longer?" she asked.

"He'll be discharged later today. We'll send you a text to let you know the time."

"It's fine, Emily. You go have fun, go swimming or fishing. I'm good here. They have very good cake," Michael said.

Emily left with a promise to return in a few hours. She wandered the grounds of the small hospital, past the long-term care unit, and found a beautiful rose garden. It had an expansive view of the lake, and the roses were in full bloom. She sat at one of the picnic tables and pulled up the information on Melanie Zane. She knew if the girl went to such lengths to stay off the radar, she would be suspicious of any stranger calling out of the blue. She lived in Eureka, near the Oregon border.

Emily had been to Eureka on one of her first CARD cases looking for a runaway teenager who had been lured there by an online predator posing as a young, hot marine just out of the service. In truth, he was a paunchy, balding fifty-two-year-old pedophile. Back then, Eureka reminded her of a town in a Jack London novel, dense fog, clapboard homes and businesses that had the haunted look of a coastal town forgotten by time. She dialed the number and was about to hang up when a voice came on the line.

"Hello?"

"Melanie Zane?" Emily asked.

"Who's this?" The young woman's wariness sharpened.

"My name is Emily Ray, I'm in Lake Arrowhead. I'm an FBI agent." She paused, hearing Melanie's sharp intake of breath. "I've met a girl named Lillian Knox who knows your sister, Melora."

"How do you know about Melora?" Her tone was accusatory.

"Lillian told me she disappeared from foster care."

"How do I know you're for real? How did you find me anyway?" Her anger and fear felt like electricity coming over the phone line.

"I have FBI resources that most people don't have. You covered your tracks very well. I know it's weird to have a stranger call you like this. You can google me. I was kidnapped as a child and returned home eight years later. It got a lot of news coverage. I also broke a big case a few months ago, up in Arrowbear. A little girl named Josie Vance was kidnapped. It was on the news. There must be a photo of me somewhere online. I can turn on Facetime and you can verify it's me. I'll wait."

Emily heard the sounds of a computer turning on and the rustling of paper. A few minutes later, Melanie said, "Okay, put on Facetime."

Emily complied and she saw Melanie Zane on her camera screen. She was a pretty girl with dark, auburn hair and pale, fair skin. She leaned in and looked closely at Emily.

"Where did you grow up?"

"Palos Verdes."

"And who was the guy who kidnapped you?"

"James Tibbs. He also took Josie Vance."

There was a long silence, then, barely above a whisper, "Is the FBI looking for Melora?"

"No, I'm looking into the death of Hayley Hope and your sister's name came up as one of her friends."

"Hayley's dead? What'd they do to her?" she asked.

"She was found dead in Papoose Lake. The official cause of death was suicide, but Lillian Knox thinks it was something else."

"Suicide? Hayley? No way," she scoffed, bitterly. "Hayley was the one kid who was going to get out and make something of herself. I guess they were going to get her one way or another."

"I've spoken with a deputy and a few others in town, regarding possible illegal activity involving Church on the Hill. I hoped you could shed more light on what happened to Melora?"

"I'd like to know just like everyone else. She called me and said she was going to come here on a bus, from San Bernardino. But she never made it. She wanted to get away from Cody and his group. They said she ran away with a boyfriend but that was a lie."

"What exactly did Cody and his group do?" Emily asked

carefully, keeping her tone neutral to avoid leading Melanie's responses.

"Activities? Is that what the FBI calls it?" Melanie asked with a harsh laugh. "They go after the vulnerable girls in town —the ones with no one watching out for them, the ones nobody would miss. They use that church youth group as their hunting ground." She spat the words out as if they burned her mouth. "They buy off struggling parents with groceries, help with bills, all wrapped up in Christian charity while they groom their daughters."

"And Starhawk was part of this?" Emily asked.

"That bitch is nothing but a grifter!" Melanie's voice rose. "She knew damn well my grandpa couldn't take care of us with his mental health issues. So, Dede Granville—the puppet master behind all of it—sets Starhawk up as a licensed foster parent. Gets her out of her car and into a real house for practically nothing. But there was a price: take in specific girls—pretty ones, vulnerable ones—and deliver them to Church on the Hill where Cody and his perfect little wife could work on them."

Emily hesitated before asking the question she dreaded most. "Was Vannah Granville actively involved?"

She had hoped Jamie might be wrong about this part, that perhaps Vannah was merely turning a blind eye.

"She was a main part of it. Her husband is a freak, and she helped him. First, they came after me and I was stupid, I got caught up in it."

"What is it exactly?"

There was a long silence on the other end, Emily could tell she was deciding whether to reveal anything further. When Melanie spoke, her voice was small and thin, filled with shame that didn't belong to her.

"They gave me stuff. A new phone, some earrings, a few hundred dollars to spend how I wanted. I'd never had that before. And then it was going places to eat and hang out, which was good 'cause Starhawk just gave us those ramen noodle cups. And then... Cody wanted more."

"More what?" Emily asked, carefully.

"He wanted to make out in his truck, to park way out of town and do stuff. He'd say how pretty I was, how I was unspoiled, and he would... teach me everything I needed to know... to become a woman."

"How old were you? When it started?"

"Fifteen." Emily's stomach turned over.

"The next step was... intercourse in the truck," Melanie continued, her voice hollow now. "Then empty houses his mom had listed—she's in real estate. Eventually, Cody wanted me to... do it with his friends, too. Roger Kupp. Jackson Miles. Others." Her words came more slowly, as if each one had to be forcibly extracted. "They'd use rooms upstairs at the church. Pastor Jim had cameras set up. They filmed everything."

Emily's stomach clenched. She gripped the phone tighter, struggling to maintain her professional demeanor as rage boiled inside her. This wasn't just opportunistic abuse—this was an organized operation for producing and likely distributing child pornography. Multiple perpetrators, multiple locations, careful coordination. The scale and systematic nature of it was staggering, sickening.

"I know this is hard to talk about, Melanie, I appreciate you speaking with me. Did you run away to get free from them?"

"Yeah. I wanted to take Melora with me since they were starting to focus on her, but she didn't want to come. She was special needs, you know? She thought they were her friends, that they were giving her gifts because they liked her. She had no idea what was coming. So, I left and then I had a hard time getting in touch with her. Starhawk wouldn't let me talk to her. I think she told her I had died in a car crash."

"And she knew Hayley since they were kids, right?"

"Yeah, with Lillian, they were in school together. Those

assholes like Danny Granville and the Kupp boys used to bully Mel all the time. Then Hayley started telling them that she was a witch, and she was going to put a curse on them if they didn't stop. Then Mark Miles fell and was run over by that truck, and they thought Hayley caused it, so they got scared. They're as stupid as a box of hammers, all of them," she said.

"When was the last time you spoke with Melora?" Emily asked gently.

"About nine months ago." Melanie's voice cracked. "I'd saved enough for a bus ticket. Mailed it to her through a friend who still lived in town. We had it all arranged—she'd slip away during a church outing, catch the Greyhound to Eureka." The pain in her voice was palpable. "I waited at that bus station for seven hours. Checked every arrival. Called everyone I could risk contacting." Her breath caught. "She never showed up."

Emily's mind flashed to herself at ten years old—Danica Hansen then—waiting at the Redondo Beach bus terminal for a mother who had promised to come. Hours passing, hope fading with each arriving bus that didn't bring the person she longed for.

"I'm going to find out what happened to her," Emily promised, the words coming from somewhere deeper than professional obligation. "Whether she's still there or elsewhere, I won't stop until we have answers."

"Please," Melanie whispered. "She's just a kid who has a hard time, you know? She's sweet and trusting. She wouldn't have run away with anyone else. She was coming to me."

"I'll call you in a day or two with updates," Emily assured her. "Until then, don't take calls from anyone in Lake Arrowhead—not even people you think you can trust. They have connections everywhere."

"I understand," Melanie said. "I'll be waiting to hear from you."

As Emily ended the call, her phone immediately alerted her

to a new message—an audio file from Kathy Warne. Her pulse quickened as she played it.

"Agent Ray?" Kathy's voice was breathless, frightened. "I think I'm being followed. There's a car—it's been right on my tail since I left San Bernardino. I think it's Roger Kupp! I was scared, so I left the evidence at my storage—"

The message cut off abruptly, leaving only silence. Emily's blood ran cold. She immediately tried calling back, but the call went straight to voicemail. Her mind raced through worst-case scenarios—Kupp forcing Kathy's car off one of the mountain's treacherous curves, or worse.

She needed those bindings and falsified reports to build her case. But more urgently, she needed Kathy Warne alive and able to testify.

TWENTY-TWO

Dina Hope dug around her kitchen for the piece of paper with that writer's name on it. She wanted to talk to her about Hayley. She'd just woken up from a drugged-out dream and her daughter was in it. Hayley was happy and smiling but there was something wrong. She was dripping wet, there was pond weed wrapped around her slender throat. A bruise on her forehead. When she opened her mouth to speak, water poured out. It kept coming, relentlessly, until it flooded the room and Hayley's eyes rolled back in her head. Dina jerked awake, on the cigarette-burned couch, terrified.

Her mouth felt like cotton and her head pounded. She was coming down and she needed something to pull her through. She knew there was nothing in the house, she'd already torn the drawers and cabinets apart. Yesterday, she'd found a ten-year-old bottle of children's oxycodone from when Hayley had a major mouth surgery at age six. Dina poured the thick, cloudy mixture down her throat, but it provided little relief. She'd have to wait for Glenda to come by, she had the connection. Dina had no idea how she did it, but Glenda Kupp could get hold of painkillers that no one else could. She figured it was that she seemed like a nice, white church lady and the pain clinics didn't suspect her.

But she got enough to keep a lot of mountain people in opioids.

Glenda had become Dina's main source in the past year. It started when Hayley got that job at the church. Suddenly, Glenda came around regularly with her little brown bag. The best part was, she did it for free. Dina didn't have to pay anything, and Glenda was reliable, not like the dealers she'd met down the hill or the skinny bearded guy up in Arrowbear. He thought she'd have sex with him for drugs. It was so much easier with Glenda Kupp. Dina laughed to herself; it was a public service of the Church on the Hill.

But today, she was in a vile mood, after that dream of Hayley. She wanted to know how and why her daughter died. It didn't make any sense. That writer lady said she wrote true crime books. Maybe she'd write about Hayley's death. Or maybe about the crazy drugs on the mountain. There were a lot of weird things that went down. Like Joannie Dietrich and Karlie Ann Smith. Dina used to babysit her, years ago. Hayley said they just up and disappeared. A lot of kids did. Some ran away, some were chased off when their parents didn't approve of them. A boy wandered away from a youth rehab in the winter and fell off the rim, right over the guardrail, and they didn't find his body until the snow melted. Too much bad shit happened. No matter what people were saying about her daughter, Dina knew the truth—her girl hadn't ended her own life. The question that haunted her, that she couldn't escape even through the oblivion of the drugs, was who had wanted her bright, beautiful daughter silenced? And why?

She called Glenda, but it went to voicemail.

"Glenda, it's Dina Hope... I'm having a hard time over here and I need a little something. You need to come soon... and I want to know what happened to Hayley." Her words slurred, and she stumbled over her own feet walking around the house, in a growing stupor. "I want to know 'cause I don't believe that shit. I think Lillian is right... so when you come, you tell me what happened... or there'll be trouble..."

Dina hung up, barely remembering what she had just said. She was getting dope sick, and her mind was hazy. Soon her whole body would hurt, and she'd be nauseous. She took a framed photo of Hayley from an end table and clutched it to her chest. Her girl. Her darling girl was gone. She drifted into a heavy sleep, the photo wrapped in her arms.

Emily called Jamie, willing him to answer the phone. It went to voicemail, and she left a message.

"Jamie, this is Emily Ray. I got a message from Kathy, saying she thought she was being followed up the hill. She was scared and then it cut off abruptly. Just checking to see if everything is okay."

She was so impatient for an answer, she couldn't sit still. She paced the rose garden, looking out at the lake, shimmering in the midday sun. Boats were bobbing peacefully; a man was fishing with his young son. It looked like a postcard from small-town America; she wondered if they knew what seething, prurient corruption was bubbling away just below the surface.

She had to do something productive; waiting had never been her strong suit. She dialed her superiors in the Los Angeles office of the FBI. It was time to go back to work, officially.

Chief Edmonson's assistant put her on hold and then passed her through.

"Agent Ray, nice to hear from you, I hope you're enjoying your time off," Edmonson said.

"Yes, thank you, sir. I've stumbled into a situation up in Lake Arrowhead, where I'm vacationing. It appears a complex criminal group is involved in multiple illegal activities. Trafficking of minors, intimidation and possible murder."

"Murder? How did you come across this?"

"A teenager died a few weeks ago, the local police ruled it a suicide, but I heard from several people that they suspected it was a homicide. And I looked into it and discovered a ring of predators. Some are in the sheriff's office; they are affiliated with a fundamentalist church as well. And there appear to be previous victims who've disappeared."

"If you'll wait on the line, I'm going to get SAC Powers to join us," he said.

When SAC Powers joined the call, she explained in detail what she had discovered, from Kathy Warne's revelations to Melanie Zane's, and that she'd reached out to Agent Griffith in the Riverside office since she was still under review. They listened quietly with no response. She finished presenting her case and there was a long silence.

Then SAC Powers asked, "Aren't you supposed to be on a vacation right now?"

"Yes, sir. I am on vacation right now," Emily replied.

"Well, you have a strange way of relaxing, Agent Ray. We'll reach out to the Riverside office, but I would say, prepare for your reinstatement. We'll be calling you back within the hour. Good work, by the way," he said, before disconnecting the call.

She hung her head in relief. It was moving forward and with any luck, by the end of the day, she'd have the power and reach of the FBI behind her. She had barely hung up when her phone rang. It was Jamie.

"Emily! What happened?"

"I don't know, her message was cut off—"

"They got to her!" he cried.

"What do you mean?"

"She drove over the railing in the narrows! I think she's dead!"

. . .

Emily raced in her car to meet Jamie at the narrows. She got as far as Lake Gregory Drive and encountered the police barricades and first responders. It was a sea of flashing red lights; people had gotten out of their cars to look on in horror. She texted Jamie.

> I'm stopped at the barricade where are you??

> I'll come to you

Ten minutes later, he pulled up in a sheriff's SUV, in uniform. He stepped out to meet her. His eyes were red from crying.

"She drove her car over the edge in the narrows," he said. "They're going to say she did it, she killed herself, but there's no way she would've ever driven off. Search and Rescue is bringing her up as soon as they can get to the wreckage."

"There's no hope she survived?"

He shook his head. "They said the car was destroyed when it hit. They think she was trapped inside. We're supposed to investigate it, but Cody and his guys will cover it up, they control the office up here and the county office doesn't pay any attention. People fall asleep or drive over the edge all the time—we have a handful of fatalities every year."

"She was going to meet me when she got back from her storage unit, she had the evidence with her. Then she called and said she was being followed, she thought it was Roger Kupp, and then it went dead."

"They figured it out and got to her! I'm going to kill these sons of bitches!" he shouted, banging his fists against the hood of his SUV.

Suddenly a young firefighter pushed through the barricade.

"Jamie! She's alive! They got down there and found her.

She's badly hurt but she's alive! They're taking her to St. Bernardines!"

"Did they find anything else in the car?" he asked.

"Just some smashed up boxes. And the keys were still in the ignition," he said, handing Jamie a ring of keys before returning to the rescue effort.

"I'm going down to the hospital, and I've got to call her kids. I don't know what to do about the evidence," he said.

"Don't worry about it. Can I have her keys?"

"Sure. You going to her place to look for it?"

"No. Do you know her storage code?"

"Yeah, it's her birthday Zero-four-two-seven."

"Let me know how she's doing. She's going to pull through, Jamie."

"I hope so."

He got into his SUV and put on his lightbar to get through the clogged traffic. Emily watched him go, praying that Kathy would survive and be able to tell them what happened.

Vannah ripped open the packed boxes in Kathy Warne's house, rifling through the contents. In the kitchen, Dede was doing the same thing. The house was packed up, the furniture bare. They had broken the window on the Dutch door to the kitchen and let themselves in, after getting Cody's call. He told them to look for nylon bindings and police reports, related to Hayley Hope's death. Vannah knew what the bindings looked like; she'd seen them before. She felt a fury burning through her as she ransacked Kathy's home. She knew Cody had been carrying on with her, a woman a decade older than she was. And divorced, an apostate before God. Sleeping with Cody made Kathy Warne an adulteress as well, condemned in the eyes of the Lord. He was not to blame, Vannah knew that. Eve was the one who tempted Adam to eat the forbidden fruit, and women carried that original sin of disobeying God's command. The seductress, the temptress, the Jezebel.

But knowing that Cody had spent time in this house, in her bed, made Vannah red with rage. She ripped up documents and left them scattered across the floor.

"We have to find the bindings!" Dede shouted from the next room.

"I'm not finding anything, just tax documents and warranties," Vannah replied.

Hayley Hope was like a dark shadow that hung over them. She wished she had never met the girl. She remembered the day Cody pointed her out, in the Pizza Arcade. He said she would be good for watching the kids at church. Bella said she was a weirdo, who made strange movies and didn't play sports or go to parties.

Vannah hadn't thought anything of it; he'd done the same thing with Joannie, Rachel and Karlie Ann. She was a little jealous at first. They were so young and pretty, with lean, lithe bodies when she seemed to spend all her time pregnant and bloated. But after a time, all of those girls left the church and moved on. And life would go back to normal. Cody wouldn't be stepping outside to take phone calls; he wouldn't come home with the scent of other women on him. But it was different with Hayley Hope.

In frustration she knocked over a pile of boxes and watched in satisfaction as they crashed to the floor. She stormed into the kitchen to Dede.

"There's nothing here!" Vannah screamed. "How could he be so stupid and reckless to give her anything!?"

Dede reached out and slapped her hard across the face. It made Vannah's eyes water, and she felt Dede's fingernails digging into her arm.

"This is your doing! And you are never to disagree with or hold your husband to judgment!" she hissed in Vannah's face.

"Look at you! As big as a walrus, worn out all the time, your face looks like a moon. What man wants that? Cody is a good man, he is not to blame for any of this!"

Vannah turned back to the boxes, a wave of hot shame washing over her for her trespass. She began searching anew. She was lucky to have such a Godly mother-in-law to guide her.

Emily drove down the back way through Crestline to avoid the rescue vehicles. She was haunted by the last message from Kathy.

"I'm being followed... I left the—"

But now Emily had her keys, and the code to her storage unit. Kathy Warne was a smart woman, she knew they could be looking for her and she left the evidence where they couldn't get to it.

The drive down to San Bernardino took half an hour; the storage facility was in a rough neighborhood of empty lots and homes that looked like they were held up with construction scrap metal and wood. In contrast, the storage units were new, with fresh paint and cinderblocks, and a shiny electric gate. Emily pulled around the corner and left her car, just in case. She walked up to the gate, entered the code and it opened. She debated whether to ask the attendant in the office for the unit number, but she worried about attracting attention. She looked at the ring of keys and found a small one with a red silicone key cover, imprinted with the name Cube Smart, the storage facility. The number 201 was written in black marker. She found the unit and the key slid easily into the padlock. She pushed the door open and stepped inside.

It contained a few heavy boxes, some skis and an artificial Christmas tree. In the corner, a tall antique dresser leaned against the wall. Emily looked around in dismay—there was no manila envelope, no plastic bag of nylon bindings. She was about to leave when she checked the dresser drawers. In the second drawer down, she found them, under a crocheted afghan. She pulled them out and shone the flashlight from her phone on them. The plastic bag still held condensation inside it from the wet bindings. There was a pale bloodstain on one. They spoke of the brutality of Hayley Hope's death. Emily could only imagine the terror of a young girl, bound and tied and thrown into the dark, cold water of Papoose Lake, subjected to the ancient, sadistic ritual of swimming the witch.

TWENTY-THREE

Eddie carefully took Hayley's steam punk watch camera and hung it from a chain around his neck, then tucked it into his T-shirt. He pulled a hoodie on over it and placed the second camera that looked like a Bluetooth earpiece into his ear. His dad was doing odd jobs at Church on the Hill today; it would be the perfect time to help him and blend into the background, the way he always did. He texted Caine.

Coming by church to help today R U there yet?

No I'm at the FBI lady's house The one who knows Vannah G

Eddie was surprised and a bit concerned and replied:

????

Dede says the security cameras aren't working I'm checking them out

Eddie guessed that Emily had disabled them, but he didn't want his dad to get the system working again so he made quick time getting there. He pulled up to find Caine on a ladder, inspecting one of the cameras.

"Hey, Dad! Let me help," Eddie offered.

Caine came down the ladder and handed the camera to Eddie.

"I know about basic electrical and plumbing and stuff, but I don't know how these new types of things are wired," Caine said.

"Don't worry, I do." Eddie fiddled with the camera, checking wires and opening the back panel. He saw right away that the panel had been removed and it was deliberate.

"Everything here looks fine. They might need to send it off to the company for a repair. Or get a whole new system," Eddie lied. He didn't want the Granvilles or any of their group seeing what Emily was doing. Eddie moved around the exterior of the house, checking the cameras.

"They all seem fine, Dad. It must be some system problem, maybe it's their internet connection?"

"Well, I'll ask Dede at church. I've got a lot of jobs over there today, glad you're interested," Caine said, slapping Eddie on the back. He watched as Eddie moved off to check the internet cables running from the electrical pole.

Caine was happy that his son was showing some interest in helping out at church. He knew it wasn't the most comfortable place for him, being gay, but Caine hoped it was a phase that might pass. He'd heard lots of kids go through stuff like that in high school. It didn't really bother him, he just wanted Eddie to be happy, but part of him still held out hope that he'd meet a nice girl and do all the things that young people do, get married, start a family.

Pastor Jim and the church leadership took a hard line on it, though. They spoke to him all the time about it, how he had to bring Eddie closer to Jesus through prayer, that he was destined to burn in hell if he didn't "get right with God" as Vannah said.

So, he tried. He put Eddie in the Christian school where they'd encourage traditional gender roles and didn't cotton to any of that LGBTQ stuff. He tried to get him into sports, but Eddie had no interest. He'd gotten him into Scouts, but Eddie said he didn't like or trust the Scoutmasters. In fact, he'd told Caine that he should be more worried about them being around young boys than about his son being gay.

Eddie did well in school and planned on college. He was interested in U.C. Riverside, maybe for engineering, but Pastor Jim advised Caine to send Eddie to a California Baptist College or BIOLA, a place that was rooted in the Bible teachings and would help safeguard against any more of this identity exploration that he was going through. Caine wasn't sure what was best. He'd never gone to college, he'd gone to work in his dad's gas station right after high school. But Eddie was smart, the smartest kid he'd ever met. And he was good, kind to everyone and never got into any trouble with drugs or drinking. He wasn't sure what to do so he just let things roll. He'd always done that in his life, just sit back, smoke a blunt and let the complicated things pass him by. It suited him fine.

They drove to Church on the Hill where Pastor Jim and his inner circle were holding some kind of meeting in the community room. Caine got to work with Eddie helping him, taking down the ceiling squares in the hallway to fix a small leak. Pastor Jim had given Caine a long list of jobs, they'd be there all day, which was just fine with Eddie, more time for him to move quietly and get what he was after.

Emily opened the manila envelope and found the false copies of the police report on Hayley's death. Cody had changed key details to cover up the evidence that made suicide unlikely. With the binding removed from her body, the lacerations on her ankles and wrists could be considered part of her fall into the water, especially after several days submerged. Emily knew it was hard to decipher the truth after underwater decomposition had begun. She figured that Cody and the others were watching everything and everyone; she had to get the evidence to Agent Griffith in Riverside since she hadn't heard back from Edmonson and Powers yet about her own status.

She was about to close the padlock when she heard male voices coming down the hallway.

"I don't know why we have to come all the way down here to look for this shit."

Emily recognized Roger Kupp's voice and froze. She had no time to secure the lock and instead hurried quickly and silently down the hall, trying doors to other units until she found one that was unlocked. It was empty, three spaces down from Kathy's unit. She pulled the door shut behind her, knowing there was no way to secure them from the inside, just as Kupp's voice came around the corner. He was with Jackson Miles.

"You're sure this is the right one?" Miles asked.

"Yeah, I found the paperwork at her house. This is it. Look, she didn't even close the lock!" Kupp said. She heard him pull the door open while she stood completely still, barely breathing. She heard them moving boxes around, grunting and breathing hard.

"When did you start following her?" Miles asked.

"Cody told me to track her down, so I went all the way down the 18 and then I caught up with her coming up Old Waterman Canyon."

"Did she see you?"

"Not at first but I pulled her over and checked the car. I let her go and I guess she thought that was it. But I caught her again on one of the curves and kaboom!" Kupp laughed.

"Did anyone see you?"

"Fuck no! Do you think I'm an idiot? There was no one on the road. It happened super-fast," Kupp said, disagreeably.

"Do you see anything like what Cody described? He said he gave her the stuff in a plastic bag."

"Nothing..." Miles mumbled.

"Fuck! There was nothing at the house, either."

"They found her alive, you know. Took her to the hospital," Miles said, nervously.

"She won't make it, no one can survive that kind of plunge. Cody said she's unconscious, probably won't wake up," Kupp said. Miles just murmured in response.

"Maybe she didn't hide it here. Maybe Cody's just fucking paranoid. I don't think she kept any of it—Cody told her to get rid of it and she did. That old broad was desperate to keep him happy. Let's get out of here," Kupp said.

She heard them close the door and walk down the hallway, passing the unit she was hiding in. Their footsteps stopped just outside the door.

"You know, I ought to tell Cody about this. This would be a good place to bring the girls for some fun; no one's here, no one would know. And there's enough room in each one of these for all of us..." Kupp said.

Emily heard his hand on the knob of the unlocked door. She tried to still her breathing as she reached her gun.

"Wouldn't work, Kupp. They have security cameras on the ceiling, see? They could be watching us now," Miles said.

"Let's go," Kupp said, suddenly nervous.

Kupp continued complaining as she heard his voice disappear down the stairway. She clutched the manila envelope to her chest, afraid to move until she was sure they were gone. She waited a long time before emerging. She texted Jamie.

> I found it taking it to FBI now

> Great! Kathy's still not awake, she's in bad
> shape hoping she'll hang on

Emily drove to the nearby city of Riverside, a twenty-minute trip by freeway. She texted Agent Griffith and pulled into a nearby Walmart parking lot to wait. Griffith arrived ten minutes later; Emily handed her the manila envelope through the open car window.

"I'll be emailing the other information later today. This is the evidence removed from Hayley Hope's body before forensics arrived," she said.

"What kind of sick creep does something like this?" Griffith asked. "I'll review the police reports and see if I can get authorization to pull the autopsy report from the coroner. We'll need enough evidence to launch an investigation to get that approved."

"I'll get the sworn statement from the other girl up north as soon as I can," Emily said. "And I'm waiting to hear about my reinstatement later today."

"Good luck. It'd be great to work together on this."

Emily drove away, hands steady on the wheel even as her pulse raced.

She recognized this moment—that pivotal point in an investigation when scattered pieces suddenly align. Disparate facts connected into revelatory patterns. Random encounters revealed themselves as carefully orchestrated moves in a larger game.

In her years with the FBI, she'd learned to trust this sensation—this clarity emerging from chaos. The investigation had reached critical mass, gathering momentum like a boulder breaking free from a mountainside. She could feel it accelerating, unstoppable, crushing any obstacles in its path. Nothing Cody Granville or Pastor Jenkins could do would halt what was coming for them now.

On the way back home, Emily pulled up at the hospital to check on Michael. He was sleeping comfortably in his room, he had no fever, and his UTI had calmed down significantly. The doctor was still waiting for the final test results to come back. She was on her way out when a young vocational nurse flagged her down.

"Oh, I'm sorry! You must be Mr. Ray's daughter?"

"Yes, I'm Emily Ray."

"We've been keeping a close eye on him. It's a good thing you brought him in. His sodium levels were very high, he could've suffered a stroke. I really wanted to be his caretaker for your vacation up here, but Lynne Smenck beat me to it. She kind of pushed everyone else off the list," she said, her voice tinged with resentment.

"The realtor put me in touch with someone in your long-term care unit who recommended her."

"That was Mary Louise, she handles all the caretakers that contract out. Several of us were on the list ahead of Lynne but I guess Vannah used her connections to get her mom the job."

"Savannah Granville?"

"Yeah, she and Mary Louise go to the same church. A few of us were slated for the next private caregiving contract but we didn't get it."

"What does Vannah have to do with Lynne Smenck?" Emily asked.

"That's her mom. Didn't she tell you? Lynne's first husband is Vannah's dad."

Emily returned to the car in a daze. She kept seeing the young LVN's face.

Lynne Smenck is Vannah's mother... his sodium levels were really high...

She felt sick at the knowledge that they had orchestrated everything, from the moment they heard she was renting the Maison du Lac. Maybe they had planned to deal with Lillian soon after Hayley's death but having an FBI agent next to the intended target made that a bit too risky, especially when fate threw her and Lillian together that first day. They had Lynne in the house every day to watch them, to listen to every conversation. She began to wonder about all the random things that had happened from Starhawk suddenly knocking on the door, the late-night prowler, a lady telling Evelyn that Lillian was lost. Had they been behind all of it?

Lynne Smenck had purposely made Michael sick, risking his life. How many times had she suggested the trip was too much for him? That Lillian was a bad seed? For Lillian, Emily's arrival had been more than fortunate—it had been salvation. Had Emily rented any other vacation home, chosen any other week to visit, Lillian might have faced these predators alone.

Emily glanced at her phone to check the time. Michael would be discharged soon, and she couldn't risk taking him back to the Maison.

Thank God she'd had the foresight to book that second hotel room. She'd collect him from the hospital and bring him straight there, well away from Lynne Smenck's deliberate sabotage.

The thought of what might have happened if she hadn't discovered the over-salted food made her stomach clench.

She took a deep breath to control her anger and texted Lynne.

> Hi Lynne! Just an FYI, my dad is going back home when he gets released you were right it's just too much for him but I'll pay you for the whole contract. I'll be back in a day or two since the rental is paid for the full ten days

Lynne responded right away.

> You're cutting your vacation short? Give your dad a big hug for me! Do you want me to pack your stuff up for you?

Emily didn't want her anywhere near the house and replied:

> no problem I'll take him back to Los Angeles right away. and come back in a day or so to get my things, don't know if the family will be coming now

> I hope they can it would be too bad if they miss being on the lake!

"Too bad, indeed, you old bitch," Emily muttered.

Back at the Maison, Emily was packing up Michael's clothing and toiletries when the phone rang. It was a Facetime call from Dolores. She never used Facetime, Emily answered immediately.

"Hi! Is everything okay with the girls?" she asked.

"Yes, they're fine. I want to talk to you about something else," she said, stealing a glance over her shoulder. She was in a bedroom, with the door closed behind her. "It's about Antonio, I don't like how he's acting."

Mystified, Emily asked, "In what way?"

"There's a friend of his cousin's, his name is Marcos. He's the brother of a girl Toño dated briefly in high school, Anjelica Romero. Marcos has been here at the house with the family, he keeps bringing that woman around and she is sticking to Toño, with him all the time. And he's going along with it!" she said, obviously upset.

"I'm sure it's nothing. He's probably just happy to see an old friend."

"No, mija. It's not that! He's with her all the time, even in the evenings. They've gone to movies alone, the day Inez took the girls to the water park, he was with her. She's the type that hangs all over him, treats him like he's the center of the whole world. She laughs even when his jokes aren't funny, she's always bringing him a beer, or a plate of food. She's a *metiche sin verguenza!*"

Emily wasn't sure what she said but she knew it wasn't good. Each new revelation felt like another tiny fracture in her marriage. She pictured Antonio at the water park, laughing with their daughters—except he hadn't been there at all. That had been another lie, another omission. Why hadn't he mentioned Anjelica even once in their conversations? The answer was obvious, but her mind recoiled from fully accepting it.

"And the worst, he let the twins stay over at her house, and I know you are against that. She has two teenaged sons!"

Emily felt the wind go out of her. He had lied. He'd told her they were at his cousin Tito's house and Dolores was with them. The no sleepover rule was a non-negotiable in their home.

"Were you there? He told me you were, and it was at Tito's?" Emily asked.

"I wasn't there—he told me I didn't need to go. That he would be with them, and he was gone the whole night. They were all at her house. Juli and Liza told me they stayed in the guest room."

"With Toño?"

"No, they said he slept in a different room! Where did he stay if he wasn't with the girls?"

Emily felt nauseous. Dolores' account of what had happened was a scenario she had never expected to face. Her husband had lied, put their girls in a situation that was completely out of bounds. He had spent the night at another woman's house and left their girls alone in a room, unsupervised. She thought of his drunken phone call. He said the girls were at a sleepover that evening. She wondered, did he call her out of some kind of guilt over what he was doing? She guessed he might've been in contact with Anjelica before the reunion.

He might have planned to meet her, which made a mockery of their heartfelt goodbye, their loving phone calls checking in.

Dolores was so upset and angry, Emily did her best to cover her own shock and hurt.

"I'm sure it's nothing, Dolores. I don't want you to ruin your trip over this. I'll talk to him about it," she assured her.

Dolores shook her head. "His father was like this, you know? He was a cheater, just like my husband was. They were all like that back then. My poor sister suffered, and I never thought Toño would do the same. It's that Marcos, he's a troublemaker. A typical macho, he wants Toño to do the same things he does. He brought her around!"

Emily felt her stomach doing somersaults. She had to get off the phone. She knew she wouldn't be able to keep her composure much longer and she didn't want Dolores to see her break. They hung up; Emily felt totally detached from herself. She looked around the room, unable to place herself in it. Everything suddenly looked strange. Infidelity from Antonio was something that had never entered her mind. She'd trusted him. He knew her, he knew the trauma she had lived through as a kidnapping victim, the heavy weight of living as Emily since her escape from James Tibbs. He was the cornerstone of her life, her sense of security and safety in the world, in her work. The idea of him being with another woman, of lying to her, felt like her whole universe was imploding.

Just a few months earlier, she had told him the truth of her real identity, taking the biggest risk of her life. Had he been hiding his discontent all this time? Had he been unhappy or lonely and never told her? Had she driven him away from her or made him feel diminished in some way? She covered her face and curled up, falling to her knees on the floor. She cried silently, just like she had learned to do all those years ago with Tibbs. She felt as if she were splitting in two. Her breathing became shallow; she was lightheaded.

She wiped her face with her sleeve. She had to pull herself together. There was work to be done with Agent Griffith and Jamie. They needed to compile ironclad evidence against Jenkins, Cody, and their entire operation. And above all, she had to ensure Lillian remained safe until this was over.

Emily closed her eyes, drawing a deep breath that did nothing to ease the tightness in her chest. She felt herself reverting to the woman she had been trying so hard to leave behind. Moving away from the softer version, the trusting one who could let go of that tightly wound, compartmentalized core that had defined her life for so many years. The woman Antonio wanted her to be.

But that woman was a luxury she couldn't afford now. She needed to become the survivor who'd emerged from captivity—hypervigilant, untrusting, calculating three steps ahead. The agent who'd found Josie Vance when others had given up. The woman who'd pulled her weapon and shot her former captor, watching him writhe and die on the floor in front of her.

That was who she truly was. That was who these young victims needed.

As she stood, pain lanced through her back—the familiar muscle spasms that always accompanied extreme stress. She straightened despite the discomfort, feeling a strange hollowness spreading through her center, as if her body were creating space for what was to come.

Whatever happened next—with the case, with Antonio, with her career—she was ready.

TWENTY-FOUR

Eddie helped his dad, who worked methodically on the electrical outlets in the community room. He was careful to seem focused only on the task at hand. Across the space, Pastor Jim huddled with Dede, Lynne, Vannah, and Kristen, their heads bent close together in tense discussion.

Eddie strained to catch fragments of their conversation while pretending to check a wall socket. Their voices remained frustratingly low, though he caught Dede's sharp tone cutting through occasionally. The group's body language suggested urgency—Vannah kept glancing nervously toward the door, while Jenkins repeatedly dabbed sweat from his forehead with a handkerchief.

Whatever they were planning, it couldn't be good.

"Pastor, we're going to head over to fix the benches in the preschool," Caine said.

Pastor Jim waved him away. Eddie hung back as his dad gathered his tools.

"Dad, I left a screwdriver in the office, when we were doing the air vents."

"Okay, son, go get it, and I'll see you in the preschool," Caine said.

Eddie hurried toward the office, where he had indeed left a screwdriver. He wanted a reason to go back alone and search for the flash drives where Pastor Jim kept his video recordings. He slipped into the office and quickly opened the drawers of the desk, except for one. It was locked. Eddie searched the other drawers for a key as he heard Jenkins approaching from the hall-way, his resonant voice echoing like a foghorn. Eddie ran his palm along the sides of the drawers and found it, held in place with tape. He pocketed the key just as Jenkins entered with Dede and Lynne.

"What're you doing in here, boy?" he asked.

"I forgot my screwdriver in here earlier, when we were working on the vents. I'm going to help my dad. Excuse me, Pastor."

Pastor Jim eyed him for a moment, then said, "Well, get along. You have no business in here."

Eddie walked quickly down the hall, the key like a hot coal in his pocket. He would come back later, when the church was empty, to retrieve the drives. As he crossed the parking lot, he saw that Danny and his friends were skateboarding. When Danny saw him, he nodded briefly then circled away from him. Usually, he and his gang would've gathered around Eddie and given him a hard time, but not today.

Roy Bishop pulled his old truck in, almost hitting the boys. He was dressed in the same dirty, disheveled clothes as always, and his white hair stuck up as if it were electrified. He got out of the car, with a long wooden shovel, and stood in the middle of the lot.

"Jim Jenkins!" he bellowed, rigid as a marble statue in the middle of the lot.

Eddie froze, terrified and captivated. His father watched from the window of the preschool.

Roy yelled again, "Get out here, Jim Jenkins!"

A moment later, the office door opened, and Jenkins stepped into the doorway.

"What can I help you with, Roy?" he asked, keeping his voice even as he kept his distance from the wild-eyed old man.

"I want my girls, and you've got 'em! I know you do! Give me my girls!" Roy shouted.

The neighbors looked out their windows. Danny and the boys watched, transfixed at the daring of Roy Bishop. Jenkins smiled nervously, his eyes darting back and forth, to see who might be watching. He didn't want a scene.

"Now, Roy, you just get on home. You know I don't have your girls here," he said.

"You've got 'em or you know where they are. Get Cody Granville to come out here and tell me to my face that he don't know where my girls are!" Roy yelled.

Dede stepped out in front of Jenkins. "You keep my son's name out of your mouth, you crazy old fool! Get out of here, we've already called the police!" she said, moving toward him. He took a menacing step forward. Jenkins grabbed her by the shoulder and pulled her back.

"You want a problem with me, Dede? You're gonna get it if you don't give me my girls!"

"Dede, we don't want any trouble. The police should be here any moment," Jenkins said, quietly.

"You better watch yourself, old man!" she shouted as the first of several sheriff's SUVs arrived.

"Careful, Dede. I know what you done, all the things you've done all these years!" Roy warned her as three deputies hand-cuffed him and shoved him into a car.

"What're you all staring at? Go on, get back to what you were doing!" Jenkins barked at the boys. Danny and his friends left while Eddie hurried inside to join his father, a faint smile on his face. Soon, he'd have evidence for Emily to bring them all down.

Emily received a text from the doctor to say that Michael was ready to be discharged. She drove to pick him up and headed toward the hotel.

"Aren't we going back to that big house?" he asked.

"No, Dad. That house had some problems so we're going to the hotel, where you and Mom stayed. And Lillian will be there, also," she explained, hoping the change wouldn't cause him too much anxiety.

"Oh, that'll be much better. The hotel is very nice. Is that lady coming? The one from the big house?"

"Lynne Smenck? No, she's not coming back," Emily said.

Michael nodded and smiled. "I didn't care for her," he said.

Emily laughed. "Me either."

At the hotel, Emily got Michael settled into the room next to Lillian's, who had spent the day with her grandma, watching movies and ordering room service. She was so happy and relaxed, Emily figured it was the first time in months she'd been able to let her guard down. She could only imagine the weight she lived under, feeling responsible for her grandmother with an organized group of criminals harassing and threatening her in the wake of Hayley's death. Being at the resort seemed almost like a mini vacation. Michael was quite sleepy from his meds, so he climbed into bed and quickly fell asleep. The whole scene was so peaceful, Emily was tempted to stay. She might have been able to enjoy it if her entire world hadn't imploded with Antonio's betrayal. The revelations had left her emotionally flayed, every nerve ending raw and exposed. She needed solitude—space to process what this meant for her marriage, her family, her future.

"I'm heading back to the Maison. I have some stuff to take

care of, but I'll be back soon. I'll keep you posted on everything and remember, do not open the door!" Emily instructed Lillian as she left. Driving back toward the Maison, her mind was running wild, imagining all the ways Antonio might have deceived her, how long he'd been in touch with Anjelica, how far it might have gone. She never even considered that one day she would be sneaking into her husband's social media or email accounts to check up on him but now she was seized with the desire to find out.

Since she'd told Lynne that she had left, she parked her car in the lot at the hospital, where no one would look for it. She crossed the road and hurried down the path to the Maison, passing Lillian's house on the way. It was locked and dark, with no sign of anyone there. Emily wanted Cody, Vannah and the rest of them to believe that all danger of being found out was gone. She slipped into the Maison and drew the curtains.

On her laptop, she mapped out all the links between families in Jim Jenkins' inner circle, the girls who had disappeared and Hayley's death. She connected the foster kids with Alice Boone and Starhawk to Dede Granville. Glenda Kupp to Dina Hope. It was a circuitous maze of people and predators. It helped her to have a visual, like the whiteboard she used with the CARD team. She pulled up the videos of Hayley that she had downloaded. She went frame by frame through the video of her with the grown men, trying to decipher where it was. She made a list of all the clubhouses in the area, the Elks Lodge, the Masonic Lodge, the Rotary Room, from Crestline to Arrowbear. She had a hunch it was local, easy to get in and out of. She called Melanie Zane again.

"Hello, Agent Ray?" she answered, her tone desperate.

"Yes, are you okay, Melanie?"

"I'm fine but my phone's been ringing a lot today. The number calling is blocked, or it says unknown. I've been afraid to pick it up. Do you think it could be them?" she asked, her voice sounded thin and small.

"It could be. Is there any place you can go for a few days?"

"We're packing now to go to my boyfriend's mom's house in Eugene. She lives in one of those neighborhoods with guard gates and security."

"Good. I also need you to print out your sworn statement and have it notarized as an affidavit. Then I need you to email and fax it to my office. You can get all of that done at one of those mailbox places. I'll text you all the information," Emily said.

"I'll get everything submitted today," Melanie promised, her voice steadier now. "And could you... would you check on my grandpa when you can? With everything that's happening, I'm worried about him. Those people know he's connected to me."

"I'll look in on him," Emily assured her. "In the meantime, stay vigilant. Don't take unnecessary risks. I'll be in touch very soon."

Melanie paused, and when she spoke again, her voice trembled with emotion. "Agent Ray... one more thing." The words caught in her throat. "Please find Melora. Even if—" She couldn't finish the sentence. "I just need to know what happened to my baby sister."

Jim Jenkins sat heavily in his desk chair. He was sweating through his dress shirt again. Dede and the others had just left; he hated dealing with all those women. They were the ones causing problems. Vannah Granville couldn't accept the boundaries of her life—she kept getting angry and pushing back. He was sick and tired of counseling her and Cody, of praying with them over their marriage. Cody Granville was like an unneutered dog; he'd been that way since he was a teenager. It wasn't like young Vannah Pratt hadn't known what she was getting in him. Jim scoffed inwardly; she must've thought, like so many women do, that she was different, that he would change. Now Vannah couldn't accept her role in their arrangement. With each pregnancy, she seemed to grow more resentful, more unstable—challenging Cody's authority in ways that undermined everything their church taught about a wife's proper submission. And Dede only made matters worse, constantly coddling her son, assuring him he had every right to seek satisfaction wherever he found it.

He felt like an old mother hen with all these women that had to be managed and contained. Lynne was the low one in the hierarchy, and she resented the others. She resented Cody, hated kowtowing to Dede. He wished they could be like his wife, Mary, who was so calm and easy to deal with since her rehabilitation. She'd come back with a nice prescription drug cocktail to keep her mood steady and calm, and he watched every morning as she washed it down with her orange juice. He knew that Cody would soon have to do something similar with Vannah.

But the incident with Roy Bishop had shaken him. The old man was not in his right mind, but he was still as strong as a bull and could do some serious damage. When he showed up, even neighbors had come to their windows to see what was going on. Jenkins couldn't have that. He didn't need any suspicion or hostility from the community. The church was already on thin ice, after Hayley Hope's death, with that crazy Lillian Knox causing so much trouble. No, Roy Bishop had to be taught a lesson, never to trespass and confront Jenkins again. He dialed Cody's number. He would know the best way to handle such a delicate situation.

Emily paced nervously in the kitchen. She wasn't hungry, her stomach was in a knot, but she hadn't eaten in hours, and she knew she needed to stay on an even keel to deal with everything she was facing. She opened a can of tuna fish and grabbed some mayo and pickle relish from the fridge. She wanted to call Antonio and confront him, but she held herself back. She needed more information first. Emily stared at Antonio's email login page, her finger hovering over the keyboard. Was she really going to do this? Invade his privacy, search for evidence of betrayal? A voice that sounded suspiciously like her therapist's whispered that healthy relationships were built on trust, not surveillance.

But another voice—the one that had kept her alive all those years with Tibbs—insisted that uncomfortable truths were always better than comforting lies. With a pang of guilt that quickly hardened into resolve, she began typing potential passwords. After several failed attempts, she tried his mother's nickname and birthday, chayito 222.

It worked and pulled up two different email accounts, which she was aware of. He used one for work emails and one as his personal account. She scrolled through the personal account, until she found an email from Angel88, dated a few days before Antonio and the girls left for Arizona. From the message she guessed it was Anjelica.

Hola Papito! Can't wait to see you at Tia Yaya's house! It's going to be so great to catch up. You have to come by the restaurant to see my folks and my brother, they ask about you all the time!

Papito? The tuna fish sandwich suddenly felt like pond scum in her mouth. Emily spat it into the sink. Anjelica Romero referred to her husband as "*papito*" days before he left to go to a family reunion. He knew she would be there. He never mentioned her, even as someone he dated as a teenager. Emily read his messages in response.

Hola guera! Can't wait to see you all, it will be great to catch up! You'll meet my girls, Juliana and Eliza. They are adorable! It'll be great to go to Cocina del Charro. I bet it looks the same!

She looked up Cocina del Charro and discovered it was a restaurant run by Anjelica's family. From her work, Emily knew enough about human behavior to know that people reveal themselves not only by what they say but what they leave out. There were a handful of messages between Anjelica and Antonio going back several months. There was no mention of his wife of thirteen years, the mother of those adorable girls. If she had read his messages and didn't know him, she'd assume he was a single dad with two kids. That was how he presented himself and she could only guess how he described the undeniable fact that he was married. Perhaps he had cast her as the driven career woman who had no time for him? Maybe she was detached and obsessed with work, not fawning over him the way Anjelica did? Emily felt a fury building up inside.

The foundation of her marriage, the rock upon which she had built her life, was cracked and broken. The facts were right in front of her on a computer screen. Antonio had been planning on meeting up with this woman and never mentioned it to her, not once. Was it an emotional affair? Or a physical, sexual affair? Was it love or did he believe it to be? Or was it a dalliance meant to boost his ego and confidence?

Whatever it was, Emily would deal with it when she saw him face to face, not in a phone call or on Facetime. Not when the girls were enjoying a vacation. As if on cue, her phone pinged, and she saw an audio file message from Antonio. He never sent audio messages, and she knew now that it was a way of avoiding a person-to-person conversation.

"Hey babe, I wanted to know how it's going with your dad? I'm thinking of staying here with the family a little bit longer, the

girls are having such a good time. So, let me know if that works..."

She bristled, feeling the sharp sting of knowledge that he didn't know she possessed. She wondered how Dolores would respond to his plan when she found out.

She texted back.

> Got your message. No problem. My dad fell ill with a UTI so it's probably for the best. And I'm busy working on something also. Stay as long as you want. We can always bring the girls up here another time.

He texted back.

> Working??

She waited a few minutes before replying:

> Yes. Working.

TWENTY-FIVE

Evening had fallen. It was the dinner hour when everyone was home, and the church was locked up tight. Caine was busy watching a crazy YouTube news channel, the kind that convinced him that aliens walk among us, so Eddie had no problem slipping out the door. The electrical panel was in the back of the building and once he'd switched it off, the cameras that Jenkins had placed everywhere wouldn't work. He pulled a dark hoodie and knit cap on in his car; they would never know it was him.

Eddie secured the cross-body bag under his hoodie, checking that Hayley's hidden cameras were properly positioned. Both were perfectly concealed—innocent-looking objects transformed into his weapons of truth.

He drove through the quiet streets, his heart pounding. He felt powerful, for the first time. He'd stood up to Danny at Emily's place and the next time they saw each other, Danny didn't harass him. He'd ducked his eyes and gone the other way. Now Eddie would get the evidence that Emily needed, and they would find out what had happened to Hayley and the other girls. They could put a stop to the terrifying things that people suspected and were too scared to talk about. He pulled onto a side street and entered the property from the back. There was one camera as he moved to the panel to shut off the main switch. The whole place went dark.

He entered the community room side door. It was unlocked, just as he had left it. Once inside, he used his phone flashlight and made his way to Jenkins' office. With the key he had taken earlier, he opened the locked drawer and reached inside. There were stacks of papers and photographs and, in a plastic box, a pile of flash drives. Eddie grabbed the box and emptied it into his cross-body bag and stuffed as many photographs as he could fit. He was closing and locking the drawer when the lights of a high beam flashlight shone from the open doorway.

"Who's in here? What're you doing?" Jim Jenkins shouted. With him were Dede and Vannah Granville. Their flashlights illuminated him, his shadow falling across the wall.

"I came back... because I forgot one of my tools here..." Eddie stammered.

"You came back at this hour for some tools? In the pitch dark?" Jenkins roared at him.

Dede moved in on him, grabbing him roughly by the arm. "What're you up to, faggot? What's a pervert like you doing snooping around the pastor's office? What're you looking for?"

"Nothing, I swear... I left some tools that I needed at home," Eddie protested.

Dede slapped him hard across the face. "Don't lie to me, you filthy animal. That's what you are, aren't you? A disgusting pervert, an abomination before God!"

She hit him again and it was as if Vannah and Jenkins were suddenly freed from some hidden constraints. They circled him, like dogs going in for the kill, and began hitting and punching him, venting all of their pent-up fury and fear upon him.

"You're a liar and a sin against God!" Vannah shouted at him.

Jenkins grabbed him roughly by the collar, twisting it tight. "You need to have the sin beaten out of you, boy! You need to be made clean in the eyes of God!"

Jenkins landed a punch to Eddie's gut and turned to pick up a wooden rod. As he moved toward the boy, Eddie pushed back, hitting Dede in the face with his forearm, knocking her into Vannah. He grabbed the rod from Jenkins and ran for the community room. He shut the door behind him and jammed the rod into the long handle, blocking it from opening. Then he ran out into the night.

Caine March realized Eddie was gone when he got up to refill his Dr. Pepper. He called out to him in the house but got no answer. He checked Eddie's location on his phone and saw that he had gone to the Church on the Hill. He couldn't figure out why his son might be there, and it didn't sit right with him. He was driving the streets near the church when he saw Eddie running as fast as he could toward the highway.

He pulled over and shouted, "Eddie! What're you doing out here? Get in the car!"

Eddie saw him and relief washed over him. He climbed into Caine's truck.

"Drive, Dad. Just get out of here!"

"What's happened to you, son? Why're you out here? Are you hurt?"

"Just drive, Dad! Please!" Eddie shouted, looking over his shoulder in fear.

Caine hit the gas and took a series of turns, leading away from the church.

"What's going on, Eddie?"

"There's bad stuff happening at church, Dad. And not just

there. But it's related to Hayley's death and the other girls and... just bad stuff."

"Should we go talk to Pastor Jim about it? I'm sure he can do something," Caine said, gripping the steering wheel tightly.

"No!" Eddie shouted. "He's part of it!"

Caine was silent for a moment. He blinked his eyes rapidly, as if trying to see through dense fog. Then he said, "I don't understand what you're saying, son."

"Here, I'll show you. Pull over," Eddie said.

Caine stopped the car in a cul-de-sac with a view of the lake through the trees. In the distance it looked like a shiny, black jewel. Eddie opened his cross-body bag and pulled out a handful of flash drives.

"These are Pastor Jim's. He records everything and I think there's stuff on here that's related to Hayley and the other girls. I'm giving it to Emily Ray."

"The FBI lady? Vannah's friend?"

"Yeah. She's looking into all of this with another deputy and even some FBI people from Riverside."

Caine shook his head. "I don't like you being involved with all this, Eddie. These people are outsiders, they don't live here..."

Eddie interrupted him. "Let me show you what just happened."

He plugged Hayley's watch camera into his phone and the video began to play. Caine stared in silence as Jenkins discovered Eddie in his office. On the screen he saw Dede and Vannah circle him and Dede slapping him hard across the face, *"Don't lie to me, you filthy animal. That's what you are, aren't you? A disgusting pervert, an abomination before God!"* and Jenkins shouting, *"You need to have the sin beaten out of you, boy! You need to be made clean in the eyes of God"* before landing a punch.

Caine pushed the camera away and covered his face with his weathered hands.

"I don't need to see any more of that, Eddie," he said weakly.

"I think there's a lot of stuff they're doing and..."

Caine cut him off with a hand on his arm. "I want you to listen to me, son. I... was wrong, dead wrong about a lot of things..."

He sat in the darkness for several minutes, struggling to find the right words, his own guilt and shame overwhelming him.

"What those people did to you... said to you... is a lie. You're not a sin, you're not a mistake. You're not an abomination before God. You're... perfect, Eddie, just the way you are. And I couldn't be prouder of you. God blessed me with a son like you. You're the best thing in my life. And those sons of bitches are going to pay for what they did to you tonight!" He pulled Eddie into a hug, the tears running down his face.

"It's okay, Dad. I got out, it's okay."

"No, it's not. You tell me what we have to do, and I'll do it."

"Let's go find Emily."

Emily was just stepping out of the shower when her phone rang. She'd had it off for an hour, not wanting to see or hear anything from Antonio. Now it was SAC Powers from the L.A. Bureau. She wrapped a robe around herself.

"Hello, sir," Emily said.

"Hello, Emily. I hope you managed to get some downtime in because you are now officially back at work, Special Agent Ray."

"Thank you, sir. I will reach out to Agent Griffith so we can proceed. I'll have the signed affidavit from one victim within twenty-four hours and it is also being faxed to my office in Westwood. Another victim is unconscious in the hospital. I'm hoping we can get some hard forensic evidence within the next twenty-four hours," she said.

"Keep me posted. As soon as we have enough, we will launch a full-scale investigation and make arrests."

Emily felt a surge of adrenalin shoot through her body. The chase had begun. She dressed quickly and checked her email. Melanie Zane's affidavit had come through as an attachment and she forwarded it to SAC Powers. There was a loud pounding at the front door, and she froze. She grabbed her gun from her duffel and crept toward the door. Outside, she heard Eddie's voice.

"She has to be here. I checked with Lillian at the hotel, and she said she was coming back."

Emily quickly unlocked the door and ushered Eddie and Caine inside, surprised to see the older man.

"What's up, Eddie?" she asked.

"I got the flash drives! I went to Church on the Hill and got them!" he said, excitedly handing Emily a pile of them. She looked nervously at Caine. "Don't worry about my dad. He's one of us now."

"Eddie told me everything," Caine said, his voice tight with barely contained rage. His normally easygoing demeanor had vanished, replaced by the protective fury of a father who'd discovered his child had been harmed. "He went to the church and they—they put their hands on him. Called him terrible things. He recorded the whole ugly scene."

"So, you have a video of a hate crime being committed against a teenager? Good work but it was way too risky, Eddie. Was this the plan Lillian talked about?"

Eddie nodded. His eye was swelling badly, and he had a gash on his collarbone.

"Let's get you cleaned up and some ibuprofen into you. Have a glass of water and sit down," she said. She handed Caine her first aid kit and turned on her laptop, sticking one of the flash drives in. The first video was of a sermon, with Jenkins at the pulpit raging on about Satan and his helpers, waiting at every turn. He spewed lies about the dangers of vaccines and the government putting tracking devices into babies. Emily was about to put a different drive in when the screen went fuzzy and came back with a video of a pretty teenage girl, drinking a canned cocktail, in the same place where Hayley secretly recorded her insurance video.

"That's Melora!" Eddie said.

"Where is this place? It has to be some kind of clubhouse," Emily said.

Caine looked at the screen, his face lighting up with recognition.

"That's the American Legion Hall, in Sugar Pines Park!"

Emily felt a flood of relief; she knew the location. She knew where to look. She texted Griffith.

> Been reinstated. Have one victim affidavit and now reviewing a pile of video evidence. We need a warrant ASAP!!

Dina Hope heard a racket outside. She was sick and exhausted, hot and cold. She didn't know if she would be able to get through the night. That bitch, Glenda Kupp, hadn't returned her message. She stumbled to the bedroom window and saw a black SUV out front; two men were going into Roy's house next door. She blinked. Roy never had any visitors. He didn't have any friends. She thought she heard a scream, but she couldn't be sure. Sometimes her mind played tricks on her, especially when she was dope sick. Once she thought she saw a mountain lion jump over the hood of her car. And once she swore a bear charged her in the driveway, but Hayley said there was nothing there.

There was a lot of noise next door. It sounded like furniture was being tossed around and she heard some shouting and then another scream. She was sure this time. She stayed at the window and peeked out. It was a long time before the two men came out, one with blood on his shirt. He kicked at Roy's truck before he got into the SUV and the other guy drove off. She thought she knew them, she had seen them before, but she couldn't remember where. Then Glenda pulled up and Dina rushed to the top of the stairway on wobbly legs to meet her.

"Hi there, honey!" Glenda said, sweetly.

"Hi, Glenda, thanks for coming. I'm in bad shape," Dina said.

"I figured as much. I got your message and here I am. All ready to make you feel better, okay? I brought you some pills and also something to help you right away," Glenda said, climbing the stairs slowly and leading Dina back into the bedroom.

"Thank you, thank you..." Dina said, taking Glenda's hand in hers. She sat in a semi-stupor as the older woman pulled on a pair of plastic gloves and took an old shoelace from her purse to tie off Dina's arm. Then she prepared a syringe before inserting it into a small vial. Dina watched, rapt, as the clear liquid filled the syringe and Glenda turned to her.

"Now this will be the end of all your suffering, honey. This will make you feel much, much better," Glenda said, injecting it into Dina's vein, the swirl of blood mixing with the drug. Immediately, Dina felt the warm rush of relief wash over her. Her body relaxed, her mind stopped jumping from one thought to another like a ping-pong ball. Glenda stood watching her for a moment, making sure the drug took effect. Then she gathered up the drugs, shoved them into her purse and left without a word or a glance back. Dina floated into a space of complete release, she felt as if she were riding on a cloud. She saw Hayley reaching out for her. She was smiling and it felt so good to know that her daughter forgave her for that last bad fight they had. She lay back on the bed and as she lost consciousness, she remembered where she'd seen the two men at Roy's. She knew them in high school. They were Roger Kupp and Jackson Miles but now, they were all grown up.

TWENTY-SIX

It was early. Emily was still asleep when she was awakened by the sound of voices. She slipped out of bed and listened at the bedroom door. She heard footsteps, people moving about and then, "When did she say she was coming back?" It was Vannah.

Lynne responded, "She said in a day or two. Her dad had to go back since he was sick with a UTI. I thought it would come on him sooner—he's a tough old guy."

Emily grabbed her purse and gun and hid in the closet. Vannah and Lynne came into her bedroom.

"I wish she'd just left for good. And the Knox kid is gone?"

"Emily said that she and Evelyn went to join her parents someplace in Africa. Maybe they'll stay there. But she and Emily Ray aren't meeting up again anytime soon."

"I can't believe she didn't even make the bed before she left. There are dishes in the sink, too. I wonder what her house looks like," Vannah said.

"Her father said the husband's aunt lives with them and takes care of a lot of the house responsibilities. She's so busy with her work," Lynne said.

"Whatever. She's not fulfilling her role as a wife and mother, that's for sure."

Emily stood still, willing them to leave the room. They pulled back the curtains and looked out at the lake.

"How did you and her become friends anyway? Years ago?" Lynne asked.

Vannah stared at the water, the village across the lake, the small marina, the winding shoreline and the weathered water tower. These familiar sights made up her whole world, she'd never seen anything beyond it except for the occasional trip to Arizona and Lake Havasu.

"I don't know. It was different back then. She was so smart and daring, she wanted to do all kinds of things and when I was with her, I felt like I could do those things, too. Like I could be... more," Vannah said, quietly. "But then Cody noticed me at the homecoming dance and... that was it."

"We should go. Ask Dede if she can have Caine install those cameras again, here in the house."

"Okay. Maybe he'll do it today. I think Glenda took care of that little tramp's mother, Dina. And Cody sent Jackson and Roger to deal with the old man. I can't believe Roy came by church yesterday..." Vannah's voice trailed off as she and Lynne went downstairs and left.

Emily emerged from the closet and listened; she heard a car driving off, then grabbed her clothes and dressed quickly. She unlocked her thirty-eight revolver and packed pepper spray, her Taser Bolt 2 and her HyperStrike knife into the fanny pack that she clipped into place around her waist. She hoped she wasn't too late for Roy and Dina. She made it to Crest Park in a few minutes and as she approached Roy's house, she saw the front door was slightly ajar. She took her gun from her pack and pushed the door open.

"Roy? Roy Bishop? Are you here?" she called out.

There was no answer. She stepped in and saw a beat-up

easy chair knocked over onto the dirty carpet. Newspapers were piled up in stacks along the walls. A plastic trashcan was filled with frozen food boxes. She heard the water running and had a sinking feeling as she hurried up the narrow stairway.

"Roy? Are you okay? Are you here?"

He was in the bathroom, splayed out on the floor, his upper body dripping wet from the tub that was overflowing. His face was badly beaten, his left arm and hand appeared broken. There was a smear of blood from the bathtub to where he was laying—it looked as if he had dragged himself out and collapsed. She thought he was dead until she leaned down to check his pulse, and he sputtered water out of his mouth. His breathing was labored but he was alive.

"Don't worry, Roy, I'm getting help right now," she assured him, dialing 911 on her cell.

He opened his eyes briefly, they were glassy and blank, as she gave the emergency dispatch operator the address. She crouched beside Roy, her back against the bathroom wall in case Cody or any of his cohorts arrived before the paramedics; she steadied her gun on the doorway. Roy moaned in pain and shifted his body slightly.

"Don't worry, help is coming. And Melanie is okay. She's safe, I spoke to her yesterday," she said.

He slid his badly injured hand toward her on the wet tile floor and grabbed her pant leg with his gnarled fingers. She reached down and gingerly patted his hand, afraid to hurt him further, but he gripped her fingers and held tight.

"I'm here with you, Roy. Don't worry."

He tried to speak but only a garbled sound came from his bruised mouth.

Emily heard the siren approaching. A minute later, two EMTs barreled up the stairway to attend to him. She stepped clear and wiped the blood on a tattered towel that hung on the door. She heard them talking on the walkie-talkie; they were sending him down to St. Bernardine's hospital which could handle the critical care that the local hospital couldn't.

Her legs wobbled as she descended the stairs and went outside. She looked at Dina Hope's house, which was quiet and dark. Her car was parked in her driveway. The exterior lights were still on.

Emily walked to the house, knocking on the front door loudly. There was no response. She knocked again.

"Dina? Dina Hope?" she called out. The only sound was the twittering of birds in the trees. Emily looked around the entrance area, under a frayed rubber welcome mat and under a couple of cracked masonry pots with dried weeds poking out. Under a cinderblock she found a key. She opened the door and, again, drew her weapon as she stepped in. The house had been ransacked. Furniture was knocked over; drawers were pulled out and emptied. Paper and trash were strewn across the floor. It was clear that someone had been there, searching for something. She knew it was Hayley's track phone. They'd been looking for it since she died. Emily made her way up the stairs and pushed open the door to Hayley's room, but it was stark and empty.

"Dina? Are you here?" she called out.

She stepped into Dina's room and saw her laying across her bed. She was still and her eyes were open. Emily could see from the doorway that she was dead. She had a tie-off tight on her upper arm. A hypodermic needle lay on the bedspread next to her. Dina had mainlined and overdosed but Emily knew it was Glenda Kupp who'd been sent to handle her. With Hayley gone, Dina was an inconvenience they didn't want to deal with any longer.

Emily closed the door behind her and dialed Griffith.

"Hayley Hope's mother, Dina, is dead from an overdose. Her house was ransacked. And Melanie Zane's grandfather was attacked, probably last night. He's on his way to the hospital now. I can't call the local 911 operator for Dina. It's a suspicious death and it'll go to the local sheriffs, who are probably responsible," she said.

"Jesus! I'll call it in to the San Bernardino PD and tell them it's part of an FBI investigation, to keep it off the local mountain law enforcement radar. It might take them half an hour to get there. Are you good there by yourself to protect the scene?"

"Yeah, I'm armed and waiting. I'll hear the locals if they come. Tell the SB police, no sirens, okay? We don't want these guys up here to know what's happening," Emily said.

"No sirens. I'll be up there within the hour," Griffith said.

"Great. And I spoke to the L.A. office late last night when I received the flash drives. We'll have a team of agents up here by this evening."

As Griffith was about to hang up, Emily said, "One more thing. Can you bring me some clothes? I don't have my work stuff here, I'm on vacation. And there's no store up here that sells a plain dark women's suit."

"Sure, what size?"

"Eight. The usual, you know. Dark suit, white shirt. Size six shoe. And an extra bulletproof vest."

"I've got you covered," Griffith said. "We do want to look the part when we bust their asses."

Emily locked the front door and pushed a cabinet in front of it. She drew the blinds on all the windows so no one could see inside. Then she sat with her back against the wall, facing the doorway with her weapon drawn.

Mary Jenkins sat quietly, watching an old episode of *Murder She Wrote*. Jim always chose her television shows now. She heard him in their bedroom, moving things, opening drawers. He'd come home from the church late last night, carrying a big box of papers and his laptop computer. He hadn't slept, he'd been up all night, mumbling to himself and calling different people in the congregation. She didn't know what had happened and she didn't care to ask. It wasn't her business any longer. She stayed in her own world, showing up at Jim's side for church events and at every Sunday service. She sat like a mannequin behind him at the pulpit, in her pale, cream-colored suits, her hair like a spun sugar confection of blue-tinged silver.

But most days, she just stayed home in their big house and watched her shows. Except for the days that she walked the trail by the lake and made plans. She'd been moving small amounts of money from their church accounts to her own, set up in a credit union, apart from anything she shared with Jim. Over time, it had grown, and she had a good amount of money saved and stored away where no one could find it. Or get their greedy, dirty hands on it.

She knew about his sordid activities with those degenerates: Granville, Kupp and Miles. She knew about the girls and how angry the wives were. She knew about her husband's proclivity for illegal images and videos that could get him locked up for the rest of his life. That was what had caused her breakdown years earlier. But she had used her time at the Angel Voices Rehabilitation Center wisely. She'd learned a lot about things. And she decided exactly who she would be when she returned to the fold of the church and her marriage. The docile, obedient helpmate, living the scriptures. Now they saw her as the paragon of Christian womanhood. Now she had earned their trust.

Jim was banging around in the next room cursing and muttering under his breath. He came into the den, half dressed, sweating like a barnyard pig.

"Mary, where's my passport at? Didn't you keep them in the top drawer of the file cabinet?"

"What did you say, sweetheart?" she asked, turning to him with her perpetual sweet smile.

"My passport. I'm trying to find it. I thought it was in the top drawer of the file cabinet here at home but it's not there. You've always been in charge of those things. Do you know where it is?" he asked, trying to manage his impatience.

"Are we going on a trip?" she asked.

"No, no... we're not going anywhere. I just want to know where it is."

"Well, darling, that's the last place I saw it. You know we do have a lot of church people in the house all the time. Maybe one of them put it in a safe place?" she asked, in her practiced, little girl voice.

"Oh, for fuck's sake..." he said, turning back to the bedroom.

Mary took a sip of her green tea. She knew where the passports were. They were in her safety deposit box at the credit union. Along with the extra credit cards he'd opened in her name. She always knew the day would come when Jim would go too far and do something that would require an immediate departure to places unknown and hard to reach. She was prepared. Her husband didn't know anything about technology, he couldn't even close the apps on his phone without help. So, he had no idea she had turned on his location services and linked them to her phone. Or that she'd put an Air Tag in his suitcase. When they caught him, he'd be gone for good, and she'd be free. She pulled the plush throw that she'd knitted around her, the one with her favorite Bible verse from Proverbs 4:14-19.

"But the path of the wicked is like a dark night. They trip and fall over what they cannot see."

She was safe and warm, wrapped in the cloak of righteousness and God's judgment.

TWENTY-SEVEN

Emily stood outside Dina Hope's house as the forensic team descended on it and the coroner wheeled her body away in a heavy, black plastic bag. The San Bernardino PD had cordoned off the scene and so far, no one from the local sheriff's office had shown up.

Emily texted Melanie.

> You were right, your grandpa was attacked sometime in the last twenty-four hours but he's alive. He was taken to St. Bernardine's hospital. His vitals were strong when the EMT's took him

> Thx 4 the update no activity since we got to eugene have you found Melora? Any sign of her? Anything?

Emily could sense her desperation, needing to know what had happened to the young girl.

> No, not yet but I will let you know as soon as I do. Stay positive

She got into her car to head to the hotel and book herself a room. She didn't feel safe being back at the Maison until all of this was over. She'd requested Agent Diaz and Izzy Doqui come up as part of the Los Angeles FBI team. Griffith and her agents would be arriving soon. Emily had only reviewed a few of the flash drives but there was enough there to arrest Cody, Jenkins, Kupp, Miles and Prentiss. There were videos of Melanie Zane, dancing half-dressed and intoxicated around a firepit with all of them watching and leering at her. She was underage and under the influence. There were some with the other girls that were much harder to watch but they were viable product for anyone interested in selling underage pornography on the dark web. Watching them had been unbearable for Emily, even after many years with the Bureau. No amount of experience could harden her reaction to seeing young girls being abused and violated. It triggered the sense of helplessness she had felt in the long years of captivity with James Tibbs.

In what she had seen, there were no videos of Hayley Hope. When they reviewed all of them, they'd surely find some with her, to tie them into her murder. Emily wanted to be sure Cody, Kupp and the others paid for what they'd done to Hayley. She just had to find the hard evidence that they had done it.

She arrived at the hotel and found Lillian, doing a puzzle with Evelyn and Michael.

"Emily! Eddie came by and told us that he got the flash drives for you," Lillian said.

"Yes, he did, and it was very risky. You should've told me."

"But you would've stopped him."

"I need you to do something for me, Lillian," Emily said.

"Sure, what?"

"I need to contact your parents. They have to come home right away."

Lillian's smile faded. "They won't come back. They're too busy."

"Well, I'll have a talk with them, and I think they'll make the time to get back."

"What're you going to say?" Lillian asked.

"That's for grown-ups, but I need their number."

"Okay. You can also try their agency, they always know how to reach them when they're in some insane place," Lillian said, taking Emily's phone and adding the phone numbers.

"Thanks. There will be a lot more people up here very soon, from the FBI office in Riverside and from L.A. Keep a very low profile because this will attract the attention of Cody and the rest."

"You're going to get all of them, aren't you? They're going to pay for what they did to Hayley, right?"

Emily nodded, knowing she was making a promise she might not be able to keep.

"Yes, we will."

Kristen Griffith and the Riverside agents arrived and, along with the Los Angeles team, they booked the entire second floor of the hotel. They came in unmarked cars, dressed down in undercover clothes. They put undercover surveillance on the Granvilles, the Kupps, the Miles' and the Jenkins' families. They staked out the Church on the Hill. They pored over phone and bank records, social media accounts and emails, pulling everything related to any of the missing girls. Izzy got to work hacking into all the online accounts of everyone they were investigating. Emily knew he would sift through their online footprints like a prospector, extracting every little nugget of incriminating information they needed. With Griffith, Diaz and the others, she reviewed the remaining flash drives from Jenkins' office. There were images they knew he must've been trading in online pornography sites.

There was a video of Cody, Vannah, Roger and Dede

discussing a break-in to Lillian's house, enlisting their kids to harass her at school, to kill her crows. It seemed Jenkins wanted to be sure he had something on everyone so he could maintain control over them. Emily and the other agents spent several hours going through all of the drives, but there was nothing on Hayley Hope, to Emily's dismay. She poured herself a third cup of coffee, Griffith joined her.

"How're we going to link this to Hayley's murder?"

"I don't know. It looks like Cody and the others must've put any videos with her in a different place. I'm sure it's the track phone they gave her. They didn't want Jenkins having them," Emily said.

"Why do you think?"

"I don't know. I have no doubt we'll find a whole ring of pedophiles that these videos were shared with. But there's something different about Hayley's situation."

"The bindings are at the forensic lab. They were in the water so it's going to be hard to get even touch DNA. And any fingerprints can be attributed to their claim that they thought they could save her," Griffith said.

Emily nodded, taking a swig of strong, black coffee. "I know," she said quietly. "We need Kathy Warne's statement, but I don't know when or if she'll be able to provide it."

Izzy waved her over. "Emily, I found Jenkins' network to share this stuff. It's like Elysium or Giftbox used to be. He's trading images and videos, all over the country."

As they investigated, it became clear that Jim Jenkins' main interest was in the pornographic side of the abuse. Cody, Kupp, Miles and Prentiss were the ones who committed the actual crimes. They had more than enough evidence to arrest them all right away, but the decision was made to wait twenty-four hours to try and find a link to prove that Hayley Hope was murdered. If they could get that, the charges would be more severe; they would go to prison for life with no possibility of parole.

Emily was heading up to the third floor to check on Lillian and Michael when her phone rang. It was Dolores.

"Emily? Antonio is on his way to you. He knew something was wrong when you spoke to him earlier and I broke down. I told him how I called you about that Anjelica Romero. He's catching a plane back to California while I stay here with the girls," she said, nervously.

"Thank you for letting me know, Dolores. I'll be ready to talk to him when he arrives," Emily said.

"I hope I did the right thing," she said.

"You did. Thank you," she reassured her.

Emily hung up, unsure how she would feel seeing him face to face. She decided that when he showed up in Arrowhead, she would make a decision about their future when she had the time and mental space, which wouldn't be until the investigation was over. They were strategizing the final stages of planning and execution to catch a ring of criminals who were well armed and desperate, living in a small, resort town filled with residents and tourists. There were a million ways it could go wrong and turn into a disaster. She couldn't be pulled into an emotional hailstorm because of Antonio's indiscretions. There was too much at stake.

Cody was at the station when Deputy Larry Laime came back from patrol.

"Hey, did you all see the San Bernardino PD out in Crest Park? A whole mess of them with forensics and everything. I stopped by but they said it was a special investigation. It was a trip!" he said.

Cody looked around the office, checking to see if anyone was acting strange. The door to Sheriff John Chelsea's office was closed. He wanted to go to Crest Park and see for himself, but it was too risky. He saw how Kupp and Miles had left Roy

Bishop—he didn't think the old guy would survive but he wasn't going to leave his fingerprints on anything. He'd gone to Dina Hope's place, too, looked everywhere for that fucking track phone that he'd given Hayley. They should've found it by now. There was something going on, he could feel it. Jenkins was acting strange, Vannah and his mom were hiding something from him. It was like all the threads of his life that he held so tightly in his grip were breaking free and being carried by the wind in every direction. And he could not gather them again, not fast enough.

Behind the closed blinds of his office, Sheriff John Chelsea sat motionless at his desk, the phone call from the FBI's Los Angeles office still echoing in his mind. The allegations against his deputies—men he'd known since they were boys—turned his stomach.

Though part of him wanted to dismiss it all as impossible, Chelsea wasn't naive enough to risk his thirty-year career protecting anyone, no matter their history. Cody Granville, Roger Kupp, Jackson Miles, Mike Prentiss—they'd been the backbone of his department for years. Everyone knew they operated by their own code, bending rules when it suited them. But what the feds described went far beyond cutting corners.

The Bureau had warned him to expect a federal presence in town.

His job was simple: don't impede their investigation. Don't alert anyone. Chelsea hadn't even told his sergeant, unsure who might be involved in Granville's inner circle.

Through the slats in his blinds, he observed Cody at the water cooler, laughing with the dispatcher as if it were any normal day. When Cody's gaze suddenly shifted toward his office, Chelsea quickly closed the blinds. Whatever was coming, he wanted no part in it.

TWENTY-EIGHT

Emily took a quick walk along the hotel lake path to clear her head. She had to get outside and move, breathe fresh air and reset her system. She was restless and impatient, wanting to make arrests, but they had to wait. She stood on the hotel beachhead, looking out at the water, stretching out the tight muscles in her back. Her phone rang, she saw it was Lillian's mother, Caroline Knox, returning her call.

"Special Agent Emily Ray," she answered.

"This is Lillian's mother, Caroline Knox. I want to know what this is about?"

"Hello, Mrs. Knox. I met your daughter on my first day of a vacation up here. She was being harassed and threatened by a group of aggressive, intoxicated teenage boys. She's also been targeted by a group of people suspected of very serious crimes. We are in the middle of an investigation, and she cannot stay alone any longer with her grandmother. She needs proper adult supervision," Emily said.

"Lillian is very mature for her age and she can take care of herself. Her grandmother is there to watch her," Caroline said, casually.

Emily felt a surge of anger at Caroline's indifference to her daughter's suffering. "Someone threw an incendiary device onto your property which could've started a fire. She cannot 'take care of herself', as you describe! Evelyn is more and more confused. Your daughter has had to take on the responsibilities of an adult and she is fifteen years old!" Emily said, her voice rising.

Caroline Knox sputtered a response, "I had no idea that was going on! We figured she was fine there while we were on assignment. She's been fine in the past."

"I doubt that. She's been staying at the Lake Arrowhead Resort the past two days for her safety. This is where it stands: you need to come and join Lillian until this is over. If you leave her alone again for any extended period of time, I will report you to Children's Protective Services. You will be charged with the abandonment and endangerment of a child, and you will lose custody of her."

There was silence on the other end of the line. Emily waited for a response while Caroline Knox realized the seriousness of her irresponsible parenting.

"I understand. We'll be there as quickly as we can. This won't happen again, I assure you," she said, her voice shaking.

"Make sure it doesn't because I will be checking. I know you're in Africa, please catch the earliest flight possible."

"We will. And thank you, Agent Ray, for protecting her," Caroline said stiffly as they hung up.

It was a relief to know that Lillian would have her parents by her side, where they should be.

Her phone pinged, with a text from Jamie Dougherty.

> Kathy's awake! She can talk and she remembers!

A wave of relief washed over Emily. Kathy's statement would help link everything they had discovered to Hayley's death. She was getting closer to holding all the missing pieces in her hand, which would allow her to close her fist and bring it down hard. She rode the elevator to the FBI floor and as she stepped off, she came face to face with Antonio. Her heart lurched toward him, but she kept her distance. He looked at her, his face etched with regret, his arms hanging limply at his side.

"You made good time," she said.

"I flew into Ontario," he said, trying to sound casual. "So, what's going on? I gather there's a whole team of agents here and police?"

"It's a RICO case, complicated by multiple victims and perpetrators. We need several branches of law enforcement to handle it."

"How d'you get reinstated?" he asked.

"I requested it," she replied simply.

He looked at her for a long beat. He was tired, with dark circles under his eyes. She wanted so much to go to him and embrace him, as if nothing had happened, but she was rooted to the spot.

"Can you explain what's going on?" he asked, finally.

"How about you explain how our girls slept over at Anjelica Romero's house with two teenage boys there?"

From his reaction, it was clear he didn't know Dolores had shared that information with her.

"I should've checked with you..."

"No, you shouldn't have done it! If you'd checked, I would've said no and you knew that!" she snapped at him.

"She's an old family friend. It was nothing. We went to watch a movie at her place, and it got late."

"And where did you sleep that night? Don't say with the girls because I know you didn't."

If someone ever looked like a deer caught in the headlights, it was Antonio realizing that she was aware of more than he'd expected; this was not going to be an easy fix. It would take more than him showing up, handsome and exhausted, his eyes soft with a sweet, boyish smile.

"What exactly do you know?" he asked.

His question hit Emily like a sharp stab in the heart. He didn't immediately deny that he'd slept with Anjelica, he didn't insist that nothing had happened. He asked how much she knew, to gauge his response and how much he could hide.

"I know that you've been spending a lot of time with an old girlfriend, who's been inappropriate in her attention to you, as a married man. That you've never mentioned her to me once, that you lied about the sleepover, and you didn't sleep in the same room with the girls to keep an eye on them. People don't lie unless they have something to hide."

He covered his face with his hands for a moment, rubbing his eyes.

"It's not anything, Em. It was just hanging out with an old friend."

"Then why did Dolores call me? And why did you rush over here to do damage control?"

"Can we go somewhere to talk about this? Not in a hotel hallway?" he pleaded.

"Not now. I have an investigation to run and arrests to make. We'll talk when this is over," she said.

"Is it too much to ask that this might come first?"

"Yes, it is. I'm in the middle of a murder investigation, of a fifteen-year-old girl. I cannot and I will not put your probable infidelity first! I'm not the reason you're standing here!" She spat the words at him, surprised by her fury.

He moved closer to her, touching her arm tenderly. "I think you're making too much of this..."

She pulled away. "No, I think you forgot who I am."

TWENTY-NINE

Emily joined the other agents. Her hands were shaking, her heart beating wildly. The warrants had arrived for Church on the Hill as well as the American Legion Hall in Sugar Pines Park. She was eager to get out of the stuffy, crowded hotel suite. She signaled to Diaz from the CARD team to join her.

"We're going to go check this place out. It's about twenty-five minutes away. We'll need several officers as backup. Not sure what we'll find out there," she said, holding the Legion Hall warrant.

She rode with Diaz in his car. They hadn't worked together since the day she was put on leave by the FBI.

As they drove toward Crestline, he said, "This is some intense shit, Emily!"

"I know. I was on vacation but that went south real fast."

"How do these weirdos end up in these out of the way places? There's nothing up here. It looks so peaceful."

"That's why they come up here. They want to be off the radar from all of us in the big city. You won't believe the number of people on the sex offender registry who live in the mountains. And there's some swingers compound up here, too!"

Diaz laughed. "Swingers? Is this the seventies? What the hell?"

"I know. If you're that bored, read a book." Emily laughed with him.

"Or change the oil in your car," he added.

They headed into Sugar Pines Park. Diaz scanned the area. The San Bernardino PD officers were following behind.

"This is way the fuck out here. The warrant is for the American Legion Hall? Do those still exist?" he asked.

"Yes, there's one in L.A. but it's become a cool special venue."

"Oh yeah, it's by the Hollywood Bowl, right? I went to a performance art thing there once. It was a date, and she had tickets."

Emily looked over at him with his neat crew cut, his crisp polo shirt and FBI vest.

"You went to see performance art? What was it?"

"It was some kind of play, and we had to be participants in the story, we had to walk through these rooms. I lost my date, and I had to wait outside for her at the end."

"Was there a second date?" she asked.

He cracked a small smile. "She's my girlfriend now. I'm cultured, you know."

They pulled up onto the small commercial strip, then into the parking lot of the Hall.

"How're we going to get in?" Diaz asked.

"The last known listing agent is one of our targets so we can't ask her to come out with the keys."

"So, we bust in. Fine by me," he said with a smile.

He knocked on the door in case anyone was on the premises. There was no response. They walked around to the back of the property and found a sash style window that was wobbly. Diaz picked up a piece of rebar from a pile of old construction materials and jarred the window open.

"And so it goes!" he said, hoisting himself through the window. A moment later he opened the front door. Emily and the officers stepped into a room that was frozen in time, filled with vintage furniture and décor from the early seventies. She pulled up the video that Hayley had on her phone and showed it to Diaz.

"It's the same place!" he exclaimed.

They walked through the building. There was a kitchen, dining room and a main hall with a small stage for presentations, and several smaller rooms, probably used for storage, adjacent to the main hall. Emily pushed the door open to one of them and stopped cold; there was a mattress on cinder blocks in the corner of the room, a thin checkered quilt thrown over it.

She walked into the room. There were a couple of folding chairs in the corner and plastic storage bins against one wall. She flipped the light switch and a broken fixture in the ceiling illuminated only one bulb, giving the room a greenish pallor. It sickened her to imagine Hayley, Melanie or Melora in this dank, depressing place, drugged or incapacitated by adult predators. There was a plastic trashcan next to the bed. Inside, she saw a pair of women's underwear. She slipped on plastic gloves and pulled them out. They were torn, with visible stains, which she knew could hold the DNA evidence to bring this case full circle back to Hayley Hope.

"We need forensics out here right away!" she called out to Diaz.

She had the video Hayley had shot, that placed her in the Hall with Cody, Kupp and Miles, pressuring her to drink alcohol. Now that Emily had walked the scene, she could only imagine what Hayley had endured in this sordid place. But someone had forgotten to clean up after themself and Emily hoped that might give them the missing piece.

They stayed at the scene until the forensic team arrived. As they moved meticulously through the premises, Emily saw a few scattered neighbors wander out to see what was going on. Her phone rang; it was Lillian.

"Hi, everything okay?" Emily asked.

"Yes, we're fine. My mom called, they're coming home. But the videos are up! Hayley's videos are up!" she said excitedly. "Check her Instagram account! She did it! You have to go get her track phone! It has everything on it!"

Emily had no idea what she was talking about and pulled up Hayley's Instagram account as Diaz joined her.

"What's up?" he asked.

"Hayley Hope posted new videos. Lillian said they just went live!"

"How'd she post them? She's dead."

"IG has a feature that allows you to set a release date for videos, so you can set them up ahead of time," Emily explained. "Let's step outside, where it's quieter." They left the forensic team to work in the hall.

"You think she postdated them in case something happened to her?" Diaz asked.

A video close-up of her filled Emily's phone screen.

"This is Hayley Hope and if you're seeing this video, that means they killed me..."

Diaz and Emily froze. She had answered his question. It was as if Hayley was speaking from beyond her grave. In a way, she was.

"I'm Hayley Hope. I'm making this video as a record of what's been happening, in case I go missing or something worse. I've gotten into a bad situation that I can't control. I thought I could, I thought I knew what I was doing but I didn't. It started with the job, babysitting the kids on Wednesday nights at Church on the Hill. I know Vannah Granville from school, she's one of the moms who volunteers. I thought it was easy, just keep an eye on the kids when the grown-ups were busy. But then it changed when Cody Granville started dropping by. He'd ask me to help

him do stuff at their house and Vannah was there, she knew about it. Then it was going down to Home Depot with him to pick up something. And we'd stop to eat or he'd give me money to go into a store. Then he... changed and he said he wanted to teach me how to be a woman..."

They stood in the growing twilight, the forest closing in on them like a heavy cloak. The air was crisp, a smattering of bats beginning to swoop and dodge in the sky above. In the video, Hayley was sitting in her bedroom—Emily could see the altar piece in the background, the posters of her favorite bands on the walls. Her pretty face was scrubbed clean, her hair pulled into a messy topknot. She looked directly into the camera without flinching and detailed the same grooming that Melanie experienced, slowly drawing her into an intimate relationship with Cody Granville. But unlike Melanie, Cody didn't want to share her with the others.

"Cody gave me a GoMobile track phone to keep the videos he took of us together. He said it will be our secret treasure trove. Roger Kupp wanted to be part of it, but Cody wouldn't let him. He said I was special and only for him. He says he's in love with me, he wants me to move in with them and be his second wife. He says that Vannah's only good for making babies now and he's not interested in her that way anymore. I don't want to, I'm afraid of him and the whole thing is... gross. I hate it when he does it. The whole thing is sick and I want it to stop. I told Cody and he said it's not my decision, that he's the man, the head of the household. Vannah hates me now and she says I've bewitched her husband, 'cause of how Lillian and I talk about being witches. The videos of what they did are on that phone and only Lillian will know where to find it. It's in the Witch's River," she said cryptically, then the screen went black.

Emily's mind raced wildly, searching for the time and place she had heard those words.

"What does he mean? Where's the Witch's River?" Diaz asked.

Then it hit her. It was Hayley's altar piece, with the circle of women in white, standing at the river's edge.

"Let's go! I know where it is!" she said, racing to the car.

Half an hour later they were in Lillian's house. Emily moved directly to the altar piece headboard she had taken from Hayley's room.

Hayley and I did the decoupage from an old poster she got at a garage sale. We call it the Witch's River...

Emily ran her hands along the paisley fabric that covered the upholstered side of the headboard. She found a small, four-inch incision that had been stitched up and took a kitchen knife to rip through the heavy brocade. She reached in and worked her fingers through the stuffing until she found it. A white track phone, the evidence that Lillian had been targeted for. Dina Hope had died for it. Cody had given Hayley the phone, believing it would bind her to him, create an intimate connection only they shared. Instead, she had transformed it into the instrument of his destruction. The videos she'd secretly recorded—evidence of grooming, drugging, abuse—would put Jenkins, Cody and their entire operation behind bars for the rest of their lives.

Emily called Griffith and alerted her to the newly posted videos. Back at the hotel, Izzy went through Hayley's track phone, which contained a mountain of evidence. Once they had the coroner's review of her autopsy, they would have a better idea of exactly how she was murdered. It turned out that they didn't need the report to make that discovery.

Someone else had their own video to post.

THIRTY

Amber Kupp stood outside one of the FBI hotel suites, accompanied by a hotel security guard. When an agent opened it, she asked if she could speak to Emily Ray privately. Emily led her into an adjacent room. She sat in a chair and handed Amber a bottle of water and a cup of coffee.

"You probably want to record this," she said.

"Is this a formal statement?" Emily asked.

She waited before responding, "Yes, it is."

Emily left the room and asked Griffith to join her. They Mirandized Amber and set their phones to record what she had to say.

"I was there when they killed Hayley."

Amber's voice was barely audible, her hands trembling so violently that her coffee sloshed over the rim of her cup. She couldn't meet Emily's eyes as she continued.

"It was Vannah and her mother who planned it all. There had been other girls before—but Hayley was different." Her breathing grew shallow, her skin ashen. "Cody was obsessed with her. Wanted her to live with them, become his... second wife. Vannah couldn't take it anymore."

She swallowed hard, her fists clenching. "They lured Hayley to the church, said it was for babysitting. But it was a trap. We were all waiting for her." Amber's voice cracked. "Vannah injected her with something. Made her disoriented, compliant. She didn't even understand what was happening to her."

Emily and Griffith exchanged a stunned look as Amber continued.

"Vannah ordered me to record it all. Said they'd want to watch it later." Amber's chin quivered. "I... I just posted the video online. YouTube. The account is 'OGMamaBear.' You need to get it before they take it down."

Emily bolted from her chair, adrenalin cutting through her exhaustion. "Izzy!" she shouted, rushing to the door. "Pull up a YouTube account 'OGMamaBear'—now! Download whatever's there!"

Agents crowded around as Izzy's fingers flew across the keyboard.

The large monitor flickered to life, and Griffith led a visibly distraught Amber to join them. When the video began playing, Amber turned away, her shoulders hunched as if trying to make herself invisible.

On screen, Hayley Hope's face appeared—flushed and disoriented, pupils dilated to black pools.

Vannah, Glenda, Dede, and Lynne circled her like predators, forcing an oversized hoodie over her head in what appeared to be the church parking lot.

"That's right," Vannah's voice hissed from the speakers. *"This is what happens to witches who mess with things that don't belong to them."*

"What time was this?" Emily asked Amber.

"Late. About midnight," she replied.

The video continued, with Dede Granville tying a rope around Hayley's wrists.

"You know what we're gonna do, you little whore? We're gonna put you to the test. You say you were just playing with that crazy friend of yours, that you're not really a witch. It was just a game," Dede said.

Hayley giggled, unaware of what was happening.

"It was a game, we played a game..."

"We're going to play a little game, too. It's called swimming the witch," Vannah said, pushing Hayley into the back of her Suburban as the others climbed in next to her.

The video cut off at this point and resumed at Papoose Lake.

A group moving as silently as a snake, prodding the girl forward as she stumbled, unsteady on her feet. They guided her, keeping her upright as a key slid into the padlock and the gate was pushed open...

The group stopped and settled, some feet shifting in uncertainty. The ropes around Hayley's wrists were fastened tightly; one of the others stooped to wrap the line around her thin ankles. Then a hand lurched out and shoved her over the concrete edge, her body hitting the surface with a sudden splash. They stood watching her thrash against the depths, her voice struggling as the water rushed to fill her open mouth. She sputtered and writhed, freeing her legs and kicking hard to stay afloat.

"She's floating." It was Vannah Granville who spoke.

"I think... she's trying to keep from going under..." Glenda whispered, barely audible.

"She's floating," Dede insisted.

The camera panned the faces of the women who stood watching Hayley Hope fight to stay above the water. Glenda Kupp, Lynne Smenck, Dede Granville and Vannah Granville, who grabbed a ling metal pole and pushed it against Hayley's body, holding her down below the surface. When the water went still, she put the pole back and turned to the others.

"She was a witch, you see? We are free of her now. She float-ed," she said in a lifeless monotone, her eyes empty, devoid of any emotion.

The screen went black. Some agents turned away in distress. What they had witnessed wasn't a test of witchcraft; it was a brutal murder of a helpless teenager. Amber Kupp cried softly.

"We did it, we all did. It was Vannah and Lynne who set it up, but we all did it..." she said.

"You need to remove the video now. We can't have that kind of evidence out there where anyone could see it. It's going to be part of this court case," Emily said.

Amber sat at Izzy's laptop and deleted the file from her YouTube account, but he had downloaded it. Emily worried that Lillian might see it; she didn't want her to go through that trauma. She looked around the room of officers and agents.

"We have what we need. Let's get ready."

Two hours later a fleet of black SUVs pulled into the parking lot of the resort. A slew of agents had come up as well as SWAT since they didn't know if Cody, Kupp, Miles and Prentiss would be armed or who else in the sheriff's department might be involved. They had a team of CPS social workers ready to take in any minors that would be left unattended. They planned to arrest them all simultaneously so they could not alert the others. Emily hoped that going after them in the very early hours of the morning would catch them off guard. They didn't need a standoff on their hands with heavily armed fundamentalists bringing about their own Armageddon.

It was just past two a.m. when they rolled out to hit multiple targets at different addresses across the community. The police presence would be stepped up in Oak Lane Flats, given the militia-vigilante character of the area. It was where

Glenda Kupp and Dede Granville lived, and Emily fully expected them and their relatives to put up a fight. She was waiting for Diaz to bring the car around when she saw Antonio step out of the elevator. He looked around, stunned at all the police presence. He was tired, his shoulders slumped.

"What's going on? I saw all the commotion from my window," he said.

"We're going to make arrests," Emily replied, not meeting his eyes.

"It's a lot of agents. I can't believe you uncovered all of this," he said, with a small smile.

"I guess these things just find me," Emily said.

"Be careful," he said, reaching out to touch her arm.

"I always am," she replied, drawing away.

Diaz pulled up, the car idling.

"Come back to me safely," he whispered, a routine they had followed for years when she went off to a take down. Normally she would respond, "I always do" but this time, she could only look at him, thinking of everything she had learned in the past few days. She feared that nothing would ever be the same for them and she couldn't pretend. She climbed into the passenger seat without a word, snapping her seatbelt into place. A caravan of other officers and agents followed behind it as they drove away, their taillights disappearing into the darkness of a moonless night.

Emily and Diaz pulled up outside Cody and Vannah's house and waited while the SWAT officers swept out around the perimeter. A county van from CPS parked behind them. Emily's nerves were on edge; so much had happened in the last twenty-four hours, she couldn't calm her nervous system down. She felt the sense of overwhelm threatening to overtake her.

Silently, she did her box breathing practice, wishing she still had a rubber band on her wrist to snap her focus back.

When all the officers were in place, Diaz and Emily went to the front door, flanked by Griffith and the others. They'd debated whether to bust in with the battering ram but decided against it since there were children in the house.

Diaz knocked hard on the door and announced, "FBI! We have a warrant."

A moment later a hallway light came on and Vannah opened the door, wrapping a bathrobe around her huge belly. They had caught her unaware; she had a half-asleep look of confusion and annoyance on her face.

"What's going on? Emily?" she asked.

"We have a warrant for your arrest and to search your home," Diaz said, pushing past her with a group of SWAT officers who took up tactical positions on the stairs and in doorways. Vannah gripped the doorframe to steady herself, her eyes scanning the scene, uncomprehending. Griffith headed upstairs as Emily took Vannah's wrists to put her in handcuffs. Vannah resisted and pulled away, but Emily's grip was stronger as she locked the cuffs into place. Vannah leaned against the door to keep her balance.

"What're you talking about? What's going on? Emily?" she cried.

"You're under arrest for the murder of Hayley Hope, you have the right to remain silent..." Emily said, reading her Miranda rights as Diaz shouted, "Cody Granville isn't here!"

"Where is he, Vannah?" she asked, letting Vannah watch as the CPS workers led her children out to the waiting van.

"Where're you taking my kids? What're you doing?" she screeched. "You can't do this!"

"Where is Cody, Vannah? It's two o'clock in the morning—is he at work?"

"The kids need to go to my mom or... to Dede's house!" she shouted.

"Not possible since they should be in police custody by now. Your kids are going to county, they'll go into foster care, but you're so concerned about those poor kids, aren't you? Like Melora and Melanie Zane? Rachel Carson?"

She looked at Emily, stricken. "What do you know about them?"

"Quite a bit since Melanie's already given her statement to the FBI. And when Roy Bishop recovers, I think he'll have some things to say also, like who attacked him and left him for dead. He's a tough old guy, he made it."

"I don't know what you're talking about," Vannah protested, her eyes wild as she struggled against the handcuffs.

"Don't resist, Vannah. Tell us where Cody is so this doesn't escalate."

"I don't know where he is! I haven't done anything!" she cried.

"We have a video of you murdering Hayley Hope in Papoose Lake, of you committing a hate crime assault against Eddie March. Stop bullshitting and tell me where Cody is!" Emily shouted at her.

Suddenly a gush of water ran down Vannah's legs, puddling on the floor.

"My water just broke. The babies are coming!" Vannah cried.

Emily rode with Vannah in the ambulance to the community hospital; she was handcuffed to the gurney. She whimpered and shifted her weight in discomfort.

"What's going to happen to my babies?"

"They're going to be just fine. CPS will be on hand to take

them since you're under arrest and you'll be taken to the county jail upon your recovery," Emily said coolly.

Vannah's eyes filled with tears, and she turned her head away.

"How can you do this?" she whispered.

"How could you drown a fifteen-year-old girl?" Emily replied.

"You have to let me have a little bit of time with the babies!" Vannah pleaded.

"Tell me where Cody is." Emily stared at her, unmoved.

Vannah closed her eyes, tears spilling out, and whispered, "They're all out at the Legion Hall. In Sugar Pines Park. It's Cody, Kupp, Prentiss and Miles. No one else."

Vannah was loaded onto another gurney, uniformed officers flanking her as medical staff wheeled her through the double doors of the maternity ward. Emily watched her disappear, a storm of emotions churning inside her. That this woman—this mother—could orchestrate the drowning of a teenage girl was beyond comprehension. That she could do so while carrying new life inside her seemed almost demonic.

Emily's hands shook as she texted Griffith:

> Cody and the others are at the Legion Hall in Sugar Pines Park. Must get out there ASAP!

She stared at the message after sending it, suddenly struck by the gravity of what they'd uncovered. This wasn't just a corrupt sheriff or an isolated case of abuse. This was a systematic network of predators who had been operating with impunity for years, sacrificing vulnerable children without consequence.

She thought of Lillian, who'd tried to tell anyone who would listen. Of Hayley, who'd fought back in the only ways she could. Of Melora, whose body might still be lying somewhere beneath the mountain soil. They deserved justice. And Emily would not rest until they had it.

THIRTY-ONE

The Riverside agents showed up at Jim Jenkins house as he was loading his suitcases into his car. Mary stood on the front porch, nonplussed when he was put into a black SUV. He was ready to talk. Knowing they had a warrant to search the church premises, he handed over two large boxes of flash drives containing videos that he used to blackmail members of his congregation. He admitted that Cody, Kupp and Miles had killed young Melora Zane to keep her quiet and to prevent her from leaving to reunite with Melanie. She was buried in the fenced-off garden area behind the church. Jenkins had a video of the whole thing, implicating everyone. He hadn't participated in many of the crimes, but he knew he was facing the rest of his life in prison so he was ready to make any deal he could.

Emily pulled up to the American Legion Hall in Sugar Pines Park as Cody, Kupp, Miles and Prentiss were being put into a police van. They were all being transported down to San Bernardino to be processed and booked; the local Twin Peaks Sheriff's Department was under investigation to see if other officers were involved. The quiet neighborhood was ablaze with flashing lights, multiple police vehicles, FBI and SWAT.

"Hey! Emily!" Diaz waved her over to where he and Griffith were with the head of the SWAT team.

"Did they give you any pushback?" she asked.

"Hell, yeah! They were armed and ready, but they were no match for what we showed up with. They fired a couple of shots but when SWAT came in with the flashbangs, the AR-15s, they folded. I think the Miles guy peed himself," Diaz said.

"They had no idea the place has already been swept by forensics. I think they came here to get rid of evidence," Griffith said.

"Once we get their DNA, we'll test it against what we found here yesterday. That should give us some answers."

"Or maybe a lot of new questions. I think these guys have been dirty for a long time. I won't be surprised if now that they've been caught, more victims come forward," Griffith said.

Emily made a note to reach out to Manuel Heredia so he could let Ernesto's family know that Kupp and the others had been arrested. Perhaps they would return to the town they had called home for so long. She walked to the police van and opened the door to see Cody, Kupp, Miles and Prentiss cuffed and restrained, under the watch of two burly cops.

"Vannah's at the hospital, in labor," Emily said.

Cody didn't even look up to meet her eyes. The others were silent as well, staring at the floor.

"And Roy Bishop regained consciousness, as did Kathy Warne. I'm sure both of them have a lot to say to us. She already gave me the bindings you took off Hayley's body when you pulled her out of the lake." Emily leaned into the van, for emphasis.

Cody shifted. She could see the fear coming over him, like water rising in a flooded room.

"And Hayley Hope posted a video to Instagram, detailing

your whole trafficking operation. It went live earlier this evening. She told us where the track phone was hidden so we've got that, too."

Prentiss looked up, confused and angry. He squinted his small, close-set eyes at her.

"What're you talking about? She's dead!"

"You can load a video to Instagram and postdate it. She knew something might happen to her, so she set it up to go live today. Smart kid. A lot smarter than any of you," Emily said.

Cody glared at her now. "I don't believe it."

"It was up on the site. We copied it and removed it, since it'll be used as evidence. But even if we didn't have all of that, Amber Kupp handed us the video of Hayley's murder before we took her into custody. And Jenkins gave you all up. They're digging for Melora Zane's body now. Jenkins has videos of everything. Pardon my language but you four are royally fucked," Emily said, closing the van door with a hard shove.

She rejoined Griffith and Diaz who were seated on a low retaining wall, drinking down the last dregs from a hotel coffee cup.

"Did you bring that coffee with you?" Emily asked.

"Yeah, it's gross now but I need the caffeine," Griffith said. "We have a long night of interrogations ahead of us."

"They arrested Glenda Kupp with no problem; everyone in that neighborhood was asleep so we didn't have any nutcase militia types to deal with," Diaz said.

"The social worker, Alice Boone, and that Starhawk character were also picked up without incident. They had no idea what was coming," Diaz said.

"What about Lynne Smenck and Dede Granville?" I asked.

"They had to tase Smenck and Dede is on the run. They didn't get her; she drove off and they lost her. They think she went toward Silverwood Lake and the Cajon Pass," Griffith said.

"She could take the 15 straight to Nevada. She might have family there, so we need to check that out. See if she has anyone all along that highway 15 corridor—there are so many little weird pop ups out there," Emily said.

"Like Zzyzx Road?" Diaz asked. "What the hell is that? I see it every time I drive to Vegas!"

All the agents would be heading down to San Bernardino within the next hour. Emily was mentally and physically exhausted. She texted Lillian and Eddie to let them know that everyone had been apprehended, except Dede Granville. Lillian responded immediately.

You got the track phone from my house?

Yes, it has the evidence we need. Don't worry about Dede, she's long gone. You can all come home.

She sent back a thumbs-up emoji. Next, Emily dialed Melanie, dreading the news she had to deliver. Melanie answered immediately.

"Agent Ray? What's going on?"

"We've arrested everyone, we have a ton of evidence against them. Your grandpa is all right. He has a couple of broken bones and a concussion but he's going to be okay."

"What about Melora? Did you find her?"

Emily paused. She hated this part of her job, being the one who would be seared into someone's memory as the person who delivered the worst pain of their life.

"We think so. I'm sorry to give you this news, but Jim Jenkins admitted that Cody, Kupp and Miles killed her to keep her from leaving and going to find you. We have a search team digging for her remains."

Melanie let out a sharp gasp, then she began to cry.

"No, no, that can't be what happened! I should've taken her with me, I should never have left her behind!"

"You had to get out, Melanie. You saw a chance and you took it. You did nothing wrong. If you had tried to force her, you would both be dead now, most likely. They did this, they created this situation," Emily said.

Melanie continued to cry. Emily waited on the line until her tears subsided.

"When can I go see my grandpa?"

"Anytime. I'm sorry to give you such painful news."

"At least now I know what happened to her. The not knowing is worse sometimes. I... have to go."

They hung up, and Emily felt the inevitable crash beginning. The adrenalin that had sustained her for the past forty-eight hours began to ebb, leaving her physically hollow and mentally depleted. Her muscles screamed in protest with each movement, joints stiffening as if someone had replaced her tendons with rusted wire. The familiar post-case migraine pulsed at her temples, threatening to engulf her entirely.

She allowed herself thirty seconds of complete surrender to the exhaustion. Thirty seconds to feel every ache, every doubt, every emotion she'd compartmentalized during the operation. Then, as she'd trained herself to do throughout her career, she straightened, squared her shoulders, and pushed forward. There would be time for recovery later. She was walking back to her car when she received a text from the agent at the Mountains Community Hospital.

Vannah Granville wants to speak with you

Now?

Yes. She just gave birth. Twins.

She was surprised that Vannah had given birth so quickly

and was curious what she wanted to say at this point. Emily headed back toward Arrowhead. Fog had blown in, turning the winding road into a narrow ribbon of moonlight, barely visible.

Dede drove her Subaru at top speed, her brain swimming in panic. She had never expected police and FBI agents to show up at her house. She had always been protected, her son was a cop. He always covered for her, and she had his back. They had a bond, an unbreakable bond. He was her baby, the light of her existence. Even after he married Vannah Pratt, Dede remained the most important woman in his life. Dede drove the back way, towards the Cajon Pass. She had to get away, she couldn't let them catch her.

She had no idea how anyone had found out anything. No one talked, no one dared to. They knew that she'd come after them. Like Vannah, she'd lived her whole life on the mountain, she didn't need anything more. Her thoughts ran like frightened rats hiding in the dark, when a bright light flashed on them. She wished Cody had never met Hayley Hope, she was his downfall. The girl bewitched him, made him lose himself. Just a skinny little slip of a girl to have such power. Dede slowed down as she passed Silverwood Lake, much bigger than Arrowhead. She pulled her car off the highway, into the shadows of the lake campground. She sat in the dark weighing her options.

They would catch her. They probably had the road blocked at the 15 freeway. With the cops and the FBI, there was no way she was escaping. And then what? The rest of her life behind bars, knowing that her precious son was living the same nightmare? She couldn't bear it. She put the car in reverse and headed back home. Twenty minutes later she came roaring up through Crestline, heading straight for Highway 18. There were cops everywhere and she saw that their SUVs lit up in pursuit when she passed them. She didn't care, pushing her foot down against the gas pedal, gaining speed. She knew the spot she needed to hit, in the cutoff that wound its way toward Lake Arrowhead. Once she was in the narrows, it was a two-lane road.

She checked the rearview mirror. A small smile crept across her face, and she entered the twisting stretch of highway. Ahead, she saw a blockade of patrol cars. In pursuit, multiple CHP and FBI vehicles were gaining on her. She couldn't let them cut her off and block her path. She looked out at the sprawling city lights of the San Bernardino Valley below, like a million diamonds washed up on the shore. They were beautiful. She pushed the gas pedal to the floor and swerved the car over the low railing, plunging against the rocks and scrub brush, the manzanita and mountain laurel as it disappeared down the steep cliff.

When Emily got to Highway 18 from Lake Gregory Drive, she saw that it was shut down with police, paramedics and a search and rescue team. Two of the black FBI SUVs were there as she pulled up. An agent from Riverside leaned in her window.

"It was Dede Granville. We picked up her vehicle heading back up toward town from Highway 38, by Silverwood. We were keeping her under surveillance but holding back since the road is so narrow, but she just gunned it, straight over the edge."

Emily had little sympathy for her, after seeing the vitriol and violence she'd unleashed on Eddie March and Hayley Hope. She was one less criminal that they would have to spend time and money prosecuting. Emily drove to Mountains Community Hospital; two San Bernadino police cars were parked outside. She checked in and found Vannah in her room, pale and exhausted from labor, but sitting up in bed when Emily entered.

"They said you want to talk to me?" Emily asked.

Vannah glared, her eyes filled with resentment. "The CPS worker came in already. They're planning to take the babies tomorrow."

"I've read you your rights previously, for the record," Emily said, calmly.

"I know my rights, I don't need a lawyer to talk to you right now," Vannah muttered, crossing her arms.

"Just so we're clear on the law," Emily said, sitting in a hard, vinyl chair against the wall.

"Right! The law! What about the laws of God? They trump the laws of man," Vannah said, with a self-satisfied smirk.

"Not in this world, they don't. I don't know what you think is going to happen when you die and quite frankly, I don't care. You're a murderer. Your husband is a rapist and a pedophile. And you're all going to be in prison for a very long time," Emily said.

"Cody is a good man! A godly man who loves his family and upholds the Word!" Vannah snapped, clenching the thin sheet in her fists.

"That's why he groomed teenagers and other women to have sex with him. In his truck, at the church, at the Legion Hall. He was ready to do it anywhere, wasn't he?" Emily said, hoping to provoke more information out of her.

"That's not true. Those women threw themselves at him, they tempted him. They were full of Satan's lust. It's in James 1:14 *'But every man is tempted when he is drawn away by his own lust. He is enticed'*. She enticed my husband, through witchcraft!"

"Are you talking about Hayley Hope now? The young girl that he desired more than you? He wanted her to move into your home as his second wife, didn't he?"

"She wanted what was mine. She was the one who used evil to influence and corrupt him," she whispered fiercely.

"And that's why you killed her? You and your mom, with Dede and Glenda? Why you drowned her in the lake?"

"It was a test and to teach her a lesson! To warn her to stay away from Cody."

"No, it wasn't a test. Swimming the witch isn't a test now and it wasn't five hundred years ago. It was murder. You held her under the water. We have it all on video," Emily said.

She turned white and went perfectly still. Then she whispered, "Who betrayed me? Who betrayed God's servant?"

Emily sat back and watched her for a moment. She clutched at the sheets, her eyes darting around the room in paranoia. Her silent rage was palpable. Emily realized that this was more than religious fervor. She had slipped over the edge into madness, hidden behind a façade of being the perfect wife and mother.

"Hayley wanted what was mine," she repeated.

"No, Hayley was scared of Cody and all of you. She was an easy target, and you knew it. You brought her around for your husband, like a lamb to the slaughter. You knew what would happen. You knew about Melanie and Melora. He was starting with Daila, wasn't he? That's why Ernesto showed up at your barbecue, to put a stop to it."

"Shut up! You don't know what you're saying. You don't know him, he's a good man, a good man. He's a godly man, who upholds the Word..."

THIRTY-TWO

The San Bernardino Police Station hummed with activity as separate interrogation rooms filled with the day's arrests. Emily observed through one-way glass as Griffith, Diaz, and other agents from the Los Angeles and Riverside offices conducted initial interviews.

Jim Jenkins broke almost immediately, his bluster collapsing at the first mention of potential sentencing guidelines. He offered names, dates, locations—anything to secure a more favorable deal. Glenda Kupp followed suit, her grandmotherly demeanor dissolving into panic as she detailed her role in procuring drugs and helping dispose of evidence.

In the adjacent room, Alice Boone initially maintained her innocence, insisting she had only ever acted in the best interests of her assigned children. Starhawk adopted a similar strategy until confronted with financial records showing payments from Dede Granville. Their stories unraveled in parallel, revealing the carefully constructed pipeline that channeled vulnerable foster children toward Church on the Hill and into Cody's orbit.

Most surprising was Roger Kupp's reaction. The man Emily

had pegged as an unrepentant brute dissolved into tears, blaming Cody and Prentiss for masterminding the operation while portraying himself as a reluctant participant. Miles, still wearing standard-issue pants after wetting himself during the arrest, proved even more forthcoming. He described a criminal enterprise dating back three years, encompassing not only trafficking but also the murders of Joannie Dietrich, Karlie Ann Smith, and Rachel Hogan—all silenced when they threatened to expose the operation.

As night deepened, Emily prepared to face Cody Granville. She downed a double espresso in the break room, fighting to maintain focus after nearly twenty-four hours without sleep. The caffeine jolted through her system, providing a final, tenuous boost of clarity before what promised to be the most challenging interview of the day.

When she sat down across from him in the interview room, he leaned back in his chair, cocky and sure of himself.

"Let's start with Melanie and Melora Zane," Emily said.

He grinned. "Nice looking girls, both of 'em."

Emily fought back the instinct to gag at his response. He was repulsive and just to look at him made her queasy, but she forged ahead.

"We know you started grooming Melanie and then moved on to Melora. We've arrested Sherry Snyder as well as Alice Boone. Sherry just gave us a detailed account of how your mother made a financial arrangement with her to siphon vulnerable girls to you."

"She's nuts. Everyone up here knows that. Ask my mom."

"Unfortunately, we can't do that. Your mother took her own life earlier after evading the police who came to arrest her."

She watched that information hit him like a bulldozer. He

sat up in his chair and laid his palms on the table between them, as if trying to steady himself.

"No way. She'd never do that," he said, angrily.

"She drove over the edge on Highway 18. The same way Kupp tried to kill Kathy Warne. Dede knew the police and FBI were after her and she drove over intentionally."

"She didn't! You all chased her; you pushed her to do it!"

"She gunned that engine right over the railing. The agents at the scene told me. No skid marks, she never hit the brakes."

He laid his head on the table, his breathing becoming ragged. Emily guessed that his entire life Dede had enabled and protected him from the consequences of his maladjusted, anti-social personality, his aggression and violence. Underneath his carefully curated persona, he was like a malignant man-child who needed to dominate and control everyone around him with his mother running interference for him.

Without raising his head, he said suddenly, "I didn't kill Hayley. I was in love with her. I wanted her to join our family. It wasn't me."

"But you groomed her and committed statutory rape of a minor," she replied sharply.

"She was smart, she knew what she wanted. She was happy with me. Vannah got upset, she wasn't satisfied being the mother of my children. She wanted all of me," he complained.

"Most wives don't expect their husbands to have sex with little girls who are underage."

He slapped the table, his rage exploding. "Hayley wasn't a little girl, she was a beautiful, grown woman who wanted me! She wanted me, no matter what she said on that fucking video!" he shouted.

"Did you know about the video she recorded? Did she threaten you with it, so you'd leave her alone? Is that why you were so desperate to find her track phone?"

"She was confused, because Vannah got so upset. She was just confused!"

"So, what is it? She was a grown woman who knew what she wanted, or she was a teenager who was confused after being coerced and raped by an adult man? And she was frightened of his religious fanatic wife and his unstable mother?"

He let out a strangled cry. Emily had the impression he expected to be comforted for this outburst, as if he were a child. She waited silently. After a few minutes, he sat back and regained his composure, his tears gone.

"I didn't do it, you can't pin it on me. I wasn't even at Papoose Lake that night. It was Vannah," he said calmly.

"Even after you put the whole thing in motion, you're ready to throw your wife under the bus? She's the only one to blame?"

"That's right. I wasn't there. She did it."

"You're going to let her take the fall, just to protect yourself?"

"That's a wife's job. To take care of her husband, the head of the family."

Emily felt a pang of sympathy for Vannah, looking at his self-satisfied expression, knowing she would pay the highest price for a nightmare that he'd dragged her into. She had birthed six children for this sad excuse for a man, sacrificed her life to uphold a toxic narrative that would now put her in prison for the rest of her life, leaving her children as orphans in an unforgiving system that she and Cody had been so ready to exploit.

A wave of sadness washed over Emily, seeing how everyone involved in this sordid ring of criminality had chosen their role to play. It confirmed a hard truth that she had learned, working with the FBI in the shadows at the edges of human decency, in the dark places where greed or depravity broke loose and ran unchecked. Payback always comes no matter how you think you've escaped it. It hits like a lightning strike, when the consequences of your actions come back around and turn on you with a ferocity you did not expect. Or it comes like a stalker, hunting you from behind, making you fear exposure, forever looking over your shoulder, never knowing a moment of true peace. It always comes for you.

The police and FBI had finished with the first round of interrogations. There would be more, and the suspects would be arraigned. Emily was certain there would be no bail allowed for any of them so they would stay safely behind bars until trial. She felt Griffith was right in her expectation that more victims would come forward. She headed back to Arrowhead; she still needed to pack up her belongings from the Maison and deal with Antonio. St. Bernardine's Hospital was on the way back, so she stopped in to check on Kathy, Jamie and Roy.

She found both Roy and Kathy on the critical care floor. When she entered her room, Jamie was seated beside her bed. Kathy was awake, sipping a juice box through a straw.

"They stopped the brain bleed late last night. She's doing good and she'll be able to give a statement later today or tomorrow. She remembers everything," Jamie said.

"We arrested all of them, they're in custody. Hayley Hope postdated an Instagram video that exposed them all."

"Hayley was really something, everyone in town saw that. She was gonna be somebody important if they hadn't killed her," he said sadly.

"I think she was pretty important, even the way it turned out. She provided the missing piece that shut these monsters down. And we couldn't have done it without you. And Kathy. I was just grasping at straws on this until I met you."

"That was all Kathy. She took the biggest risk," he said.

Emily moved to her bed and sat beside her. She was hooked up to machines, two IVs and her head was wrapped in bandages. One eye was covered with gauze and she had broken both arms, which were set in plaster casts. She had a neck and spinal brace helping her to sit up.

"We got him. We got all of them. The whole thing has been shut down," Emily said.

Kathy nodded, a tear falling from one of her eyes, rolling down her bruised cheek.

"Then it... was worth it," she said quietly.

In Roy Bishop's room, Emily found him peacefully asleep. A nurse came in and told her that he was improving, he would be able to go home within a week. Emily explained that his grand-daughter would be coming soon to look after him. When she left, Emily took his hand. She didn't know if he could hear her or not.

She leaned in close to his ear and whispered, "They've all been caught, the people who hurt your granddaughters. Melanie is coming as soon as she can. And we know what happened to Melora. It's all over now, Roy."

He didn't move, there was no change in his monitors to show that he'd heard anything. But she felt in her heart that he did. That he finally had an answer he had been searching for.

As Emily pulled out of the parking lot at St. Bernardines, she realized she was across the street from the Mt. View Cemetery where Hayley was buried. Emily pulled in and asked in the office for her grave location. She walked across the neatly kept lawn, passing a large fountain. Hayley's headstone was under a willow tree. There was a fresh bouquet of flowers; she wondered who had placed it there. Someone who cared for her, someone who missed her.

Emily stood motionless before the headstone, the finality of

Hayley's name carved in cold granite finally overwhelming her professional detachment. This girl—this bright, creative spirit—had been silenced before she'd barely begun to live. All her plans, her films, her potential future contributions to the world —erased.

A sudden breeze rustled the leaves overhead. Emily looked up to see a black crow settling on a branch, its intelligent eyes seeming to study her. Though logic told her it couldn't possibly be one of Lillian's trained birds, something about its presence felt deliberate, as if it had found its way here and would watch over Hayley in this peaceful garden of death and remembrance. Emily felt an unexpected comfort wash over her. Hayley wouldn't be forgotten. Lillian would ensure her friend's memory endured, just as Emily had kept alive the memory of the real Emily Ray all these years.

Perhaps there was a heaven, after all. Maybe loved ones do meet again. In that moment, Emily desperately hoped that was true.

Once she finished at the Maison and she'd locked the door behind her, she texted Antonio.

I'm back and it's done. Are you free to talk?

Yes, at the hotel, I'll order breakfast

She made the short drive to the resort. She wasn't going to sit across a table from him eating scrambled eggs and pancakes, as if this was a simple disagreement over landscaping or buying a new appliance. She knew she looked like hell, but she didn't care. She rode the elevator up, thinking back to how, just a few days ago, she and Michael had been here, looking forward to a relaxing getaway. She found Antonio's room and knocked. He opened right away, wearing a pair of old Levis and a white button-down shirt. He knew she loved that look on him.

"I ordered coffee anyway," Antonio said with a half-hearted shrug.

"I drank a whole pot at the police station," Emily replied flatly. "I'm wired enough."

The silence stretched between them, a physical presence in the room.

"This was a pretty big case, I guess," he finally ventured, his tone carefully casual.

"RICO," she said, her voice catching slightly. "Blackmail, extortion, sex trafficking of minors, murder." Her hands trembled as she listed each crime, the reality of what she'd uncovered still raw. "Children, Antonio. Girls barely older than our daughters."

"God, Em. Who would've thought something like that could happen in a vacation town?"

"Let's not do this," she said, her jaw tight. "I'm not here to discuss the case. I'm here about us." She sank into a chair, suddenly exhausted beyond measure. "How far did this go with your old girlfriend?"

Antonio's face flushed crimson. The color spread down his neck as he shifted uncomfortably.

"She's not my old girlfriend," he protested, voice rising defensively. "We just went out a few times in high school. It wasn't serious."

"Whatever. You reconnected, you behaved in a way that prompted Dolores to call me, concerned and angry about it. You lied about taking our girls to a sleepover with a woman you hadn't seen in years, with teenage boys in the house. You know that is prohibited. It's not just me, Dolores told me she was the same way, so was your mom."

"Her boys are nice kids..." he began.

She cut him off. "They're all nice kids until the day they

sneak into a little girl's room at night or into the changing room at the local pool or wherever. You don't know them, you barely know her, but you took our girls there and stayed over."

He nodded and turned away before answering, "Nothing really happened, Emily. We went to watch a movie at her place, we had a few beers. The girls slept in the guest room."

"And you?"

He looked at her, his eyes pained and embarrassed. "I stayed in her room. In her bedroom with her."

She felt her heart lurch and a trembling in her solar plexus. "You mean you were intimate with her?"

"No, I didn't have sex with her. I just slept in the same bed."

She gave a hollow laugh, trying to stop the tears from forming in her throat.

"You slept in the same bed with a woman you'd been flirting with for days, but you didn't do anything? You expect me to believe that?"

"I didn't say that. I didn't have intercourse with her, it didn't go that far. But I did other things that I'm really ashamed of now."

The thought of him engaging in any kind of sex with anyone made her feel sick. She fought back a retching in her throat.

"But you weren't so ashamed when you called to extend your trip, right? This shame only started when you got found out."

He didn't respond. He sat stock-still, like a statue, frozen and immovable. She got up to move, unable to stay seated across from him. She couldn't even look at him.

"So, what the fuck is going on with you? What is this? We've been good, really good. This kind of thing was never an issue. We have a good marriage, we do everything right. We have amazing sex even after all this time together. We laugh, we lay in bed and make plans. What the hell was this?" she shouted at him, fighting back tears.

"I don't know, Em. I really don't. I didn't expect it, it just... happened."

"Bullshit." The word came out as a hiss. "Nothing 'just happens.' You were emailing her for months. You presented yourself as a single dad. You deliberately kept her existence from me." Her voice rose with each accusation. "Don't you dare minimize this with 'it just happened.'"

His eyes widened. "Did you get into my email?"

"Yes!" The admission burst from her like a physical blow. "After Dolores called me. After discovering you'd lied about our daughters sleeping over at some strange woman's house." She paced toward the window, needing distance. "Was my checking your email the real betrayal here? Worse than you sleeping with another woman while our daughters were under the same roof?"

White-hot rage coursed through her; she clenched her fists to contain it. She moved to the far corner of the room, afraid of what she might do if she remained near him.

"I fucked up!" Antonio cried, his composure finally cracking. "It was all me. You've done nothing wrong—nothing. It's me." His voice broke. "I don't know why... maybe it felt good to feel like the smartest person in the room for once. Like someone thought I was brilliant, amazing, the center of the universe."

"And I don't? You're a rocket scientist, for God's sake! You're brilliant! Don't I show how much I love you?" The question came out as a whisper. "Do I belittle you? Make you feel inferior? Have I ever once made you feel less than me?"

"No, you don't. You're always there for everything I'm doing. I know you go out of your way sometimes to make sure that I don't feel overshadowed by your work. And what you do is something so important, it's not building rockets and rovers, doing calculations. Sometimes it's just hard... you burn brighter than I do, you run hotter and you're so driven and obsessive with your cases. I'm not like that," he said.

The fact that he couldn't articulate clearly what he felt scared her. It was much deeper than a simple fling. It was a symptom of something bigger.

He continued, "You get so passionate and involved with your cases, I wanted you to slow down. To let go of that thing inside you that's always wound so tight. I just wanted it all to be easier and more... relaxed. I hoped that after you told me the truth about your identity, that you would be ready to leave all of this behind. Like maybe you were finally free of it."

She sat down on the edge of the bed and took a deep breath. She saw him with sudden, painful clarity—not the partner she'd believed in for thirteen years, but a stranger whose insecurities had been festering beneath the surface of their marriage. After Emily's death, when she took on her identity, she became the perfect daughter, student, FBI agent, wife and mother. Her whole life had been defined by always holding everything together, working to make it all fit. It was exhausting and desperate; she felt as if she had to work so hard to earn the life she had taken on, to deserve everything that she had after surviving Tibbs. She couldn't do it anymore.

Antonio was right in one thing, she did need to let go of all that struggle, to be the best, to be enough, to prove that she was worthy of any happiness she had. But she had learned on Hayley Hope's case that she would never be able to be the way Antonio wanted her to be. She would never be able to unwind that coil inside her, that made her take on the Cody Granvilles of the world, to help a young girl in pain like Lillian Knox, to deliver justice for victims like Melora Zane. They were the kids who didn't stand a chance against the adults who abused them. There were never enough people to protect them, to speak up for them. But Emily knew that she would always be someone who did. If it made her too intense, too driven, too obsessive, then so be it. Those kids existed in a reality defined by danger and exploitation. To help them, she had to be willing to enter that darkness—as someone who understood its terrain, who could navigate it without flinching from its horrors.

Antonio thought he wanted something different and perhaps he did, after thirteen years. People change. Maybe he wanted a quiet existence with a woman who didn't make life and death decisions every day, who never visited the disturbing places where predators hide. But Emily was not that woman.

She felt the rage and hurt seep out of her body and looked up at him, standing against the picture window with the mid-morning light pouring in.

"I don't know that I can get past this, Toño. I just don't. I never thought we would be in this situation, with another woman and all of it. I trusted you, completely, but I can't any longer. I don't know that I ever will again."

He came to sit next to her, but she recoiled from him, pushing him away. The hurt in his eyes almost broke her, but she remained stoic.

"Emily, you have to forgive me, you have to trust me again. It was me; it was some bullshit for my ego or something. I'll go to counseling, I'll figure it out," he pleaded.

"I'm not like other women, you know that. I'm not like Anjelica or the wives of your friends. James Tibbs took all of that... normalcy from me. You don't survive captivity like that and come out unscathed, no matter how much I pretend that I'm unscarred by it. I am deeply scarred, and I don't think I can be the easy, relaxed version of me that you want."

"It's not that, I know how you are, I love how you are..."

She interrupted him. "No, it's a problem for you. You want me to be less than I am. That's why a sweet, old-school girl-friend who brought you plates of food and a cold beer, was appealing enough for you to break our marriage vows," she said, her voice cracking at the realization that they would never be the same, ever again.

"Please let me fix this, Emily. You have to give me a chance to fix it!"

"I'm letting this go, Antonio. I don't know how it will work out, but I don't want to be with you the same way any longer. I don't want to disrupt the girls' lives, so I don't want you to move out or anything extreme. We have four guest rooms; when we go back, please quietly move into one of them. We'll keep the same schedules and such but consider us separated."

"No, Emily! I don't want this," he cried.

"It's what I want. You should go visit Anjelica, you should see if that is really a better fit for you. Maybe it is. But I can't be anything other than what I am. I can't be less intense, less driven, to make you feel better. I can't hear about a girl like Hayley Hope being murdered and not jump in to try and help. Or Josie Vance being abducted and not try to find her. This is who I am."

He was crying now, with his face buried in his hands. Part of her wanted to rush to him and embrace him, to pull him close and whisper promises that it would all be okay because she wanted so much for it to go back to what she believed it was before. But it had all changed.

She left him that way, walked to the door and got in the elevator. In a daze, she found her car in the parking lot. Her whole world had shifted, and she had to find a new way to live in it.

EPILOGUE

Emily sat in the fading light as the sun went down on the deck at Lillian's house. Her parents were grilling a feast, the aroma of meat and vegetables filling the air. Eddie and Caine were there. Evelyn was content and happy with her whole family together. Michael played with Sammy, tossing a toy for her to fetch. Emily looked at the few remaining boats on the lake. She heard the laughter of children on the shore. With the evil gone, it felt like paradise again.

Lillian ran out to get them. "C'mon, come inside. I have something to show you all!"

They went inside to the living room where Lillian had projected a video up on the big white wall.

"I found this, you all have to see it!"

She started the video. In it, Hayley, Lillian, Eddie and Melora were at the lake's edge, splashing and laughing.

"This is our dream circle! So, what's your dream, Eddie? Tell us, we want to know," Hayley asked.

Eddie looked uncertain, then said, "I want to be a teacher. A history teacher. I want to be that guy who gets a lost kid to find the right path. I want to be the guy they think of later when they grow up. The one who changed their lives."

Hayley turned to Melora. "And you, Mel?"

Melora was hesitant and shy, afraid to look directly at the camera.

"I want to work in a vet's office. To help with the animals," she said in a quiet, husky voice.

"Lillian? My bestie?" Hayley asked, throwing her arm over her shoulders.

"I want to... be a neuroscientist. Or maybe a fortune teller. Or perhaps an astronaut!" she said, laughing. "And you, Hayley?"

Hayley Hope looked at the camera, her pale eyes as clear as glass.

"I want to go far away and make movies and tell stories and be very famous and very rich and then I want to come back here, when I'm old. Back here to the mountains, and the crows and the bobcats. The coyotes yipping at night and the snowstorms. Back here with you three, sitting at the lake, living our best lives, in the town where we grew up."

The four teenagers linked hands and spun in a circle, gaining momentum until they were like a wild, spinning top, all arms and legs and laughter. When they stopped, they put their hands in the air and shouted, "The Houdinis!"

The frame froze, on all the smiling, hopeful faces, their bodies in motion, filled with the energy and exuberance of youth. It was almost as if Hayley Hope knew to capture this moment with her camera. That the dreams of those taken too young will be carried on by those who remember, the survivors.

Like Lillian Knox and Eddie March.

Like Melanie Zane.

Like Danica Hansen.

Dear Readers of the Emily Ray Suspense Series,

Thank you so much for your support of the first book, *My Name Is Emily Ray*, and for your continued interest in book two, *Hayley Hope Is Gone*. I feel tremendous gratitude to all the readers who took the time to write reviews; it has been such a pleasure for me to see how much you enjoyed the book. If you want to stay in touch with other readers, please sign up for my email newsletter, which will have updates and information on the Emily Ray Series.

www.stormpublishing.co/michele-dominguez-greene

If you enjoyed *Hayley Hope Is Gone* and can spare a few minutes to write a review and share your thoughts with other readers, it would be a great help to me. Positive reviews from other readers in this genre are really the way a book's success is built; it is all about how someone connects with the story, and sharing that experience is the most important support of all. Thank you so very much!

I wrote book two in this series, *Hayley Hope Is Gone*, out of the desire to explore what lies beneath the surface of a place, of a person. Emily is adept at looking beyond appearances, a skill hard won in her years of captivity, and just when she thinks she will be able to let go of that drive and vigilance, she stumbles upon a dark corner of humanity in a place that looks like paradise. I wanted to explore the ways in which people present a public persona that can be so far from who they truly are and what they are capable of. The place, Lake Arrowhead, is a resort community nestled in the mountains in California and at first glance, it seems to be a peaceful, tranquil hamlet, defined by small-town charm. But like the lake itself, which harbors dangers that are unseen, the culture of the town and its people hide disturbing secrets. Despite her attempts to appease her husband and shift her focus away from high-risk, high-intensity work with the CARD team of the FBI, she finds herself unable to turn away from a troubled girl in need of help, and in doing so, she must face the reality of who she is, who she will always be. There is no easygoing, relaxed version of Emily Ray, and that is her strong suit. The mystery of Hayley Hope's death forces her to see the things she does not want to see in people she trusts, to face the unsavory truths about corruption and criminality in law enforcement and the tragic ways that religious fanaticism can destroy lives. At the same time, she faces betrayal and loss in her personal life which, solidifies her commitment to stay true to herself, her nature and her character with all of her flaws and failings. She sees that she cannot find happiness or fulfillment by making herself smaller to suit others, and she has to burn as hot and brightly as she was meant to. This, again, is emotional territory that I feel a lot of women can relate to, the cultural expectation that they must make others feel happy and secure above all else. They have to be careful not to be "too much"—too driven, ambitious, intelligent, courageous. I feel that Emily's emotional journey in this second book takes her deeper into understanding who she truly is as a woman, wife, mother... and high-level agent in federal law enforcement with a calling she cannot ignore.

KEEP IN TOUCH WITH THE AUTHOR

Michele-Greene.com

 facebook.com/MGreeneArtist
 x.com/MicheleDGreene
 instagram.com/micheledgreene

ACKNOWLEDGMENTS

I would like to thank everyone at Storm for their tremendous support of this book series and giving me the opportunity to work with them to bring Emily Ray to life. My amazing book agent, Jill Marsal, continues to be one of the best things that ever happened to me as a writer, and I am appreciative of her support and encouragement. My dear friends Trina and Jeffrey Foster gave me so much help in managing my home life with a pressing writing schedule. And, of course, all my love and gratitude to my son, José Daniel, for his help and maturity as I delved into this project and spent many hours holed up in my chilly, first-floor office in the woods.